The
COVERUP

RUE DOOLIN

PAGE PUBLISHING, INC.
New York, NY

First originally published by Page Publishing, Inc. 2018

ISBN 978-1-64424-353-4 (Paperback)
ISBN 978-1-64424-354-1 (Digital)

Printed in the United States of America

PROLOGUE

**Los Angeles, 1947
(Fifty years before the killings)**

Ivan Josef Crenski wasn't the brightest kid in his class, but he was very good at two things: numbers and sitting still. If they ever held a sitting still contest for twelve-year-olds, Ivan was certain he would win it, hands-down. Ivan kept a folder of arithmetic tests, each marked with a bright-red B+ or an occasional A-, under the mattress of his mother's bed, hoping someday to show them to her.

Ivan was anxious to leave his mother's bedside before Greg got home, but sometimes if he so much as took a sip of water, Mama would wake up and grab his hand, hard, and say things in Russian—things Ivan didn't understand—but she always looked really scared when she said them. Ivan didn't like for Mama to be scared, so he would talk to her in his softest indoor voice until she wasn't scared anymore, then he'd sit very, very still until she went back to sleep.

Ivan loved Mama. Mama had told him many times that she loved him too, very much, even though he had nearly killed her getting born. Ivan had weighed over ten pounds at birth. Pearl said he was stocky like Papa. Ivan liked it when people said he was like Papa. Ivan knew that birthing him had caused Mama to be sick because once he heard Papa tell Mrs. Holloway that Mama was never right again after Ivan was born. Ivan was sorry he had made Mama sick, and was always going to take care of her. He sat by her bedside every day when he got home from school, except when she was asleep. Even then, he would stay close by, in case she woke up and needed a drink of water or something. On Saturday afternoons, though, Pearl would see to Mama and give Ivan a dime so he could go to the picture show. Pearl was a good sister. Gladys was nice too, except she didn't come around much anymore since she married Tony Giatti. Pearl said Tony thought he was too good for the Crenski family.

At last, Ivan could tell from her heavy breathing that Mama was sound asleep. He slipped off of the tattered red velvet chair and tiptoed soundlessly across the worn linoleum and out of the room. He was relieved to see that Greg wasn't home yet. Gregoe, Ivan's older half brother, had the same name as their papa, but everyone called him Greg. Ivan wished he could have the same name as Papa too, especially now that Papa was dead, but Mama once told him that three Gregoes would have been too many.

Ivan waited patiently for Pearl to leave for work then hurried into the room he shared with Greg. He removed one of Greg's detective magazines from under his mattress, and took it into the closet. He was engrossed in a story about Elliott Ness when the magazine was suddenly yanked from his hands and a sweaty palm covered his mouth, pressing hard.

A raspy voice whispered, "You know what happens when you touch my stuff." Greg was home.

Ivan could tell from the beer smell and slurred speech that Greg was drunk, and he braced himself for the inevitable pain his brother would inflict upon him. His heart beat wildly, and tears streamed down his face as he fought back the bile forming in his throat.

Greg snarled, "So now, you creep, I guess I'm going to have to rip your arm off."

That was to be the last threat Greg would ever make to Ivan. The dynamics between the brothers would be permanently altered on that day, exactly one week before Ivan's thirteenth birthday. As he moved to shield himself from Greg's blows, something exploded inside of Ivan, filling him with a rage so powerful it frightened him. Helpless to stop himself, Ivan stood, squared his shoulders, and slowly turned to face his brother. Body shaking, hands clenched into fists, and face contorted. Ivan heard his own voice growl, "I AM YOUR

BROTHER! ONLY MONSTERS DO BAD THINGS TO THEIR BROTHERS! DON'T EVER RAISE YOUR HAND TO ME AGAIN!"

Then, as quickly as it had come, the anger subsided, leaving Ivan drained and aghast at what he had done. He fell to the floor, threw his arms across his face, and waited for Greg's retaliatory onslaught. When nothing happened, Ivan uncovered one eye and watched in disbelief as his brother staggered away. Then Greg did something that amazed Ivan even more. He stumbled back to the closet and dried Ivan's tears with a dirty sock. Next, he wrested a quarter from his pocket and placed it in his brother's hand.

Ivan was dumbfounded. He had never before threatened or raised his voice to anyone, especially not to Greg, nor had he ever owned a quarter. He could see two picture shows, buy popcorn, and still have a penny left from a quarter.

Greg stopped tormenting Ivan after that. The boys at school still talked about how mean and crazy Greg was and how he stole things and liked to torture animals. Ivan saw a gun under Greg's mattress once, next to a pile of money.

Greg continued to be generous with Ivan though, frequently giving him quarters. On two occasions, he had given Ivan a whole dollar. Greg even fixed up a used bicycle, which Pearl said was probably stolen, and presented it to Ivan on his fourteenth birthday. When Greg got himself a switchblade knife, he gave Ivan his pocketknife. Ivan kept his growing treasure trove in a coffee can beneath two floorboards he had loosened under the pile of galoshes and rain boots in back of the hall closet.

Ivan was pretty content with his life now. Mama slept most of the time and he only had to see to her medicine and feed her dinner each evening. He had a brother who was good to him. Pearl had given him her radio when she married Erik, and he got her bedroom as well. He could read Greg's detective magazines whenever he wanted, and the kids became friendlier to him after he began bringing bubblegum and candy to school to share with them. Once, Nancy Marquardt, the prettiest girl in school, told him he was nice.

On the whole, Ivan's life was better than he had ever imagined it would be.

CHAPTER 1

Laughlin, Nevada, 1997
(The morning after the killings)

Assured by a quick glance around the room that Greg wasn't lurking about, Capri Olindo emerged from the ladies' room and hurried through the nearly-empty casino. Her visit to the ladies' room had been a waste of time, serving only to confirm what she already knew. She was a mess. She'd applied a fresh coat of lip gloss, ran a comb through her wilted hairdo, and given up.

After another Greg-check, Pree entered the hotel coffee shop, waved to the cleaning crew, and returned to the table she had vacated a short while earlier. In her absence, Charlotte had replenished her Diet Pepsi and cleared Crush and Lu's breakfast dishes from the table. Pree settled in with the latest issue of the local newspaper, the *Laughlin Weekly*, to await Bob's arrival.

Meeting Bob Kips had been the one bright spot in her seemingly endless ordeal with Greg Crenski. Pree had gone to the multiplex at the Riverside Hotel for her usual Friday morning movie that day. Despite the restraining order and Greg's confinement to house arrest, Pree could never fully calm the jitters in her stomach when she ventured out in public. But since Greg had never been an early riser, her Friday morning movie provided her with a unique opportunity to relax and suspend the ugly reality of her life for a couple of hours. That particular morning, she'd intended to catch the 8:30 a.m. showing of *Fargo*. Standing at the snack bar, debating whether or not her chubby frame could stand a box of Milk Duds with her Diet Pepsi, she heard a horrifyingly familiar voice and turned to see Greg coming toward her, sneering, "You won't get away from me this time!"

Ducking behind the counter, Pree was unaware that the sandy-haired man who'd been standing next to her in line had stepped in front of Greg and flashed a badge.

Only after she heard the command, "Stop! Police!" did she step out from behind the counter, removed the restraining order from her purse, and handed it to the officer.

"He's supposed to be under house arrest," she explained. "I don't know how he knew I was here, but I can tell by his eyes he's high on his prescription meds."

Over Greg's protests, the detective cuffed him and hauled him to the local police station to clear things up. Badly shaken, Pree sat in the theater lobby for a few minutes then went home. On her way out of the theater, she was handed a pass and an invitation to return to see the film another time.

The next morning, Pree and Detective Robert Kips were the only two people at the 8:30 a.m. showing of *Fargo* so they sat together. Afterward, they had brunch in the coffee shop where the detective insisted Pree call him Bob, then filled her in on the incident with Greg.

"He actually did have permission to leave his home," Bob told her. "His parole officer said he had a standing Friday morning appointment in Kingman for back therapy. But the poker room manager said that Greg and his friend play poker here at the Riverside every other Friday morning. I informed his parole officer of the situation, so your husband won't be playing anymore poker for a while. They've also extended his house arrest for two months for parole violation."

Relief washed over Pree.

"By the way," Bob continued, "he lives in Nevada now."

"Really?" Pree asked, surprised. "How did he get permission to move out of Arizona?"

"Apparently he claimed financial hardship and a friend is letting him live in a house rent-free, in Nevada," Bob said. "His parole officer didn't object so the court allowed it."

"That's good to know," Pree told him as he stopped her from reaching for the check. "I can't thank you enough," Pree insisted. "The least I can do is buy you breakfast."

"Let's go dutch," he insisted. "We might want to do this again sometime, and that way we won't have to keep track of whose turn it is to pay."

Pree agreed.

Their Friday morning movie and brunch became a habit. After a while, they began seeing live shows and concerts together at the casinos, and Bob came over for dinner from time to time. On two occasions they traveled to Las Vegas together, staying overnight, always in separate rooms.

From her perspective, Pree attributed the brother/sister aspect of their relationship to the fact that Bob was several years younger than she. She was a big sister to six younger brothers, and Bob was like a seventh brother. He never made a pass or came on to her, nor did she want him to. Except for saying he was divorced, he never discussed his previous relationships and Pree never asked about them. The companionship and protection he provided were enough.

CHAPTER 2

Laughlin, Nevada, 1997
(The morning after the killings)

"Good morning, Sweet Cheeks."

Pree's stomach gave an involuntary lurch.

"Clyde," she said with forced civility. She reminded herself that the idiot was Bob's nephew and that Bob actually seemed fond of him. Uninvited, Clyde hung his jacket on the chair over her beaded sweater, seated himself at the table, and called to Charlotte to bring him a cup of coffee.

Noting Clyde's jacket was dry, Pree asked, "Has it stopped raining?"

"Indeed it has, Sweet Cheeks," Clyde said, adding, "How about paying for my coffee? I'm broke."

Managing another smile, Pree said, "As a matter of fact, Clyde, I hit the progressive jackpot on a video poker machine this morning. Order anything you like. I'm buying."

"In that case, I apologize for every offensive remark I have ever made to you and for those I am destined to make in the future. Thank you, thank you, thank you. I am megahungry and megabroke, so how about a sandwich to take with me too for my lunch?"

Pree sighed. "Go ahead."

"Thanks. I'll try to behave. I'm way too hungry to screw this up." He called Charlotte over, kissed her hand, and stroked it until she poked the back of his hand with her pencil. As Charlotte left with his order, Clyde called after her, "Write your phone number on my check and maybe I'll give you a jingle sometime."

Charlotte flipped him off behind her back.

"She's crazy about me," he said, grinning and turning back to Pree.

"I can tell," Pree replied.

"By the way," Clyde said. "I think Uncle Bob may show up in a few minutes. Okay if he joins us?"

"Of course. That's why I'm here. I want to buy him breakfast and hear about his vacation," Pree replied. "Have you heard from him since he left?"

"No, but I know he's back. I spent my dinner break last night trying to contact him. Hence, my extreme hunger. Both his home and cell phones went to voice mail. Dispatch finally patched me through to Sergeant Ceja. He said Uncle Bob called in sick around nine fifteen, which is odd, because he hardly ever gets sick, and he never misses a shift, especially on New Years' Eve. It must be more than just jet lag. He rescheduled to go on duty at six o'clock this morning. I left him a message asking him to meet me here, so I hope he'll stop by at least. He's bringing me a present from my grandma. Money, I hope."

Pree returned to her paper, ignoring Clyde as he droned on about some kind of criminal justice classes he was taking at the community college, apparently assuming she would be interested in the minutia of his life.

"Don't believe anything this guy tells you, Pree," called a friendly voice, and Bob walked up to the table.

He kissed Pree's cheek, wished them a Happy New Year, and gave Clyde's shoulder a playful punch. He looked haggard.

"Welcome home," she smiled. "I heard you were ill. Are you okay?"

"I'm okay now," he insisted, patting his stomach. "Imodium is great stuff."

Pree said, "That's good, because I hit the progressive this morning so breakfast's on me. Anything your tummy can handle."

"I'm afraid I can't," Bob apologized as Charlotte walked up. "Duty calls. I have to get going."

He ordered two cups of take-out coffee.

To Clyde, Bob said, "I just stopped by to bring you this, from your grandmother." He handed Clyde a small, red velvet box.

"What is it?" Clyde asked.

"It's your grandfather's gold antique railroad watch," Bob answered. "Your grandmother wants you to have it."

"That's nice," Clyde said setting the box on the table. "Did she send me anything else?"

"No, just the watch," replied Bob.

Charlotte returned, handed Bob a paper bag and set a white take-out box next to Clyde's plate.

Bob reached for his pocket.

"Your money's no good today," said Pree. "It's on me."

Bob raised the bag in a gesture of thanks then said, "I really do have to run. We'll have dinner this evening, Clyde, and talk family."

Clyde asked, "The buffet here at Harrah's?"

"Works for me," said Bob. "I'll call you. But right now, I have to get out to the Cove."

"Cottonwood Cove?" Clyde asked, perking up. "What's going on?"

"Don't even think about it, Clyde!" said Bob sternly.

"But, Uncle Bob," pleaded Clyde. "I just finished my class on—"

Bob cut him off midsentence, and Pree saw signs of a temper she'd never seen before.

"Read my lips, Clyde! If I catch you within a mile of the Cove, I'll arrest you."

Clyde turned back to the table and glared silently at his plate.

Halfway to the exit, Bob spun around and hurried back.

"Pree, is your car here? Do you need a ride home?" he asked, all signs of anger now gone.

"I rode over with Crush and Lu last night, but I'm good," she insisted. "I'll catch the shuttle to the Riverside and take the boat across to the River Queen. Clyde said it's stopped raining. Run along and catch some criminals. I'll be fine."

"Don't be silly. Clyde will give you a ride. Right, Clyde?"

Clyde hesitated then nodded.

"No, no," Pree quickly insisted. "Clyde's tired and I'm sure he wants to get home."

Without raising his head, Clyde said quietly, "I insist."

Bob hovered, waiting for Pree's response, giving her no choice but to accept.

Clyde's silence continued after Bob left. Pree wasn't sure if his mood swing was from embarrassment at being chastised by his uncle, or disappointment at not getting the anticipated money from his grandmother. She would slip him a hundred when he let her off.

"Let's go," he said suddenly, grabbing his jacket off the chair. To Pree's surprise, he removed her sweater from the chair and helped her on with it.

"Listen, Clyde," she said, slipping into her sweater. "You run along. I can get home just fine. I can always call the sisters if need be. They'll be awake by now. And I promise not to tell Bob. Thanks, anyway."

"No, no" he said. "I insist. It's the least I can do. For the food."

She reluctantly surrendered to her fate.

"I'll pay the tab and meet you out front."

As Clyde hurried out the door, Pree laid a hundred-dollar bill on the table. She called "Happy New Year, Charlotte," gave the casino a cautionary once-over, and left the restaurant.

CHAPTER 3

Laughlin, Nevada, 1997
(The morning after the killings)

O utside, Pree stood behind a pillar to escape the wind, blowing on her hands to warm them. After two or three minutes, a very loud black motorcycle pulled under the overhang and stopped. She panicked when the rider pulled off his black acrylic spaceman helmet.

"Hop on!" Clyde shouted over the engine noise, holding his helmet out to her.

"Oh no!" she exclaimed in horror, hurrying back into the casino.

Clyde found her sitting on a stool near the door, pondering her next move.

"Look," he said. "I know a motorcycle ride in those fancy duds is a real bummer, especially in this weather, but we both know it's your best option right now."

He was right.

He added, "If you can just suck it up and hop on the back of my bike, you'll be home in ten minutes."

Pree surrendered, letting him strap the helmet under her chin, and followed him out the door.

The ride home was less dreadful than Pree had expected. The sun was peeking over the horizon, illuminating the entire valley as they rode down the hill, and the air had that after-rain freshness. When they crossed the bridge into Arizona, Pree noticed that the river was down as low as she had ever seen it. The ferryboats sat idle and she could make out the top of a rock sticking out of the water near the Edgewater Hotel.

At Pree's request, Clyde cruised the big rigs in the truck parking lot. She was disappointed not to see her son Jimmy's rig there, but it was too soon to start worrying. At last she saw the familiar words, "LAZY RIVER MOBILE HOME PARK" painted in large, bright-blue letters across the white stucco of a carport.

Home! More accurately, the place she was calling home for the time being.

Clyde shut off the engine and Pree prepared to dismount from the bike.

Clyde asked, "What are you doing?"

"I can walk from here," she said.

"Not if you ever want to wear those fancy shoes again," Clyde said, pointing to the cobblestone walkways inside the gate. He had a point.

"No problem," she said. "I'll just take them off and carry them."

"Why?" Clyde asked. "Those stones are wet and cold and slippery. Just stay on the bike and I'll take you to your door."

"And wake up my hung-over tenants?" Pree asked, again preparing to climb off the bike. "Not a chance!"

"Listen, Pree, I promise to take you to your door without waking a single tenant. Trust me."

Too weary to argue, Pree stayed on the bike as Clyde walked it forward until she could reach the keypad and punch in the code. When the gate opened wide enough for them to pass through, Clyde continued walking the bike down the stone walkway toward the front of the park.

Pree stopped him in front of a white stucco building with "WASHHOUSE" painted on it, also in bright-blue letters.

As soon as the bike stopped, Pree slipped off, her stocking-clad feet sank into the cold, wet grass. Clyde reached into the storage box on his bike and handed over her purse. She opened it and reached inside to extract the hundred dollars for Clyde.

"I'm sorry to do this, Pree," Clyde said. "But I need to ask you a favor."

Pree's chin fell to her chest.

"I'm really wiped out, Clyde," she said. "And cold, and I'm in desperate need of a bathroom, so please make it quick."

He held the velvet box out to her.

"I need you to keep this for me."

"Why don't you keep it yourself?"

Clyde hesitated and said, "I got kicked out of my apartment last week and I don't have a safe place to keep it."

Pree didn't want to know about this.

"How did you lose your apartment?" she asked, finding she really did care a little bit.

"Well, you probably know Uncle Bob got me that job as a security guard at the Colorado Belle, but for some reason, my boss there doesn't like me. Every morning when things slow down, he sends me home and lets others with less seniority stay. I'm lucky if I get in fifteen hours a week.

"A couple of months ago, I had to trade my car to a guy for this bike and a thousand bucks," he continued. "But now that's gone too. I tried crashing in my sleeping bag under the workbench in Uncle Bob's carport while he was on vacation, but the second night, I woke up and caught two guys in the carport. I yelled and they ran away, but I was too chicken to go after them, in case they had a gun or something. A guy from work is letting me sleep in his storage shed here in Bullhead City. He said I can keep my stuff in there too. For now, anyway. But I don't want to leave my grandfather's watch there."

"No, you can't," Pree reluctantly agreed, taking the watch and putting it into her purse. "I'll keep it for you for a while. Thanks for the ride, Clyde."

She again started to pull the hundred out of the envelope in her purse and send him on his way.

"I don't know why my boss doesn't like me," Clyde continued. "I'm the hardest worker he's got, and I do a better job than anyone else on my shift."

Would this nightmare never end?

"You know, Clyde," Pree interrupted. "We need to postpone this conversation until a better time. I really do need to pee."

"Okay," Clyde agreed. "But you can't tell Uncle Bob about any of this. Please. He'll tell my mom and I'll never hear the end of it. Or worse yet, he'll talk to my boss and I'll get fired."

Pree hated the idea of keeping a secret from Bob, but she did feel sorry for Clyde, and it was really none of her business. Reluctantly, she agreed not to tell then reached into her purse for a second hundred.

But still the ordeal didn't end.

"One more favor?" Clyde said. "I need to borrow ten dollars."

"No," said Pree.

"I really hate to ask," Clyde continued as if she hadn't spoken. "But I don't have enough gas to get back across the river tonight. I can pay you back Friday, and you said you won at the casino."

"You don't need to borrow money, Clyde," she said, pulling the two hundred-dollar bills out of her purse and handing them to him. "This is for you. For getting me home safely."

Stunned, Clyde spread the bills. "Three hundred dollars? I can't accept this, Pree."

Three hundred? Oh, crud!

"Sure you can," she insisted, sportingly. "Now get out of here. I'm tired, my feet are freezing, and my bladder is about to explode."

"I'll make this right with you, Pree, you'll see," he said, pocketing the money, pushing his bike down the walkway. Turning the corner, he looked back, smiled, and added, "Sweet Cheeks."

Idiot! Idiot! Idiot! Pree thought, pulling out her keys as she hurried around the washhouse and across the grass behind her trailer, desperate to make it to her bathroom before her bladder gave out. As she turned the final corner, she stopped short. An involuntary groan emitted from her throat. She stared in horror at the brown leather satchel sitting on the steps of her trailer. She began backing away slowly, heart pounding, eyes searching in all directions. Moving along the trailer wall, she felt the familiar knot form in her stomach and the trembling began.

Where to hide? Peeking around the edge of the trailer and seeing no one, she ran back around the washhouse and unlocked the door. Once inside, she fastened the dead bolt, leaned against the door, and took several deep breaths. *Safe! For now, anyway.*

It was several moments before she realized she was standing in twin puddles of her own pee!

CHAPTER 4

Bullhead City, Arizona, 1997
(The morning after the killings)

P ree stood over the floor drain in the center of the room and removed her soaked stockings and panties. Shivering, she used wet paper towels to clean herself then washed down the concrete floor, her thoughts on the satchel all the while. Greg's initials, GC, would be engraved on the strap. The normally tan leather of the satchel was brown, so she knew it was pretty wet. The rain had stopped over two hours earlier so the satchel had to have been sitting there for some time, and whoever left it was probably gone by now.

Sloshing her unmentionables around in the sudsy water, Pree's tired brain was besieged with questions. *Who left the satchel? Why? What was in it? Had Greg finally found her?*

As usual, she evaded the big question, which was, *How had she come to be hiding in fear for her life in a trailer park in Bullhead City, Arizona?*

It had started six years earlier, when she and her network of friends from her office, "The Lovelies," Pat Nestor had named them, had gathered at the restaurant at the Bicycle Club in Bell Gardens, California, to celebrate Barbara McCaughin's dreaded fortieth birthday. It was an evening filled with abandon and hysterical laughter, the kind that only occurs when close friends and good wine come together.

After the others left, Pree and Peggy Tamaki stayed on for a free poker lesson offered by the casino. After the lesson, they agreed to return the next morning to try their luck.

When a family emergency forced Peggy to cancel, Pree decided to give it a try anyway. Her twenty dollars lasted for over an hour, and she actually won several pots. When her money was gone, she headed for the restaurant where she sat at the empty counter and ordered breakfast and a Diet Pepsi.

"You been playing?" Alita Smith, the server, asked as she set the juice and Diet Pepsi in front of Pree.

"Yes," said Pree. "My first time."

"How'd you do?" Alita asked.

"I lost twenty dollars. Do you play?"

"No," Alita replied. "But my husband, Brian, plays enough for both of us."

"Is he good?" asked Pree.

"To hear him tell it, he is. But let's just say if he ever lost just twenty dollars, I'd consider him a winner."

"What does he play?"

"That new game, Texas Hold'em. I'll swear the devil himself invented that game to show us what hell will be like."

Chuckling at her little joke, Alita raised her eyes and smiled over Pree's shoulder.

"Good morning, Greg," she said to the man who seated himself two stools away from Pree. "The usual?"

"Thanks," he nodded. "I see Brian has a pretty good stack of chips in front of him at the Hold'em table."

"Hallelujah!" Alita exclaimed as she left to place the man's order on a metal wheel. "I hope he can hang on to them for a change."

The man turned to Pree and asked, "Do you play Hold'em?"

"Oh dear, no!" replied Pree. "I just played draw poker for the first time this morning. Are you a Hold'em player?"

"No. Lowball is bad enough. He plays Hold'em, though, but he hardly ever wins."

"He?" Pree asked.

"Mape," replied the man. "Maple Belata, my friend. He's a deputy sheriff here in LA County."

While Alita put her breakfast on the counter, Pree stole a quick look at the guy. Late fifties or early sixties, neither tall nor short, skinny nor fat, not homely, not overly handsome. He had a pleasant look about him, but was wearing enough gold and diamonds to open a jewelry store, which she found a bit tacky. The jewelry obviously wasn't fake, so Pree pegged him as a jeweler or a gangster.

Seeing Pree looking at him, the man moved to the seat next to hers and explained, "I like jewelry."

"So I see," she replied.

The man said, "My name is Greg. Greg Crenski."

"I'm Pree Olindo. Pleased to meet you."

Alita set Greg's scrambled eggs and bacon in front of him and walked away to serve other customers who had come in.

"Are you going to play some more?" Greg asked as they ate.

"No," Pree said. "Twenty dollars was my limit. And I don't want to miss my Saturday afternoon movie."

"Oh," said Greg. "You like movies?"

"I do," Pree replied.

Greg said, "When I was a kid, I lived downtown, and I went to the movies every Saturday afternoon. For ten cents you could see two pitchers, a newsreel, a serial, two cartoons and a sing-along. Sometimes it took five hours. A kid named Liberace used to play the piano at intermission. You know what became of him."

Pree was finding that talking to this somewhat odd man was surprisingly pleasant when a voice on the loud speaker announced, "GC, return to your table."

Greg jumped up and said, "Gotta go! Listen, this was fun. Do you suppose I could call you and we could get together sometime and talk some more?"

"It was fun," Pree agreed. "But I don't give my phone number to strangers. Sorry."

Greg picked up his check and reached for hers.

"Don't even think about it," she said, putting a hand out to stop him. "I'll pay for my own breakfast. Thanks anyway."

"If you insist," he shrugged. "Enjoy your movie."

"Good luck!" she called after him as he scurried away.

That was different, Pree thought. As she turned back to the counter to finish her Diet Pepsi and toast, Greg reappeared.

"I really would like to see you again," he said awkwardly. "If I ask you politely, will you please meet me here at seven o'clock tonight and have dinner with me? I promise to be a gentleman, and you can pay for your own dinner if you want to, although it would be my pleasure to treat. I apologize for rushin' you, but I really have to go."

Amused by his shyness and his little performance, Pree agreed and watched as he hurried out of the restaurant.

He is kind of sweet, she thought. *And he certainly seems harmless enough.*

At dinner that night, Pree continued to enjoy Greg's stories, especially those about Los Angeles in more innocent times. She started seeing him almost every weekend. The more she saw of him, the less strange he seemed to her. He was kind and generous, but seemed to be a bit of a loner. His two sisters, Gladys and Pearl, were deceased and he hadn't seen his brother for decades. His only close friend seemed to be the guy named Mape.

About three months into their relationship, they had lunch in Chinatown, after which Greg took Pree on a tour of the Los Angeles of his youth. After dinner, they went to the Bicycle Club for a little poker. It was a fun day and had ended with a kiss.

Three weekends, later they went to Palm Springs together and had a great time. Pree admired the beautiful tan leather satchel Greg had bought for the trip. He'd had his initials engraved into a leather strap that fastened over the top of the satchel.

*   *   *

Leaving the laundry room, Pree proceeded cautiously across the grass to her trailer. Hearing no ticking or other threatening sounds, she decided it was safe to enter.

The satchel blocked the stoop, so she stood at the side of the steps, reached up, unlocked, and opened the door. A peek at the alarm pad told her no one had entered the trailer in her absence, so she set her shoes, purse, and a plastic grocery bag containing her wet laundry on the floor inside. Hiking up her skirt, she grabbed the doorknob and lifted her left leg until her bare foot was planted on the stoop.

All the while cursing the thirty pounds she'd gained since leaving Los Angeles, it took Pree three attempts to pull herself up onto the stoop. Inside, she locked the door, reset the alarm, and hurried to the bathroom to shower.

By the time she was snug in her pajamas and robe, Pree's body was limp with fatigue. She would open the satchel after Jimmy arrived then decide if she needed to report it to the police. She poured herself a glass of water and undid the chain on the front door so Jimmy would be able to get in. She sat on the sofa glancing at the newspaper headlines, but her thoughts kept returning to the satchel. She still had no idea why it was left there, or by whom. For reasons she couldn't explain, tears ran down her cheeks onto her terrycloth robe.

CHAPTER 5

Bullhead City, Arizona, 1997
(The morning after the killings)

Oh, crud! Pree swatted wildly at the alarm clock with her open hand. Finally cracking one eyelid, she discovered she was still on her brown leather sofa. Her head weighed a ton. Only when the recorder picked up did she realize the ringing was the phone.

"Pree?" asked the voice on the line. "Please pick up if you're there. It's important."

Bob?

Groaning, Pree dragged herself off the sofa and trudged to the kitchen.

"Bob?" she asked into the receiver. Her voice sounded like it was passing through a sack of gravel.

"Pree, I know you haven't had much sleep, but I need to speak with you right away. It's important."

She tried to clear her throat.

"Okay," she replied. "Talk."

"Not on the phone, Pree. I need to talk to you in person, as soon as possible."

Suppressing a groan, Pree said, "All right, come on over."

She suddenly remembered the satchel and realized it probably had something to do with what Bob wanted to talk to her about.

"Would you mind coming to the station?" Bob asked.

"Of course not," Pree said, a knot forming in the pit of her stomach. It had to be about Greg.

"Great," Bob replied. "How soon can you be here?"

"Thirty or forty minutes?"

"Thanks, Pree," Bob said, breaking the connection. A chill shook her body.

The stove clock said a few minutes after ten. She'd had less than three hours of sleep. She swallowed two aspirin, brushed the yuck from her teeth, gargled, and splashed cold water on her face. She pulled on her fat jeans and was putting on her yellow "I (heart) New York" sweatshirt when she remembered that the satchel was sitting unprotected on the steps. She opened the door and leaned down to pick it up, but it wouldn't budge.

With a great deal of effort and adrenaline, she managed to work the satchel into the trailer and hoisted it onto her desk chair, rolled it down the hall to a corner of her bedroom, and threw a blanket over it. Whoever had carried the satchel from the street to her trailer had to be as strong as an ox. Relieved, she realized that Greg's bad back wouldn't have allowed him to carry it. Curious but still reluctant to open it until Jimmy arrived, she made a mental note to tell Bob about it.

Returning to the bathroom, she slapped on a rudimentary makeup job. The last piece of her ensemble was a tacky yellow ruffled turban that she kept around for bad hair days. Today was the mother of bad hair days.

*   *   *

Pree gave her usual two warning knocks and pushed open the door to Louie's trailer.

"Good morning, Dora," Pree said as she patted the silky-soft hair of the beautiful Bernese mountain dog. She went to the kitchen sink and squeezed a drop of dish soap onto her hands. Pree had two obsessions: Diet Pepsi and clean hands, not necessarily in that order. "Sorry to keep you waiting, Louie. I got in late last night."

"I think you mean this morning," Louie teased.

"For a blind man, you don't miss much, Louie," Pree teased back.

"You'd be amazed at what you can see with a little peripheral vision and a good set of ears," he laughed.

Louie was sitting in the beautiful oak rocker his father had made, listening to Louie Armstrong sing "What a Wonderful World" on the stereo. He asked, "How was the show?"

Pree poured Dora's dog food, squeezed a dropper of arthritis medicine into it, rinsed and filled the water dish, and replied, "Very funny. They had all new material. Tommy Smothers still does a great "Yo-Yo Man," and I won $3,300 on a progressive video poker machine. Lunch is on me after your doctor's appointment next week. What time did you get home?"

"Around two, I think. The sisters and Barry wanted to play the slots for a while, so I sat in the lounge. They had a great band. Forties music. People were dancing."

"I need to go across the river for a little while. Will you settle for soup and a sandwich for lunch today?"

"Nothing, thanks. You know what a feed Lu puts on at the Rose Bowl party, so don't worry about my dinner tonight, either. I'll just pig out at the party."

"Oh dear," said Pree. "I forgot all about the party. Jimmy's not here yet, but I know he won't miss the party or the game. Do you want him to come by for you?"

"No, thanks. Barry's going to walk me over."

Barry Pensis lived in number fourteen. Pree didn't know him very well. Except for the sisters and Louie, he didn't mingle with the other tenants much. Louie once told her that Barry and Sal, Louie's dad, had been good friends for many years. Evenings would often find Louie, Barry, and Dora out on the dock, fishing and talking. Jo Burnett, one of the sisters in number 24, would join them when she was in town.

"Can I get you anything else?"

"I'm fine. Run along. Louie will entertain me until Barry gets here."

"Okay, thanks. Tell Lu I'll see her tomorrow at the parade party."

Pree ran home to grab her jacket and shoulder bag and hurried to the carport.

CHAPTER 6

Laughlin, Nevada, 1997
(The morning after the killings)

When Pree spotted the teal-green cab of Jimmy's rig, as she drove past the truck parking lot, she wondered why he hadn't come home. *He must have slept in his truck. Odd.*

The sun was shining, but the river was still too low for boating and waterskiing. As she crossed the bridge near the recently opened tower of the Riverside Hotel and Casino, Pree remembered Louie telling her that the bridge was relatively new. Before that, people drove all the way to Davis Dam to cross over. Pree never tired of Louie's stories of his early days in Bullhead City and Laughlin. He and his family had arrived in Bullhead City thirty years before, when the Riverside was a motel and bar owned by Don and Betty Laughlin, with a small restaurant and a few games. Louie told her steamships had sailed on the river in the 1800s when Bullhead Rock, a large rock resembling, as one would suppose, a bull's head had been a landmark for the steamship captains. Most of Bullhead Rock now lay under the waters of Lake Mohave.

Pree saw Bob's pickup and Lieutenant Keebler's red Cherokee in the station lot, but didn't recognize the blue Dodge Caravan she parked next to in the visitor parking area. She noticed in horror that someone had scratched the letters *F* and *U*, about six inches high, into the white paint of Bob's truck. He would be livid! He doted on that truck. She remembered Clyde had chased two people from Bob's carport while he was away and immediately regretted her promise to Clyde. It was, indeed, a tangled web.

Pree spun around when she heard a child's voice call out, "Auntie Pree!"

A small boy came running across the parking lot with Annette Kitagawa, Lieutenant Keebler's wife, running behind him, yelling for him to stop.

She recognized the boy as Jo Jo Belata, Mape and Laria's youngest child. He ran into her hard, grabbed her around the waist, and hugged her.

"Jo Jo?" Pree asked. "Good heavens! You're so big."

"I'm six now," he said proudly, smiling up at her. "I go to school."

"I'm sorry," Annette apologized when she reached them. She looked at the boy. "Young man, you must never run into a parking lot like that again. You could have been killed."

Then suddenly two girls appeared and they too began hugging Pree.

"Nicole? Danelle?" Pree asked, grabbing them both. "Goodness, you're growing into beautiful young women."

The girls smiled.

Reluctantly, Pree asked, "What are you kids doing here, anyway?"

"Something happened to our dad," Jo Jo said solemnly.

"I think it's something bad," added Dani.

"Really bad," said Coley. "And to Uncle Greg too."

Pree took a deep breath.

"Where's your mother?" she asked.

"We should go into the station and talk about this," said Annette, sending an eye signal to Pree. "Mrs. Belata is inside."

Pree helped Annette settle the children in the training room, where they had apparently been coloring when Jo Jo had spotted Pree through the window.

"May will be here soon with the twins and some videos," Annette told Pree as the women returned to the lobby. "I'll let Mike and Bob know you're here."

Pree had met Mike Keebler and Annette Kitagawa through Bob. The four of them had gone to dinner a few times. Once, Pree had been invited to the Keebler home for some of Annette's excellent Japanese cooking. On that visit, she had been enchanted by their delightful granddaughters Jeanette and Lynette, identical twins.

Mike and Annette had been married for thirty years, and both had been working for the Las Vegas Metro Police Department for two years longer than that. Five years before, when Mike had been put in charge of the Laughlin substation, Annette took a voluntary demotion to a dispatcher position so she could be reassigned as well. Last year, when their son-in-law Ted Lewis, a DEA agent, had been killed in the line of duty, Mike and Annette had insisted that their daughter May and her eight-year-old twins move in with them while they tried to recover from the tragedy. May was now employed part-time in the produce department at the Safeway in Bullhead City. She and the twins still lived in the family home.

"Pree, it's good of you to come," said Mike, walking up to her and giving her a quick handshake. "Would you mind joining us in here so we can get things started?"

He guided Pree through the open door of a room marked INTERVIEW. As she entered, a somber-faced Bob stood from his seat at a large, gray, Formica table.

"I'm really sorry to call you in like this, Pree," Bob apologized. "But something has happened, and it concerns you."

Pree was looking past Bob at the thin woman in jeans and a lavender sweatshirt seated at the table, her head in her hands. Had she not seen the children, Pree doubted she would have recognized her. Laria Belata's blonde waist-length hair had been cut into a stylish bob, now totally askew, and her face was red, swollen, and tearstained.

"Pree!" she cried, looking up. "Thank you for coming."

Pree looked across the table at Bob and Mike and asked, "What's going on?"

Whatever it was, she was sure it was somehow related to the satchel.

"Why don't the detective and I step out for a few minutes and let you two talk," said Mike.

The men left. Pree sat next to Laria and faced her.

"I saw the kids outside," Pree said. "I'd forgotten how much kids can grow in a year and a half. How are they taking the divorce and everything?"

"Okay," said Laria. "We're living with my mother. She's been alone in that big house since my dad died, and she's there when the kids get home from school." Laria broke into tears again. "Oh, Pree, I'm so sorry," she sobbed.

"For what?" Pree asked.

"For not testifying for you in court. I got the letter from your attorney, but Greg was our friend long before I met you, and he's always been so good to us that I just couldn't do anything that might hurt him. I'm so sorry," she repeated.

Pree leaned over and put her hands on Laria's shoulders.

"It's okay," comforted Pree. "I knew that. Actually, I didn't want you to testify against Greg. I wanted to tell you about something Greg pulled on me that I thought Mape might have pulled on you as well. But that can wait. Tell me why you're here in Laughlin, and why we're here at the police station. The kids said something bad has happened to Mape and Greg?"

"Oh, dear Lord!" exclaimed Laria. "You don't know? Mape and Greg are dead! They were shot last night."

Laria burst into tears again, and Pree too became misty-eyed.

"I went to Greg's cabin in Cottonwood Cove this morning to pick up the kids," Laria said between sobs. "That's when I found the bodies. It was horrible! I think they suspected me of killing them, Pree. They read me my rights and fingerprinted me and checked me for gunshot residue."

Laria began sobbing again, and Pree noticed a baby carrier on the chair behind her. It was covered with a pink blanket, and the blanket was moving.

"What's that?" she asked.

Laria let go of Pree's hand, looked behind her and smiled; her swollen, blotchy face making it look more like a grimace.

"That's Lauryn. My daughter. She's seven weeks old. Can you believe I'm pushing forty and a baby carriage at the same time?"

"I didn't even know you had remarried," said Pree. "Congratulations!"

Laria's shrug told Pree that she hadn't.

The men came back into the room. Bob set a Diet Pepsi in front of Pree and a bottle of water in front of Laria.

"Extra ice, the way you like it," he said to Pree.

Just then, the bundle in the chair moved and made a kind of squeaking sound.

"Oh, dear," said Laria. "I'll have to change my baby and feed her. I'm sorry."

"We'll wait," said Mike with forced patience. "I'll walk you to the ladies' room."

After they had gone, Bob asked Pree, "Did she tell you?"

Pree nodded.

"I didn't think it was the kind of thing I should tell you over the phone," he said.

Pree agreed. "What I don't understand is why you're interrogating Laria. I can assure you that woman didn't kill anyone. Not the father of her children and certainly not Greg. She adores Greg. As if she's not traumatized enough, you haul her in here and scare her to death by reading her her rights and fingerprinting her and checking her for gunshot residue!" Pree had to fight back her anger. "And why am I here? I have thirty people who can vouch for where I was last night."

"Calm down, Pree," Bob said quietly. "It's routine procedure. Mrs. Belata discovered the bodies which, at the very least, makes her a material witness, and she distorted the evidence which she has yet to explain. If she's innocent, fingerprinting her can help exclude her. However, she did contaminate the crime scene. And the fact that she was at the murder scene and is in the process of divorcing one of the victims certainly gives her opportunity and motive. So yes, she is our prime suspect at this time, but if she's innocent, we will be able to rule her out. I'm sorry we upset her, but she is critical to our investigation. You're here because when we asked her if she wanted an attorney, she asked to have you here instead. It's a bit irregular, but we decided to allow it, as a courtesy. Now, are you okay with that?"

"Yes. I'm sorry for getting upset, but this is a lot to take in."

"I know it is," Bob agreed as Laria and Mike walked back into the room.

Picking up the baby, Laria slid into her chair, laid the baby across her lap, grabbed two of the corners of the pink blanket and tied it around her neck like a bib. She reached under the blanket and performed a couple of maneuvers then there was a little suction sound as the baby began nursing.

"All right," she said. "I guess I'm ready to begin."

CHAPTER 7

Laughlin, Nevada, 1997
(The morning after the killings)

Lieutenant Keebler performed the necessary formalities for recording the session.

"Mrs. Belata," Mike started, after Laria stated her name and address. "You are, at the very least, a person of interest and a material witness in a double homicide. You are to answer our questions fully and truthfully. Do you understand?"

"Yes," replied Laria.

Mike nodded to Bob, who began the interrogation. "Why don't you start by telling us how you happened to be at the crime scene this morning?"

Laria nodded.

"Mape, my husband, whom I am—was—in the process of divorcing, had custody of our three children from Christmas Day until New Year's Day. Yesterday, New Year's Eve, he called and told me he couldn't bring the children home and that I could pick them up this morning at the home of Greg Crenski, our friend. Later, he called back and left directions for getting to Greg's home in Cottonwood Cove. He said it would be an eight- to nine-hour drive, and I knew I wouldn't be able to drive all night, pick up the children, then drive all the way back home with them, so I packed a few things and prepared to spend the night. I left my home in Pasadena, California, around three o'clock yesterday afternoon.

"I stopped for a burger and a Coke at McDonalds in Barstow, changed the baby, and started out again, toward Needles. By ten o'clock in the evening, it was raining pretty hard so I pulled into a rest stop and once again, changed and fed the baby. I tilted the seat back and closed my eyes while she nursed. The next thing I knew, horns were honking, music was playing, and I heard shouting and laughing. I woke up and realized that it was midnight and 1997 was here. I had been asleep for nearly two hours. The rain had stopped and I took Lauryn into the restroom where I used the facility. People had gotten out of their cars and were dancing and celebrating. I put the baby back into her car seat and left."

Annette knocked on the door and told Mike that Las Vegas Metro was on the phone and it sounded important. Mike left the room, but he told Laria to continue.

"Okay. I drove a few more miles until I came to the Las Vegas turnoff, US-95, where Mape had told me to turn and go to Searchlight, Nevada. I planned to get a room in Searchlight, but after a while I came to an area called Cal-Nev-Ari, and I stopped to fill my gas tank at an all-night station. There was a small motel near the gas station. The Tri-State, it was called. The vacancy sign was lit. I was worried that the motels in Searchlight, if there were any, might be full on New Year's Eve, and I was relieved to find a motel with a vacancy so I decided to stay there. It was close to 1:00 a.m. when I got to the room, and I requested a 4:30 a.m. wake-up call so I could pick the kids up early the next morning and get back home. I fed and changed Lauryn, showered, went to bed, and fell asleep right away."

Mike reentered the room and motioned for her to continue.

"I woke up for Lauryn's 3:00 a.m. feeding, but was asleep again when I got the wake-up call from the office. As you know, Detective Kips, I paid for the gas and the room with a credit card, and I have given you the receipts. All of this can be verified."

Mike assured her it would be.

They waited quietly as Laria put herself back together and placed the baby back into the carrier, making soothing little mothering sounds. She took a sip of water then continued.

"The road was wet and pretty deserted, especially after I turned off the highway at the Nugget Casino in Searchlight. It was still dark, and I had trouble finding the house. It's a small cabin, really, and it sits back quite a distance from the road in a stand of huge trees which makes it hard to see. I passed it and had to turn around by the lake. Mape had said there was an old three-story house across the street from the place, which I found. I didn't drive up to the cabin because there's a lot of unpaved land between it and the road, and I was afraid my car would get stuck in the mud. There were a few vehicles scattered along both sides of the road and there was loud music coming from the big house, so I figured there had been a party there and that the vehicles belonged to the remaining guests.

"Anyway, I parked in the street directly across from Greg's cabin. I wrapped Lauryn in a blanket and put her inside my jacket and zipped it over her. The rain had stopped, but it was freezing cold. The wind was blowing hard and it felt like it might snow, although I don't know if it snows here in the desert or not. As I walked toward the cabin, the mud came up over the top of my sneakers.

"Approaching the cabin, I could make out Mape's hatchback parked near one of the big trees. I walked along the enclosed porch to the steps then onto the porch. The door was propped open with a big rock. There was luggage sitting just inside the doorway, like someone was getting ready to leave on a trip. The bags looked very wet. There was a lamp on in the living room, but it was dim, and I couldn't see much."

Laria stopped for another sip of water. She looked over at Pree, who saw that there were beads of sweat on Laria's forehead, and tears on her cheeks. Sensing that the hardest part was coming up, Pree reached over and took the younger woman's hand again. Laria's voice quivered as she continued.

"I walked into the house, through the living room, and to the edge of the dining area which was all one room." Laria stopped, caught her breath, let out a small groan, and then turned in her chair to speak directly to Pree. "It was so bizarre. The dining room table and chairs had been pushed against the back wall and a large tarp had been spread on the floor. I recognized it as the tarp that Mape uses sometimes to cover stuff on the luggage rack. You remember?"

Pree gave her a nod. Laria became tense as she started speaking again, halting between sentences.

"Mape was on his back, with his head near the edge of the tarp, and his feet toward the center. Greg was on his back too. Their eyes were open, like they were staring at the ceiling, and the cabin smelled really bad. There was a gun on the tarp, to the left of the bodies. Greg was still wearing his jewelry, so it didn't appear to be a robbery. But the most bizarre thing was that Greg was lying on top of Mape! As if someone had stacked their bodies! All I could see of Mape were his face and hands. There was a hole in the left side of Greg's head, and blood. There was blood all over the tarp."

With that, Laria reached her breaking point. She put her head down and began sobbing again.

Pree asked, "Could we take a short break so she can pull herself together?"

"I need to update Bob on some things, anyway," said Mike. "Let's take a few minutes."

Pree picked up their handbags and the baby carrier and steered Laria out the door, down the hall, and into the ladies' room. Movie sounds emanated from the darkened training room. The blinds had been closed. Inside the restroom, Laria quickly wiped the tears from her face and whispered, "Pree, I need to ask you to do something for me. It's a big favor, and I wouldn't ask if it wasn't important."

Pree set the baby carrier on the counter, "What is it?"

"There's a shoebox, on the passenger floor of my car, with a thick rubber band around it. I need you to go out and move it to your car without being seen. I'll explain later, but you need to do it now." She removed her keys from her purse and handed them to Pree. "It doesn't have anything to do with the killings, I promise." Laria assured her.

Pree left the building and hurried over to the blue van. Despite Laria's assurance, her heart was pounding as she pushed the button on the unfamiliar key ring and heard the doors unlock. She knew she shouldn't be doing this, but Laria was her friend. In case there were security cameras, she covered the box with a navy-blue windbreaker that lay on the passenger seat and hurried over to her own car. She set the box in the trunk, removed the windbreaker, grabbed the sweater she kept in the trunk for emergencies, slammed the lid down, and hurried back into the building.

Pree found Laria standing outside the training room, peeking in at May and the children, who were absorbed in the movie. Pree returned Laria's keys and covered her shoulders with the windbreaker. She tied the sleeves of her own sweater around her neck as they returned to the conference room.

As Laria positioned the baby carrier on the chair again Pree said, "I hope you don't mind, but I noticed Laila shivering earlier, so I fetched her jacket and my sweater."

"That's fine," said Mike. "It is a little cold in here. Now, where did we leave off? Do you need me to play back the last part?"

"No," said Laria, taking Pree's hand again. "After I found the bodies, I used the wall phone in the cabin to call 911. The operator told me to go outside immediately and stay there until the police arrived. She told me not to touch anything. I hung up the phone and went out onto the porch. Despite what the operator had said, I had to go back into the cabin to get my children out. I couldn't let them wake up and find their father and Greg like that.

"I walked around behind the cabin, but the back door was locked and wouldn't budge. Finally, I did the only thing I felt I could do under the circumstances. I knew at the time I would probably get into trouble for it, but I couldn't let my children see the bodies. I went back into the cabin and laid the baby on the sofa. Then I placed the gun next to Mape and began folding the tarp over the bodies. Since they were lying in one corner of the tarp, I was able to wrap them in it. The tarp is waterproof, so there wasn't any blood on the floor and only a little on the wall. I went to the bedroom to get my kids, but they weren't there or anywhere else in the house. I was nearly hysterical by then. I carried the baby back out to the porch to get away from the bodies and the smell.

"Since there was no place on the porch to sit, I trudged over to Mape's car, hoping to find something that would tell me where my children were. I still have a set of keys, so I searched through the car, but found only one of Joey's T-shirts. I went back to my van and sat on the edge of driver's seat with my muddy feet on the pavement. The rain had stopped and the sun had come up by then. I was so afraid that whoever killed Mape and Greg might have taken my children that I started to cry, but that woke up Lauryn, so I tried to calm myself. I changed her and had just finished feeding her when Officer Ceja drove up and parked behind me," she said.

Laria blew her nose, wiped her eyes, and continued with her statement.

"I told Officer Ceja what had happened, and he told me to stay in the car. I asked him if he would put out an APB on my children and he agreed to do so. I'm sure he could tell I was frantic. I was watching him go into the cabin when you drove up."

Mike interrupted to say, "Let the record show that Mrs. Belata was referring to Detective Kips in the last part of her statement."

"Sorry," Laria apologized. "You, meaning Detective Kips again, began walking toward the cabin when a beat-up red pickup truck came barreling toward me, crossed the road, and squealed to a stop directly in front of my van, almost touching bumpers with me. Still holding Lauryn, I got out of my car and stood in the street, using the open door as a shield. To my delight, my kids climbed out of the pickup and ran to me. I was thrilled! Then a large, hairy, young man got out of the driver's side of the pickup and walked toward me. He was carrying a baseball bat and looked menacing, so I told the kids to get into the van. An older woman got out of the passenger side of the pickup. They walked up to me together, and the woman asked me if the kids were mine, and I said they were. The man asked if I knew where they could find a rotten slime bag named 'Mape'. Then you, Detective Kips, walked up, showed him your badge, and asked him why he wanted to know."

It was obvious to Pree that this part of her statement was much easier for Laria than the previous one had been.

"The woman said that Mape was supposed to have picked up her daughter, Mirabelle I think her name was, before midnight. They were going to take the kids to Mexico and get married and live down there. She said Mape was supposed to come into a lot of money yesterday, so they wouldn't have to work. According to the mother, at about one o'clock this morning Mirabelle's ex called to wish her a Happy New Year and asked her to meet him at a bar where he hangs out, and she was so mad at Mape for standing her up that she went and left my kids with her, the mother.

"Again, according to the mother, Mirabelle called and woke her up at a little after four o'clock this morning to say she was going to stay with the ex. She told her mother to call Bubba, apparently meaning the young man, and have him bring her and the kids over here to the cabin, and leave them with Mape's friend. I assumed she meant Greg.

"I settled the kids in the van, and I saw you take the people aside, give them a card, and write something in your notebook. Bubba set my kids' suitcase and backpacks in the road, and they left. We moved the children's things into the back of the wagon and waited for the crime scene people, who arrived about half an hour later. You talked to them and Officer Ceja for a while then asked me to follow you here, which I did."

"Thank you for your thoroughness," Mike said. "We'll have your statement typed up tomorrow and call you to come in to read and sign it."

The lieutenant continued, "The call I received earlier was from the medical examiner's office in Las Vegas. The gun used to shoot the men is registered to Mr. Crenski. Due to the plastic coating on the tarp, all the blood and tissue pooled up and ran together when you covered the bodies, soaking the gun and spent cartridges. The evidence is severely scrambled and the forensics people are extremely upset about it. Although the evidence seems to suggest murder-suicide, they can't tell for certain due to the state of the crime scene. It will be a few days before they know how much damage you've actually done after which, we'll know what charges, if any, will be brought against you. You are free to go at this time, but you are not to leave the area until we get things sorted out. Do you understand?"

"Yes, sir, I do," Laria assured him. "I'll need to stay here to make arrangements for Mape anyway since technically we're... we were...

still married. I'm on maternity leave from my job. I'll try to get a room at one of the local hotels tonight, but I won't be able to live in a hotel room for long with four children. Are there any weekly rentals in town?"

"Yes, in Bullhead City, but they're full of transients," said Bob. "You probably wouldn't want to take your children to one of them."

He hesitatated then, standing, said, "Wait here. I may have a solution."

Bob left the room and Mike told Laria. "I should let you know that the Las Vegas lab has tentatively estimated the time of death to be between 9:00 p.m. and 4:00 a.m. The door was left open, making the inside of the cabin very damp and bringing the temperature down to nearly freezing which makes the exact time of death difficult to estimate."

Bob returned and announced, "Good news. A condo unit in my building rents to tourists on a week by week basis. There are two bedrooms, a fully-equipped kitchen, and a thirty-five-inch television with cable and a VCR. It rents for a hundred dollars a day, or $550 for a seven-day week, plus a fifty-dollar cleaning fee. I play golf with Martin Jeffers, one of the owners of Hanson Jeffers Property Management, Inc., who manages the property. Jane Hanson, the other owner, owes me a few favors, since I keep an eye on the place for them, and keep an extra key in case the tenants lock themselves out. Anyway, the last tenants left this morning and I still have the keys. I just called Jane and explained your situation to her, and she said that the unit is available for the next three weeks. The cleaning people won't be in until tomorrow, so you might want to stay at a hotel tonight then rent the condo for the next week, after it's cleaned. Or you can clean it yourself, save fifty bucks and move in right away. I think there are extra sheets and towels there, and I know there's a washer and dryer."

"It sounds perfect," said Laria. "And I certainly don't mind cleaning it. I'll take it for a week, at least."

"I'll come and help you get settled," offered Pree. "Jimmy will be at a Rose Bowl party all afternoon."

"I'll go confirm with Jane," Bob said, leaving the room again.

Both women stood up and prepared to leave.

"I'm afraid we're not finished yet," said the lieutenant. "Sorry. Please sit back down."

The women looked at each other and took their seats again.

"We'll wait until Detective Kips returns."

Both women nodded.

Bob returned and said, "It's all set. You can just give me a check for $550 made out to Hanson-Jeffers Property Management, Inc. Jane will come by and pick it up tomorrow."

Laria nodded, and reached for her handbag.

"We need to conclude our last item of business," Mike reminded hlim.

"Oh yes," Bob agreed.

"We must ask you, Mrs. Belata, to stay in the building for a while longer," said the lieutenant. "And we'll need permission to search your car."

Laria agreed and handed over her keys.

CHAPTER 8

Laughlin, Nevada, 1997
(The day after the killings)

While the men searched Laria's car, Pree asked, "Do you really think Greg would shoot Mape? His idol?"

"I don't know what to think, Pree," the younger woman replied. "All I can think about right now is how thankful I am that Mape wasn't able to take my kids to Mexico."

They sat wordlessly for a few minutes, both women aware the room could be bugged. Finally, Pree broke the silence.

"So you've gone back to work?"

"Yes. I'm doing paralegal work again. I worked for a year for a private practice attorney. He was going through a divorce at the time and was miserable like Mape was when I first met him. Of course, I felt sorry for him and gave him a shoulder to cry on and, also like with Mape, we got involved. I guess I just wasn't meant to fool around. I've slept with two men in my entire life, and gotten pregnant by both of them. This time, I was taking the pill faithfully. Another baby was the last thing I needed. When I told him, he wished me luck and said he didn't want another kid, fired me, went back to his wife, and that was that."

Laria took a deep breath.

"I made an appointment for an abortion, but couldn't go through with it. Fortunately, my former law firm had been after me to come back to work for them, and I took them up on their offer. I told them up front that I was pregnant, but they hired me back anyway. Right now, I'm on a three-month maternity leave. Unpaid, of course."

"Does the father help you financially? For the baby, I mean."

"No. We haven't spoken since the day I left. He sent my severance check without so much as a note and he's made no effort to see Lauryn. I hope he never will. I gave her my maiden name, Grey."

Laria pulled back the pink blanket to peek at the baby and smiled.

"How about you? Are you working?" she asked.

"Sort of," replied Pree. "Last year, I was visiting some friends, Val and Freddie Zwirn. I worked with Valerie in Los Angeles. Freddie likes to play the horses. They used to visit us when we lived up at the house, and ended up buying a double-wide in the Lazy River Mobile Home Park for a vacation home here. One evening last April while I was visiting, Val and I sat on the dock talking with Marietta and Jo, two sisters who live in the park, and Louie, the owner. Val mentioned that I was looking for a place to live. 'To hide out, really,' I told them, 'during a messy divorce.' Laria, I know Greg was your friend, but he had changed a lot, and by that time, the Bullhead City Police had advised me to move out of the house for my own safety. To everyone's amazement, Louie pointed to an empty trailer and asked me if I would like to live in it. The park is gated, and he said, I could use one of the carports with a door to keep my car out of sight. The trailer has a river view and sits pretty far from the road. I asked him how much, and he said a thousand dollars a month. I thought that was pretty steep, but I was desperate for a safe place to stay, so I accepted on the spot. Then he surprised us all by asking if I could move in the next day, and said he would write me a check immediately to cover the first month. When I asked him if he was offering me money to live in his trailer, he explained he was offering me a safe place to live, plus utilities, and a thousand dollars a month to manage the trailer park and take care of him.

"He explained that he was going blind. Macular degeneration, he called it. He said that in a matter of months he would be totally blind, except for a little peripheral vision. He would still be able to live alone, bathe, and feed himself, make his way around his trailer, and around certain parts of the trailer park, but he wouldn't be able to do things like read, prepare his meals, or drive a car. To me, it was like an offer from heaven, so I accepted on the spot.

"He's a dear man and not demanding at all. We have an excellent handyman, who swears his name is Harry Handy. He does odd jobs and cleans up around the park three times a week. It's not a bad life, but I can't say I don't miss the boardrooms and power lunches sometimes."

"So now there'll be nothing to stop you from packing up your suits, returning to California, and rejoining the rat race?" Laria said.

"Believe it or not, that sounds pretty good to me right now although, as you've probably noticed, I don't have a prayer of fitting into my suits anymore."

The men returned and the lieutenant said, "You're free to go for now. Just be sure not to leave the local area until you're notified otherwise."

"You can follow me to the condo," said Bob. "It's not far."

"Great!" Laria replied, handing him a check.

Outside, after the appropriate thank-yous, goodbyes, and promises by the girls to call each other, May and the twins got into her car to wait for Mike to switch calls to Las Vegas dispatch and lock up while the others formed a caravan and headed for the condo.

As they drove away, Pree realized that she hadn't said anything to Bob about the satchel. She promised herself she would talk to him about it. Soon.

CHAPTER 9

Laughlin, Nevada, 1997
(The day after the killings)

At the condo, Bob set up the portable playpen in the living room and Laria laid the sleeping baby in it, covering her with a soft yellow blanket with bunnies on it.

"Thanks for all your help, Detective Kips," Laria said.

"My pleasure, ma'am," replied Bob. "And please, call me Bob."

"If you'll call me Laria."

"Deal," he replied, handing her two keys and pointing to a red phone on one of the end tables. "You can receive incoming calls on that phone, but you can't call out, so you might want to buy a phone card. There's a pay phone out by the pool."

"We may not have as much to do as we thought," Pree called from the kitchen. "There are clean sheets and towels folded on top of the dryer. Also detergent, dryer sheets, dish soap, cleanser, and sponges."

"Some of the renters do that," said Bob. "Bye, ma'am. Laria, I mean. Bye, kids. Pree."

With a quick salute, he was out the door.

"He's nice," commented Laria. "Apparently you two know each other."

"Yes, we're friends. He saved me from a physical attack by Greg in the movie theater at the Riverside last spring. I know that's hard for you to imagine, but Greg really had changed a lot. Too many prescriptions drugs, I think."

"I hadn't seen Greg for nearly two years, until Christmas Day," Laria commented. "He looked awful, and his weight had ballooned so much I hardly recognized him."

"I know. Anyway, Bob and I got to be friends after that. We talk, go to movies, have lunch, stuff like that."

"Oooh?" Laria, raised an eyebrow.

"No, no," Pree laughed. "Just friends, honest."

"If you say so," Laria said.

When they finished making beds and putting things away, Pree said, "I can stay with the kids while you go shopping if you like."

"Thanks, but I couldn't bear to leave them again so soon," said Laria. "Although the baby should sleep for another three hours. If you wouldn't mind staying with her, I could take the other kids grocery shopping with me and buy a phone card. If I pick up Happy Meals for them, I should be able to make it back within an hour, give or take. I can wait until tomorrow to get myself a few clothes. If this nice weather lasts, the kids will want to swim, so I guess I'll need a bathing suit too."

"Go ahead and shop," insisted Pree. "Even if I miss Jimmy tonight, he'll be here all day tomorrow."

"You're a real friend, Pree," said Laria. "But first, I want to tell you about that favor you did for me at the police station today."

When they were seated at the kitchen table Laria said, "About the shoebox. You said at the station your reason for contacting me was to tell me that Mape might have pulled something on me. Did you think he may have hidden away the ninety thousand dollars he told me he lost gambling?"

"I did," said Pree. "Greg pulled the same trick on me, except it was for over a million dollars."

Laria looked astonished. "Greg has – had – a million dollars? I never would have guessed. Where did he get it?"

Pree said, "I had no idea either, until after we were married. He said that during all the years he worked for the brewery he put most of his paycheck into the company's stock. As the brewery expanded into a major conglomerate, his stock kept gaining in value. But by the time we got to court, he had cashed in all but a few dollars and claimed to have lost it gambling."

"Wow," said Laria. "Who'd have thought? Did the money ever surface?"

"No," Pree said, "I'm pretty sure that at one time he had it hidden in a self-storage facility in Bullhead City. Remember when Mape's girlfriend thought Mape was going to come into a lot of money yesterday? Maybe Greg was going to Mexico with them, and taking the money he stashed."

Deciding not to tell Laria about the satchel until she and Jimmy had opened it Pree said, "Perhaps Greg didn't kill Mape after all. Someone else could have killed them both. Whoever it was, may have left Greg's jewelry for fear it could be traced back to him, and taken just the money. That would explain why the police didn't find it in the cabin. I suspect it's gone for good."

Laria nodded.

"Oh well," said Pree. "I wouldn't have gotten any of it in the divorce settlement anyway. If it ever does turn up, since I'm technically Greg's widow, I might end up with it now. But that's not likely to happen."

Laria nodded again. "Anyway, you were right about Mape hiding the money. When I checked his car this morning, I found the shoebox. When I looked inside, I was floored at first, then I was furious. He always gave me such a hard time about the child support and money for school clothes, and the shoebox was filled with hundred dollar bills. I figured I was entitled to the money since, as you know, it was originally my inheritance from my father. So I took it."

"I would have taken it too," agreed Pree.

"Mape certainly has no use for money now. I had just finished counting it when Detective Kips drove up. Bob, I guess I should call him. There are fifteen packets of bills and seven loose hundreds. Seventy-five thousand, seven hundred dollars."

"I'm glad you got it back."

"Thanks," said Laria. "Now, I need to ask you for another favor. Please say no if you don't want to do it."

"Ask," said Pree warily.

"Will you hold on to the money for me until everything is cleared up? You're not a suspect, so they won't be searching your trailer. If they were to find the money in my car or in the condo, they really would suspect me."

"Sure, I can keep it for you for a while."

"Thank you," Laria said, relieved. "Now, one more small favor. Would you mind going to your car and bringing me the seven loose bills? The rent check for the condo just about exhausted my bank account and I'll need money for shopping and expenses while we're here."

While Pree fetched the money from her car, Laria placed a pillow and blanket on the sofa. After Laria and the kids left, Pree fell asleep while recalling the first time she met Laria and Mape Belata.

*　　*　　*

"Hurry," Greg urged as he handed Pree the valet parking ticket and rushed toward the door of the Prime Rib House. "They're already here. I saw their car in the parking lot."

"Greg, honey, calm down," Pree said. "We're not late. We're exactly on time. Why are you so nervous?"

"You don't know him," said Greg. "He gets really upset when people are late."

"Well, that's too bad," Pree replied. "Besides, we're not late, we're on time. Now, slow down and hold the door for me."

Greg stopped abruptly and caught the door, saying, "Sorry. I guess I am a little nervous."

"Everything will be fine," Pree assured him as she took his arm and they entered the restaurant.

The lobby of the Prime Rib House was crowded. Greg hurried over to a slender, attractive young woman in a red dress, standing in the corner. She wore minimal makeup and had straight, sun-streaked blonde hair that hung almost to her waist.

"Laria!"

The woman turned and smiled at Greg. He rushed over, gave her a hug then turned around to Pree, and said, "This is Laria, his wife."

To the woman, he said, "This is Pree, my wife."

"I'm happy to meet you, at last," Laria said. "I've heard great things about you from Greg."

"I've been looking forward to meeting you too," said Pree.

"So how is married life?" Laria asked Greg.

"Great!" He smiled, blushing slightly. "It's like having room service twenty-four hours a day."

Pree shrugged and both women laughed.

"Where is he?" asked Greg, looking around the lobby.

"In the next room, over in the corner," said Laria, pointing. "Sitting at a dirty table."

"Why is he sitting at a dirty table?" asked Greg.

"He's in one of his snits," replied Laria.

"Uh-oh," said Greg. "What set him off this time?"

"The maître d' referred to me as his daughter," Laria told him.

"He really don't like that," Greg told Pree. "Come on, I'll introduce you to him."

"I'll wait here," said Mape's wife.

As they approached the cluttered table, Pree had to stifle a laugh when she saw the slight, cartoon of a man sitting with his arms outstretched, holding on to the edges of the table as if to prevent it from flying away. He had a fringe of gray hair that ran across the back of his head, from one ear to the other. Other than some sparse sideburns, the rest of his head was totally hairless. His large ears stuck out from his head like wings. He smiled as they approached, revealing a wide gap between his front teeth.

"Sit down," he invited.

"Why are you sitting at a dirty table?" asked Greg.

"To keep them from giving it to someone else, of course," Mape explained, his face red with anger. "They already gave tables to two other parties whose names were after ours on the list. You know how it works. They probably slipped the guy some money."

"Then I'll slip him a twenty, and we'll get the next table," said Greg.

"No, you moron," said Mape, grabbing Greg's arm. "Why do you always try to undermine me? Can't you see I have things under control here?"

Greg gave Pree an embarrassed smile.

"Who's this?" asked Mape.

"Hello, Mape," Pree said. "I'm Pree, the moron's wife. Excuse me. I'm going to back to the lobby to talk to Laria." She turned and walked away.

"Your husband said they seated two parties who came in after you did, and he wants to be sure they don't give this table to another party as well," she explained to Laria.

"They won't," replied Laria. "The other tables were for parties of two and six. This one is for four. The maître d' already said we could have it, but they won't clean it until Mape gets away from it."

"Does he know that?" asked Pree.

"Yes," explained Laria. "The maître d' told him, and I told him too. This is typical Mape behavior. You'll get used to it."

"Interesting," commented Pree.

"That's a polite word for it," said Laria. "You must have gone to charm school."

The women were smiling at the remark when Greg walked up.

"The bus boy says he has orders not to clean the table until he gets away from it, but he won't leave because he says they'll give it to someone else."

"He knows they won't," Laria told him. "He's just being his charismatic self."

"I'll go talk to him, again," Greg said, returning to the other room.

A minute or so later, Mape walked past the two women without acknowledging them, and went into the restroom. The women peeked into the next room where the busboy was wiping off the table. They saw Greg slip him a bill. Pree suspected that Greg had had lots of practice covering for Mape over the years.

When the table had been set up, the maître d' seated them and gave them menus. Laria apologized to him for Mape's behavior, and Greg handed him a twenty.

Mape's next trick of the evening was to stay in the restroom for fifteen minutes, leaving them sitting, and the waiter hovering. Again, Laria apologized, and again, Greg applied cash, this time to the waiter. A ten.

When Mape finally returned to the table, he asked, "Well, what did you order for me?"

"Nothing. We haven't ordered yet," said Laria. "We waited for you."

Throwing up his hands with an exasperated sigh, Mape whined. "For God's sake, woman, how long have we been married? And you can't order a prime rib for me by now?"

Laria just sat, saying nothing.

Shades of Stepford! Pree thought.

As the evening progressed, Mape got over his snit, and became somewhat bearable.

"I'm sorry you weren't able to make it to our wedding reception," said Pree. "We were looking forward to Mape's toast."

Mape and Laria looked at each other, confused.

"We didn't know about it," said Laria.

"Really?" asked Pree, caught off guard.

"Didn't I give you the invitation?" asked Greg, his face slightly pink. "I thought I did."

"No, you moron," said Mape. "You know you didn't. What's the matter, did you think my toast might embarrass you?"

"We set aside a large table next to ours for your family and Greg's friend Rowena's family. They didn't come either," said Pree, giving Greg a suspicious look. "I'm sorry you missed it. It was lovely. I was looking forward to meeting you and your children. And Rowena and her family as well." Rowena was a handicapped widow with two children, on welfare, whom Greg had once dated and had continued to help the family out financially.

"Those freeloaders?" asked Mape. "I don't know why Greg keeps letting that bunch of losers use him like he does."

"Oh?" Pree commented. "Greg said Savannah will graduate from college and start lab technician training this summer. Her goal is to own her own testing lab someday."

"Maybe," replied Mape. "But she couldn't have done it if Greg hadn't paid her tuition all these years and paid for that Dodge she drives. He pays for the insurance too. What a patsy!"

Greg gave Pree an embarrassed smile.

"She's just playing Greg, like her mother's been playing him and the system for years," Mape continued.

Defensively, Pree said, "I can't think of a better way for Greg to spend his money than helping this girl to avoid the welfare rolls. And I understand she's working part-time while she goes to school."

Greg nodded. Laria smiled.

"Well, are we going to order dessert, or what?" Mape asked, changing the subject. "We have a babysitter burning up four bucks an hour while we sit here and chitchat."

"I told you, tonight is on me," Greg reminded him. "That includes the babysitter too."

"So we're wasting your money. That makes it all right?" asked Mape, shaking his head at the stupidity of Greg's remark. "I'll go find the waiter."

During Mape's brief absence Pree, Greg, and Laria basked in the peace and quiet.

As they enjoyed their dessert, Mape actually became quite charming. He made a nice toast to Greg and Pree and ended it by saying he hoped their marriage would be as happy as his and Laria's. Ever the good sport, Pree had joined in the toast anyway.

*   *   *

Pree's last thought before sleep overtook her was that, with the possible exception of Jimmy; she didn't know anyone who would want Greg dead, but there were probably a number of people who wouldn't be disappointed to hear of Mape's demise.

Awake and feeling surprisingly rested by the time Laria and the children returned, Pree checked the baby and went to the bathroom to splash water on her face. She had forgotten she was wearing her 'Big Bird' turban until she looked into the mirror. She looked pretty silly.

The kids had talked Laria into making spaghetti and she invited Pree to stay. Pree had to get home to Louie and Dora, but took a rain check for three portions of sauce, promising to return the next day to pick them up.

Walking Pree to her car, Laria said that Jo Jo wanted Pree to know that he was a big boy now and liked to be called Joey.

Pree smiled. "Joey it is. And on a depressing note, I guess it's up to us to make the arrangements for disposing of the men's remains."

Laria nodded.

"I suppose we should hold some kind of memorial service for them," Pree continued, opening her car door. "We'll figure it all out."

A final hug, and Pree headed for home. It had been a long day.

CHAPTER 10

Bullhead City, Arizona, 1995
(Two years before the killings)

"Good news, Greg." Pree said as he set a bag of groceries on the counter. "Laria called. She and Mape want to bring the kids for a visit next week. They'll get to initiate the new guest wing."

Greg was delighted. He kissed Pree's cheek.

By ten o'clock Sunday morning, Greg was pacing the floor, anxious for them to arrive. He had never hosted anyone in his own home before, and was both nervous and excited by the prospect.

They were scheduled to arrive at one o'clock, but they pulled into the driveway at eleven. After the hugs and greetings, Mape announced, "As soon as we unload our stuff, we're going to go get some lunch. The kids are starved!"

"I tried to get him to stop for lunch in Needles," Laria apologized. "But he said it was too early."

"Not to worry," said Pree. She had become accustomed to Mape's tricks. "I have plenty of food, and we haven't eaten either. I'll set things out while Greg shows you around the place and gets you settled in the guest wing."

"Wow!" Mape exclaimed, looking around. "You didn't tell me you bought a mansion. How big is this place, anyway?"

"Really big!" said Greg, proudly, spreading his arms for emphasis. It was the first home he had ever owned. "Twenty rooms, countin' the five bathrooms, and the pantry and the laundry room. Oh yeah, and the spa room. It's like we're livin' on a movie set or somethin'."

"Two retired people really need twenty rooms and five bathrooms," said Mape, rolling his eyes. "The five of us manage just fine with two bedrooms and one bathroom."

"Surprisingly, we use all the rooms," responded Pree, determined not to allow the little jerk to make Greg feel guilty about their hard work and good fortune. "Today, you're going to initiate the guest wing, which accounts for three of the rooms, one of the bathrooms, and the spa room. I think you'll find it comfortable."

"I'm sure we will," said Laria, graciously. "It was so good of you to invite us."

"Greg will show you around and get you settled while I set out the lunch," said Pree.

Mape was surprisingly cordial during lunch, and the families caught up on each other's lives. The girls hurried through their food so they could go back into the guest wing and play the slot machine and video poker machine Greg had bought and filled with coins for guests to enjoy.

"This is a real dream home," said Laria.

"Greg deserves most of the credit for it," Pree told her. "He put up the lion's share of the money, and he insisted that everything should be just right. The original carpet was perfectly fine, except that it was dark blue, which didn't go with our earth tones. I thought we should live with it until it started to wear, but Greg insisted that life's too short to live with the wrong carpet, so we replaced it." She smiled at Greg, who was embarrassed, but obviously pleased by the compliments.

"Can we tell them now?" Greg asked excitedly.

"Only about tonight and tomorrow, okay?" Pree said. "Let's save the rest for a surprise."

"Tonight, the three of us are going to eat at the Colorado Belle," said Greg excitedly. "Steaks and ribs and chicken. Pree is going to stay here with the kids and we're going to see Debbie Reynolds at the Riverside, and stay and gamble as long as we want. Only not too late, because tomorrow we're going fishing at Lake Mohave in our new boat, and we need to get there early when the fish are biting"

"That sounds wonderful!" said Laria.

Pree said, "Greg tells me you're planning to retire soon."

"If you can call operating a farm and an antiques business retiring," Mape replied wearily. "Retired or not, I'll still have five mouths to feed."

"It's not for sure yet that we're going to buy a farm," Laria quickly interjected. "We're going to New Jersey next month, to look around."

Mape and Laria exchanged looks, and Pree let the conversation drop.

When the men left for the casino to gamble, Pree and Laria went to the guest wing where Pree taught the girls to play video poker.

The women were in the spa, sipping iced tea and Diet Pepsi when Laria said, "Pree, I probably shouldn't be telling you this but I don't have anyone else to talk to. Except for my mother, and I can't ever tell her about this. She hates Mape as it is."

She hesitated for a moment. "It's just that last week at the market my debit card got rejected, and I found out that Mape had closed out both the joint checking and savings accounts, opened a new checking account in his name only, and was having his paycheck deposited into it. They had no record of a new savings account. Several months ago, I inherited ninety thousand dollars from my father's estate and deposited it into the savings account Mape closed, for the children's college. When Mape got home that night, he informed me that since he was the only member of the family with a job, it was his money and he would do what he wanted with it. He said he was going to start giving me a cash allowance for groceries and household expenses. We had a terrible fight, and I told him that if the money hadn't been put back into joint accounts by five o'clock the next evening, the children and I were going to move in with my mother and that I was going to divorce him."

Laria's expression told Pree that it hadn't ended well.

"The next day, he did put my name on a new checking account," continued Laria. "And gave me a new debit card. But he told me he had lost the ninety thousand dollars in a high stakes poker game, trying to win enough to pay for the new farm. I was furious, of course, but there was nothing I could do. In the end, I decided to stay with him. At this point, I believe the children are better off having a full-time mother. Besides, they're crazy about Mape. In spite of his faults, he is a good father."

After Laria left to join the men for dinner and the show, Pree set up three folding cots in front of the television while the children brushed their teeth and put on their pajamas. They watched one of the videos they had brought from home. Pree joined them on the sofa but soon fell asleep.

It was 5:00 a.m. when Greg shook Pree awake. He held a finger to his lips and pointed at the sleeping children. Silently, they waved good night to Mape and Laria.

"I don't think any of you will want to get up in an hour to go fishing," said Pree as she crawled into bed. "What happened? You never stay out this late."

"Oh, you know him," said Greg. "He gets to losing at Hold'em and he don't want to quit. He always thinks he can get even. Laria and I went to the car at about one o'clock and laid the seats back and slept a little."

"Did he get even?" asked Pree.

"I doubt it," Greg answered drowsily. "He never does."

Almost immediately he began snoring.

Pree slept for another hour, showered, and dressed as quietly as she could, slipped through the side door of the guest wing and found the children watching cartoons. She told them to brush their teeth and get dressed very quietly and that she had a surprise for them.

Pree left a note saying she had taken the children to the Riverside for pancakes and an early movie, *Beauty and the Beast*. Twenty minutes or so into the film, Laria walked into the theater and sat down next to Pree.

"I'm sorry," she whispered.

"It's okay," Pree whispered back, patting her hand.

When the women and children got back to the house at about one o'clock that afternoon, Pree found a note on the table. "Ladies:" it began. "Since you have apparently decided to cancel out on our

day of fishing, we have gone to the casino. We'll be back for dinner."
It wasn't signed.

At six o'clock, Pree began frying the chicken she had intended to make for the picnic at the lake. Laria peeled potatoes and made a salad. The biscuits came out of the oven just as the gravy thickened. Everything was perfect. They ate in the dining room, using the good china and silver. The girls had set the table, and Laria and Jo Jo had picked flowers from the garden for the centerpiece. The women and children chatted away happily, enjoying the meal. At about eight o'clock, as Pree reached for a second piece of chicken, the door opened and the men walked in. Laria stopped talking, midsentence.

"What are we?" asked Mape. "The servants? We eat the leftovers?"

"We weren't sure when you'd be back," said Laria timidly.

"Or even *if* you'd be back," said Pree. "With your record, I wouldn't push it, Mape."

Greg stood, horrified, waiting for Mape's reaction. Pree got up and walked over to her husband. "Sit down, sweetheart," she said, kissing his cheek. "The chicken is still nice and warm."

Pree knew that as much as Greg idolized Mape, her fried chicken ran a pretty close second.

"Go ahead and eat if you want, Greg," said Mape, obviously miffed. "I'm not hungry. I'll see you later."

Greg turned to follow Mape as he stormed out of the room, hesitated, then walked into the bathroom to wash up for dinner.

The next day, Mape was up early, spurring everyone on for a day at the lake. The women hurriedly made sandwiches, wrapped the leftover chicken, and packed a picnic basket. The weather was perfect. The men took the girls out on the boat to fish while the women relaxed on blankets on the sand and Jo Jo played happily with his pail, shovel, and dump truck. When the men returned, Jo Jo pouted because each of his sisters had caught a fish, and he hadn't. The girls had brought their catches back to show to their mother and to have their pictures taken with them. Afterward Mape returned to the boat with the fish, to release them back into the lake.

Suddenly Mape shouted, "Jo Jo, come here. I think I just saw a fish swim under the boat."

Excitedly, Jo Jo ran onto the boat. Mape lifted him up and handed him a fishing pole. Immediately, the boy shouted, excitedly, "I caught it!" He reeled in a fish that looked remarkably like the one Coley had just caught. Even the girls saw through the ruse, but joined the grown-ups in cheering for Jo Jo's amazing feat. The boy beamed as his mother took his picture with his prize.

Maybe Mape actually is a good father, Pree conceded grudgingly.

"Should I tell them about the other surprise now?" asked Greg.

"Sure, go ahead," Pree smiled.

Greg said excitedly. "Tomorrow, we're all going to Las Vegas. Pree rented rooms for us at the Circus Circus. We're going to take the kids to play the games, and watch the circus acts and everything. Then we're all going to see Siegfried & Roy."

The girls started dancing around in the sand, squealing with glee. Jo Jo immediately joined in.

"Las Vegas?" asked Mape. The high-pitched whine was back. "What did you do that for, Pree? I was looking forward to spending a restful day with you guys at the house tomorrow, before we have to go home."

Greg looked crushed. Pree visualized kicking the little jerk in the groin.

"You can stay here if you like, Mape" said Laria sharply, the defiance in her tone surprising both Pree and Greg. "The kids and I are going to Las Vegas."

"Thank you, Mommy," the children yelled excitedly as they fell on their mother and bombarded her with kisses.

Mape was silent for a moment, then smiled and said, "Gotcha! You guys are too easy. Greg, you know that Las Vegas is only my favorite place in the whole world. Honestly, you guys should be able to tell when I'm kidding by now. What time are we leaving? I can't wait!"

Greg was beaming. Pree's stomach was churning.

CHAPTER 11

Bullhead City, Arizona, 1995
(Two years before the killings)

They caravanned to Las Vegas in two cars so the Belatas could leave for home the next morning. It was almost noon when they pulled into the Gold Strike Hotel and Casino for lunch.

The Circus Circus was great fun. The girls won prizes in the arcade and Greg won a teddy bear for Jo Jo. Later, they were enthralled by the magic of Siegfried & Roy. They had ice cream sundaes after the show and walked on the strip for a while. Mape contributed significantly to the enjoyment of the others by saying he wasn't feeling well, and wasn't able to join them.

It was nearly 2:00 a.m. when they finally made their way to their adjoining rooms, Greg carrying the sleeping Jo Jo.

Mape was not in their room, and there was no note.

"It's okay," said Laria, yawning. "Even if he stays out all night, I can drive home tomorrow. He knows we're supposed to meet at the coffee shop at seven o'clock in the morning. Hopefully, he'll be there."

While the girls got into their pajamas, Laria urged Pree to go downstairs and play video poker for a while.

"That does sound like fun. Maybe I'll play forty dollars," Pree told them. Forty dollars was her usual limit. "I'll see everyone at breakfast."

Greg left to look for Mape.

By six thirty, Pree had run her forty dollars up to two hundred. Exhausted, she went to the registration desk and extended their room for another day so she and Greg could get some sleep before going home, then walked to the coffee shop to get a table and wait for the others. To her surprise, within five minutes, as if on cue, Greg, Mape, Laria, and the children arrived at the restaurant. Breakfast was actually pleasant as Mape took a little break from being a jerk.

"We've really enjoyed your visit," Pree said as Greg paid the check. "We'll help you get your things to your car and say goodbye, then Greg and I are going to bed."

While Laria took the children to the restroom, Mape said, "Pree." It was his smarmy voice, and Pree braced herself. "I hate to ask you this after you've done so much for us already, but you know Laria didn't get a chance to play any slots here in Las Vegas, and I'd like to take her to play for just a little while, if you wouldn't mind watching the kids again. Just for a couple of hours."

"Mape," Pree said sternly. "I've been awake for over twenty-four hours. There's no way I can stay awake for two more."

"One hour, then," he said quickly. "For Laria."

"What's for me?" asked Laria, walking up with the children.

"Pree just volunteered to watch the kids for a couple of hours so you can play the slots before we leave."

"Oh, Pree, are you sure?" asked Laria, obviously excited at the prospect. "You must be exhausted."

"I can probably make it for one more hour," said Pree. "Just one. Not two."

"Great!" said Mape. "We'll meet you in our room in an hour or so."

"Or so?" asked Pree.

"In an hour," Laria assured her. "Even if I have to drag him up there. We have to get going soon, anyway."

"You go on to bed, Greg," said Pree. "I'll take the kids to the arcade for a while then take them up to their room."

When they left the arcade an hour later, the children had won another ten dollars' worth of prizes, which had cost Pree fifty-three dollars. Jo Jo had won a giant whistle, and was driving everyone crazy with it.

Back in the room, Pree confiscated the whistle and entertained the kids with games she had played with her own children when they were small. It was fun until the girls became bored, and began whining and complaining. Pree didn't blame them. She felt like whining and complaining herself. They finally settled down when Pree ordered a pay-per-view movie, after which she checked out of their room and took them and the family's luggage next door, where Greg was sleeping. There, she ordered another movie. Thankfully, Greg didn't stir.

At one o'clock, five hours after leaving for their one hour of gambling, Laria and Mape knocked on the door.

"Mommy!" the children shouted grabbing Laria.

Pree put a finger to her lips and pointed to the sleeping Greg. Laria took the children into the hallway.

"Pree," Mape began, in a voice so sugary it made Pree's stomach turn. She shook her head and held up both hands, indicating she didn't want to hear anything he had to say.

"Can I at least say goodbye to Greg?" he asked. "And thank him?"

"No," Pree said adamantly, setting their suitcases into the hall. "He's exhausted. Let him sleep."

Angrily, Mape picked up the bags and left. Pree blew Laria and the kids a kiss and closed the door.

Less than a minute later, there was a knock on the door. It was Laria.

"I'm alone," she whispered when Pree opened the door a crack. "I don't blame you for being angry, Pree, but we don't have any money for the trip home. Mape lost all our vacation cash and maxed out our credit card."

Pree held up a finger to indicate Laria should wait. She took a hundred dollars out of her wallet, left one of her sandals in the doorway to prevent the door from closing, and went into the hall. Still refusing to speak, she handed Laria the money.

"If it's any comfort, he left me waiting four hours at the Horseshoe," she said.

"What happened?" asked Pree, suddenly interested.

"Mape insisted on playing poker downtown," she said. "At the Horseshoe, he gave me twenty dollars and said he'd be back in half an hour which was about how long my twenty lasted. I went to get him so we could leave, but he wasn't in the poker room, or anywhere else in the casino. I had one nickel in my wallet, no car keys, and no credit card, leaving me no choice but to sit there on a stool and wait for him. He showed up after four hours, with no explanation and no apology, and told me he had lost all our money. I told him I'd seen machines in the casinos where you can get cash with your credit card, but he said the card was maxed out too, and he would get money from Greg for the trip home."

Pree's heart ached for the younger woman.

"Pree, I don't blame you for hating us," Laria said, walking away. "Thank you for everything. I'll get this money back to you as soon as I can."

"Wait!" Pree called after her. Laria stopped and turned.

Pree walked over and gave her a hug.

"I don't hate you," she said. "That 'you' is singular, however."

Laria managed a small grin.

"The money is a gift," Pree said. Then she asked, "Are you really going to move to a farm with him? In New Jersey?"

"I don't know," Laria said as she walked down the hall.

The next week, Pree and Greg received two envelopes in the mail. A pink one from Laria contained a thank-you card, with a gracious note of apology, and five twenty-dollar bills. A red one from Mape also contained a thank-you card and a note, probably Mape's version of an apology.

"That was nice," was Greg's only comment.

CHAPTER 12

Bullhead City, Arizona, 1995
(A year and a half before the killings)

The phone was ringing. Pree sat up and fumbled around in the dark until she found the receiver.

"Good morning," said the cheerful voice on the other end of the line.

"Mape?" she asked. "What's wrong?"

Greg sat up in bed.

"Does something have to be wrong for a person to call his friends?" Mape asked.

"It does at four-forty-five in the morning. What's up?"

"How would you like to have company?" he asked.

"Who?" Pree asked.

She heard Greg pick up the phone in the other room.

"Us, of course," Mape whined. "Laria and me, and the kids. Who else would I be calling about?"

"Sure," said Pree. "We'd love to see you. When?"

"In about five minutes," he said. "We're on our way home from New Jersey, and we're down at the corner. We have some good news to tell you about."

In the sincerest voice she could muster, Pree said, "Sure, Mape. We'd love to see you. I'll put on some coffee."

Surprisingly, their three-day visit passed without incident. Laria apologized for not giving them more notice, but Mape maintained he thought they would enjoy being surprised. Pree assured him they hadn't.

Mape had located a small farmhouse on a few acres of land in New Jersey that he wanted to buy. He and Jo Jo would grow crops, and Laria and the girls would can the fruits and vegetables. They would have a cow and chickens and live off the land. His antiques business would pay their other expenses. Mape's excitement about the prospect was obvious. Laria was conspicuously silent.

Their visit followed the established pattern. The women relaxed in the spa, played games, and took the kids to the park while the men gambled at the casinos. Before they left, Laria told Pree that she had decided not to go to New Jersey. She was going to move in with her mother and file for divorce as soon as they got home, so that half of the equity in their house would be put in her name, and Mape wouldn't be able to get his hands on it.

That was the last time Pree had seen Laria until she walked into the Laughlin police station that morning. Unfortunately, it was not the last time she had seen Mape.

CHAPTER 13

Los Angeles, California, 1951
(Forty-six years before the killings)

"That was a really good pitcher show," Ivan said as they walked out of the theater after watching another gangster movie. "I like the part where they said the guy was sleepin' with the fishes. I wish I could sleep with the fishes."

"You're such a moron, Ivan," Greg said, laughing. "Why would you want to sleep with the fishes?"

"'Cause they're so pretty! It would be fun. Maybe I could learn to talk fish talk, and hear what they're sayin'."

"You'd drown, you moron. The guy in the picture that was sleeping with the fishes was dead, remember? They stuck his feet in a bucket of cement so he would sink to the bottom of the river. That's how they killed him, Ivan."

"Too bad," Ivan said. "He could've had fun with the fishes."

Greg shook his head.

Greg pulled his new Buick up in front of their apartment building. Ivan missed the old Studebaker. Greg used to take him to the schoolyard and let him drive it. Greg said Ivan had a knack for driving. He could operate the clutch and shift through the gears like a pro. But Greg wouldn't let anyone else drive the Buick, not even Ivan.

Ivan got out of the car and grabbed his burger and fries and chocolate malted.

"Thanks, Greg," Ivan said.

"Sure, kid," Greg smiled. "Oh, wait, I think there's something in my pocket that belongs to you."

Greg pulled a folded dollar bill from his shirt pocket.

"Here you go, kid," he said, handing the money to Ivan.

"Wow! Thanks, Greg."

Ivan slipped the bill into the pocket of his jacket and closed the car door.

"See ya," Ivan called out as Greg pulled away from the curb.

"Ivan," Pearl whispered as he walked in. "Mama's had her dinner and her medicine. She should sleep through the night."

"Okay," Ivan whispered back.

"How was the movie?" Pearl asked softly.

"Really good," Ivan said, holding up the bag and cup to show her. "Greg bought me a burger and fries and a malted."

Pearl shook her head disapprovingly. The boy had been putting on weight lately, but she couldn't blame it all on Greg. Except for the time he was in school, Ivan was cooped up in the apartment day and night, looking after Mama. Greg did seem to genuinely care about the boy, and he was providing him and Mama with a place to live and food to eat. He paid for Mama's doctor too, and Mrs. Holloway, the neighbor who bathed her and looked after her while Ivan was at school. Pearl tried not to think about where his money came from.

"What are you going to do tonight?" she whispered to Ivan.

Ivan said softly, "Read the new detective magazine Greg brought me."

"I worry about those magazines you read," Pearl told him as she put on her coat. "Some of them look pretty gory."

"It's okay, Pearl," Ivan assured her. "I don't like the bad guys. I like the cops. I want to be a cop someday, or a G-man, and wear a badge, so people will have to do what I say, or I can shoot 'em, or put 'em in jail."

"Only people who do bad things," Pearl reminded him.

"I know," said Ivan.

"You're a good boy, Ivan," Pearl told him, giving him a quick kiss on the cheek. "Be sure to lock the door."

After locking the door, Ivan added the dollar to his cache under the floorboards in the closet. He had over two hundred dollars now. Ivan liked having money. He replaced the boards and set the galoshes and rain boots back over them, then carried his radio into the kitchen and listened to *Dragnet* while he ate his burger.

That night, Ivan dreamed that he was sleeping with the fishes. He smiled in his sleep when their fins tickled his face.

CHAPTER 14

Bullhead City, Arizona, 1997
(The evening after the killings)

Pree was somewhat relieved not to see Jimmy's motorcycle in her carport when she returned from Laria's condo. She was tired and had a lot to do. She locked Laria's shoebox in the carport storage cabinet then went directly to Louie's trailer, gave him and Dora their meds, and refilled the dog's water dish.

"You missed a good party," said Louie, patting his stomach. "And a good game. Lu gave Jim a care package for you."

"That's great," said Pree, preparing to leave. "I'm famished!"

There was a note from Jimmy on the counter when Pree got home, informing her of the food in the refrigerator and that he was going across the river to collect some money he had won on the game. He planned to join Crush and the other guys for the fishing trip the next morning. He was going to sleep in his truck again which was unusual, but he offered no explanation.

For a fleeting moment, Pree wondered if it could have been Jimmy who left the satchel on her doorstep. She quickly scolded herself for the thought. The satchel had come from Greg's cabin so whoever took it must have at least witnessed the killings, and was probably involved in them. Jimmy was strong enough to have lugged the heavy satchel to her doorstep, but as much as he despised Greg and Mape, Pree knew her son wasn't a thief and he certainly wasn't capable of killing anyone.

With or without Jimmy, Pree decided it was time to see what was in the satchel. Nervously, she removed the blanket, unbuckled the strap and pulled it open. She gasped when she saw the hodge-podge of packets of hundred dollar bills, like the ones in Laria's shoebox, mixed with an assortment of loose bills of all denominations: hundreds, fifties, twenties, tens, fives, and ones. Also quarters, dimes, and nickels. Even pennies. She had no doubt it was part of the money Greg had stashed. It was nowhere near a million dollars, but it was certainly a substantial amount. And the fact that someone had moved it from the crime scene to her doorstep pretty much blew the murder/suicide theory out of the water.

She closed the satchel and put the blanket back over it. She would have Jimmy help her count it before he left. Maybe together they could figure out how and why it came to be on her doorstep.

It was laundry day, so after Pree sampled Lu's delicious food, she gathered her dirty clothes. She picked up Jimmy's bulging canvas laundry bag and muddy sneakers from her office, where he had left them. He had cleaned up in her guest bath before the party, so she grabbed the wet towels. On her way out the door, she saw his denim jacket hanging on a peg and piled it on top of the laundry basket

In the washhouse, she sorted the clothes, removing tissues from the pockets of two pairs of her pants and two dollars, a quarter, a pocketknife, and a book of matches from Jimmy's pockets. She poured detergent into all three machines, inserted coins, slung her handbag over her shoulder, and left for the market.

On her return, Pree stopped and moved the clothes from the washers to dryers, then carried her groceries to the trailer and put them away. She showered, shampooed, and wore her pajamas, robe, and slippers back to the washhouse to retrieve the laundry. She left Jimmy's clothes neatly folded on her desk near the futon, and put his damp sneakers on the floor on top of a towel. After stuffing the money and pocketknife into one of the pockets, she hung Jimmy's jacket back on the peg from which she had taken it. The matches she put into a small kitchen drawer with other matchbooks Jimmy had picked up from various places. She stored the matches and half a dozen candles in the drawer in case of a power outage, an occasional occurrence during monsoon.

Pushing the drawer shut, something caught her eye. She reopened the drawer and retrieved the matchbook. The cover was black, embossed with a silver champagne glass. Written in gold were the words, "HAPPY NEW YEAR, 1997, from the Nugget Casino, Searchlight, Nevada." She was relieved to find all the matches intact. At least her son hadn't started smoking again. Then she noticed the number four written sideways in blue ink on the inside of the cover, just above the heads of the matches. Lifting the matches, she saw what appeared to be a phone number, with a Nevada area code. She couldn't tell if it was Jimmy's printing or not. She thought about calling the number, but it was late and she wasn't sure what she would say if someone answered. She decided to wait and check it out the next day and returned the matches to the drawer.

In bed, questions began bombarding Pree's brain. *Had Jimmy been in Searchlight on New Year's Eve? Why? Why were his pant legs and sneakers covered with mud? Was it Greg's telephone number in the matchbook?* Time-wise, it might have been possible for him to dispose of Mape and Greg, take the money, and leave the satchel on her doorstep. *Had he slept in the truck instead of coming to the trailer so she wouldn't know how late he'd gotten in?* She hadn't seen any blood on his clothes. *Had he disposed of the bloody ones?*

Again, Pree chastised herself for having such thoughts about her own son. Jimmy wouldn't kill anybody, not even Greg and Mape. Still, Pree felt herself growing anxious and angry at her son, though she wasn't sure why. She knew most of her anger should be directed at herself. She was the one who had brought Greg into their family and into their lives.

The irrational anger returned the next morning as Pree made peanut butter fudge, her specialty, for the parade party. As she poured the thick, warm fudge mixture into the platter; she could tell it was going to be perfect. She still had the touch!

"I brought fudge," Pree said, entering Laria's condo and hugging the children. "The canister is for you and the foil package is for Bob. Will you give it to him when you see him?"

"Sure, thanks," Laria said as Pree followed her into the kitchen. "I can use a sugar rush. I was awake most of the night thinking about how to tell the children about Mape and Greg today. They know something has happened to them, of course, but they don't know what. I keep waiting for them to ask, but they haven't. May and the twins are coming over to swim later, with Gage, their neighbor boy, and that should help, but I want them to give them time to deal with it a while before they get here."

Pree sat at the table. Laria handed her a Diet Pepsi and took a sip of her coffee before continuing.

"I called my mother last night after the kids went to sleep and told her what happened. She's going to get their books and assignments today and FedEx them to me. May knows a teacher, Mrs. Stapp, who is on maternity leave. May's pretty sure she'll tutor my kids, as long as she can bring her baby with her, which would be no problem."

"Sounds good," Pree said. "Any word from Lieutenant Keebler?"

"Not yet," Laria said. "He said it would take some time for the lab to process everything, so I doubt I'll hear anything before next week, at the earliest."

Pree got up from the table and placed her glass and can in the sink. "I'd like to stay and chat, but I have a lot to do this morning."

"I'll get your pasta sauce," Laria told her. "It turned out really well."

"It always does," Pree replied. "I'll call you tomorrow. Maybe we can get together Saturday or Sunday and take the kids to the park for a picnic or something."

"Sounds fun," Laria told her as they walked to the door. "Enjoy your party."

As Pree pulled out of the parking lot, Bob's white Ram pulled in. They rolled down their windows and exchanged greetings.

"I left you some fudge with Laria," she told him.

"Thanks," he replied. They chatted for a minute, said their goodbyes, and Pree pulled onto the street. As she drove home, it occurred to her that she hadn't mentioned the satchel or the money, and neither of them had mentioned meeting for their regular Friday movie the next morning.

CHAPTER 15

**Bullhead City, Arizona, 1997
(Two days after the killings)**

B y the time Pree arrived at Lu's trailer, the men had already left for the lake and the party was in full swing. Maryrose Mendez was teaching some of the women the "Boot Scootin' Boogie" on the veranda.

Pree set the fudge and Diet Pepsis she had bought on the counter and joined Lu in front of the television. Lu Aki was a successful interior designer in Las Vegas. She was married to Crush Elliott, once a famous football star, now a celebrity host at the Shooting Starr Hotel and Casino owned by his college roommate, Sammy Starr. Lu had inherited her luxury trailer and a boat from her parents, and she and Crush spent as much time as possible at the Lazy River. Each year, they continued traditions her parents had started, first by hosting the Rose Bowl party on New Year's Day. On the next day, Crush would take the men fishing on their boat while Lu and the women ate lunch and watched the Rose Parade, taped the previous day.

"We missed you at the party yesterday," Lu said. "Nobody knew where you were. Not even Jim. What happened?"

"It's complicated," Pree told her. "And pretty awful. I'll tell everyone about it later. I don't want to put a damper on the fun just yet."

The door opened, and Naomi Patterson came into the room. The hair on her neck was damp, and there were sweat beads on her forehead.

"I think they have line-dancing classes at the community college at home," she said as she headed to the bathroom. "I'm going to try to get Ross to take them with me. It's great exercise."

"You guys were looking good out there," replied Pree.

Mary Baker, one of the Lovelies who had recently retired to Laughlin, showed up with Valerie just as the dancers were coming inside, still talking and laughing which they continued to do throughout lunch. As the supply of wine and beer diminished, humorous things became funny and funny things become hysterical. They became more subdued as they watched the Rose Parade and enjoyed the homemade desserts and coffee. Afterward, Laurie Forge asked, "Why weren't you at the Rose Bowl party yesterday, Pree?"

The room got quiet and the women all turned toward Pree. She told them the entire story, skipping only the part about the satchel and the money.

"Oh, my gosh," said Val, stunned, when Pree had finished. "They're really dead? Do you think it was a murder/suicide?"

"I hope Mape's wife did it," Mary Baker said. "She should have smoked his sorry ass a long time ago."

"She didn't, though," Pree laughed. "She has a substantiated alibi. I do think somebody did kill them, though."

"You don't think it was a murder/suicide?" asked Jolie Ciko. "Why not?"

"Just a hunch, really," Pree lied. "Greg worshipped Mape. He would never kill him."

"That's true," Val agreed.

Mary nodded.

CHAPTER 16

Bullhead City, Arizona, 1997
(Two days after the killings)

"Finally!" Jimmy said, opening the door for his mother and taking the grocery bags from her. "I thought maybe you'd been abducted by aliens or something."

"Isn't this one of those pot-kettle things?" Pree asked, hugging him. "If it weren't for your dirty laundry, I could say the same about you."

"I know," Jimmy acknowledged as they put away the groceries. "Everyone missed you at the party yesterday. I won a hundred bucks on the game, and another fifty from Rob. Go, Ohio State! The fish weren't biting today, though. And how was your party?" he asked as he picked up a piece of fudge.

"Fun. And don't ruin your dinner," Pree scolded. "We're having something special tonight, and I didn't even have to cook it."

"Big Macs?"

"You'll see. But first, tell me why we were deprived of your company on New Year's Eve. You missed a great dinner and a fantastic show."

"Sorry about that," he said. "It was a last minute thing. I had to pick up some futons in Fresno. I didn't pull into the parking lot here until about 4:00 a.m., so I just slept in the truck."

He's lying, Pree realized, feeling the anger rise up again. "Wash your hands and help me make dinner," she said. "Louie will be here at six. When I said dinner is going to be special tonight, I wasn't kidding. Spaghetti with Laria Belata's sauce."

"Mape's wife?" Jimmy asked, puzzled. "You haven't spoken to her in months. What's going on?"

"There's something I need to tell you when Louie gets here," Pree said, as she washed her hands. She put some water on to boil and began pulling salad veggies from the refrigerator. "It's hard to talk about, so I only want to tell it once."

Pree studied her son for signs that he already knew what she was talking about, but he just shrugged and began chopping vegetables.

Dinner conversation focused on the game and the afternoon's fishing.

"Okay, Mom," Jimmy said as the men enjoyed their dessert, Marietta's leftover peach cobbler with ice cream. "What's this big news you have to tell us?"

When the men had settled on the sofa, Dora at Louie's feet, Pree took a deep breath and said, "Greg and Mape are dead."

"It's about time," Jimmy said, laughing.

"James Robert Olindo!" Pree scolded. "Show a little respect."

"You're serious?" Jimmy asked. "They're really dead?"

"Yes," Pree told him. "They were shot on New Year's Eve. I spent several hours yesterday at the police station in Laughlin. Laria was there too."

"Did she kill them? I hope?" he asked.

"Of course not," Pree replied. "She's the one who found them, though."

"Wait," Jimmy said. "Did it happen in Cottonwood Cove?"

"Yes," Pree replied, startled by the question. "How did you know?"

"Some people were talking about it in the casino this morning," Jimmy replied. "But they didn't know who it was. They said it was a murder/suicide."

"They're not sure yet," Pree said. She spent the next hour telling the men about the gruesome events of the previous day, omitting any reference to the satchel and the cash. When she finished, they were silent until Pree finally spoke. "I'd better get you and Dora home, Louie," she said. "It's getting late."

"I'll see them home," Jimmy offered. "I need to get going, anyway."

"Aren't you here for the weekend?" Pree asked, surprised.

"No," said Jimmy. "I'm going to spend the weekend in Riverside with Ross Jaques so I can collect my fifty bucks and rub it in a little."

Ross had been Jimmy's best friend since high school.

"Well, that should be fun," Pree said, not terribly disappointed. A restful weekend sounded pretty good. "But aren't you going to sleep here tonight?"

"Nah. I'll just sleep in my truck again. I want to get an early start, and this way you can sleep in tomorrow. I know you're tired."

"Exhausted," Pree agreed. "You go on then. I'll walk Louie and Dora home and give them their meds."

"Let me grab my stuff and I'll walk out with you," Jimmy said.

"By the way, son, where's your Harley?" asked Pree. "It isn't in the carport."

"It's in a shop in Fresno getting a new transmission. I'll be going back there next week, and I'll pick it up."

"Then how did you get to the Riverside casino this morning?" Pree asked. "Your truck was in the parking lot when I passed by."

"What is this, the third degree?" Jimmy asked, his voice a bit edgy.

"No," Pree replied, a bit resentful of the question. "Of course not. I'm just curious."

"I took the boat across, of course."

Pree nodded and pretended to believe him.

"Do you want a ride to the parking lot?" she asked.

"Naw," Jimmy said. "It's not that far and I need to walk off all that dinner."

By the time Pree returned from Louie's, she was too tired to dwell on the discrepancies in her son's story, but the next morning, she could think of nothing else. Her son had lied to her. Twice. She knew that his truck hadn't been in the parking lot at six thirty on

New Year's morning, and she also knew the boats hadn't been running last night or yesterday morning.

The anger returned, even stronger. She didn't dare tell Bob about the satchel and the money now, since it would cast doubt on the murder/suicide theory and throw the case wide open. Jimmy would be an obvious suspect. Before she could tell anyone, she first had to find out where her son had been during the time of the murders, and why he had lied.

Pree debated about calling the number inside the matchbook cover, knowing that if she heard Greg's voice on the message recorder, things could never again be the same between her and her son.

But when she opened the drawer, the matchbook was gone.

Oh, crud!

CHAPTER 17

Bullhead City, Arizona, 1997
(Five days after the killings)

The comforter on Pree's queen size bed was barely visible under the stacks of bills. The top of her dresser and the floor next to it were covered with plastic buckets of coins. Damp bills were spread out all over the bathtub to dry.

The final tally left her stunned. She had $432,000 in bills and another four or five thousand in coins. It was nearly half of the money Greg had claimed to have lost gambling during the divorce proceedings.

Each time she went over in her mind the people who might have hated Mape and Greg enough to kill them and have the strength to carry the heavy satchel to her doorstep, she always came back to one name. Her son's. She was quick to remind herself that even if Jimmy had taken the money, it didn't mean that he was the killer. But the guilt and anger would flare up anyway. She had even stopped taking her daughter Staci's calls for fear she would break down and tell her about Jimmy's lies, and the money.

* * *

Pree parked in the Safeway lot in Bullhead City, where she was to meet Laria and May and the children. They were going to Oatman, an old, historic, silver mining town on even more historic

Route 66. Pree knew the kids were going to enjoy it, and hoped it would take her mind off of what to do about the money for a while.

Laria was waiting in the parking lot with the four girls and the baby.

"May should be out in a few minutes," Laria told her after greetings had been exchanged and Pree buckled herself into the passenger seat.

She was about to ask where Joey was when Bob's pickup pulled up next to them. Bob got out, leaving the door open, and Pree noticed the scratches were gone from the door of his pickup. Joey waved to Pree from inside the truck. There was another boy with him, whom Pree guessed to be Gage, May's neighbor. She waved back and blew the boys a kiss.

"Pree," Laria said. "I almost forgot. We're all getting together for pizza tomorrow night at the condo at seven, and we'd love for you to join us."

"I'll let you know," Pree said. "It depends on how things go with Louie, and all."

"Bring Louie along," Laria urged. "Please. I'd love to meet him."

"We'll see," Pree replied evasively, as they prepared to leave.

"Look, Mommy!" Joey said excitedly as they arrived in Oatman. "Real live donkeys are walking in the street!"

As Laria got Lauryn settled into her baby sling, Bob threw the diaper bag over his shoulder. Their first stop was the old jailhouse, with dummy prisoners inside.

"Our dad used to work in a jail," Joey said.

The adults looked at each other, waiting for a reaction from Joey's sisters at the mention of their dad.

"Only not a little one like this," Coley bragged. "A big one."

There was no further comment.

The excitement and enthusiasm of the children was contagious, and the trip proved to be great fun. Each child had been given five dollars to spend, so a considerable amount of time was spent searching for souvenirs.

They had just entered the old Oatman Hotel, where Clark Gable and Carole Lombard had spent their honeymoon, and where her wedding dress was on display, when Bob suddenly groaned, cupped his hands over his nose, and hurried out of the building.

"What's wrong?" asked Pree, turning to follow him.

"It's the cat," Joey said.

"What cat?" asked Pree, turning back.

The boy pointed to a huge calico asleep under a rocking chair in the hotel lobby.

"You know," Laria said. "His allergy. He's deathly allergic to cat dander."

Pree nodded, but in fact she hadn't known. Bob had never mentioned it to her. She'd been feeling more and more like an outsider lately.

"His throat closes up, real fast," Dani said, holding her hands to her throat to demonstrate.

"And his nose too," added one of the twins. "And he can't breathe."

"He keeps an inhaler thing in his truck," Joey added. "And in his police car and in his condo too. To breathe with, if he's around cats."

"Dad told me that once a stray cat got into the station, and nobody knew it," May said. "Bob's nose and throat closed up, and he couldn't catch his breath. By the time he reached the lobby, he was turning blue. Franco Ceja grabbed him as he started to fall and took him outside. Once outside, he recovered pretty quickly. By the time the paramedics arrived, he had gone to his truck and gotten his inhaler and was okay, but Dad said it was pretty scary for a few minutes."

Pree had known Bob had allergies and kept an inhaler in his truck, but had no idea they were so severe. Somewhat miffed, she wondered what other things Bob had shared with these people that he had never bothered to share with her. But he was still her friend, and she was concerned about him. She went outside to make sure he was all right while the others took the tour.

"Are you okay?" Pree sat next to Bob on a wooden bench outside the hotel.

"Oh, sure," he replied. "I saw the cat as soon as I walked through the door and my throat started closing. It could have just been a psychological reaction, but it was scary anyway. You know how allergic I am to the little critters."

Pree just nodded.

"We missed you at the movie Friday morning," Bob said. "I kept looking for you."

"Sorry, I missed it," she replied.

"We're going again this Friday. I hope you can make it."

"I'll try."

"Please come to dinner tomorrow night, Pree," he said. "It's a surprise party for you. Laria and the kids have gone to a lot of trouble. I've invited Mary and Bart, and the sisters too."

"For me?" asked Pree. "Why?"

"Tomorrow's your birthday," Bob said.

And so it was. With all that had been going on, she had forgotten about it.

Bob bought the kids some pellets to feed to the donkeys and two of the animals followed them to the parking lot. Tired but happy, they climbed into the vehicles and headed for home.

"I'm sure I can come over for that pizza tomorrow night," Pree said as she got out of Laria's van in the Safeway parking lot. "I'll probably bring Louie too."

"Great!" Laria smiled. "We'll see you at seven."

CHAPTER 18

**Los Angeles, California, 1951
(Forty-six years before the killings)**

"Greg?" Ivan called out when the door opened, his voice husky with grief.

"Naw, it's me, kid," Zoot called back. "Greg can't make it. He sent me to take you to the cemetery."

"Why?" asked Ivan, wiping his eyes. "Where's Greg."

"Somethin' happened," Zoot told him. "He's okay and everythin', but he can't be seen in public for a few days. By the way, Ivan, I'm really sorry to hear about yer mom."

"Thanks," said Ivan. Then he started to cry again. "Will Greg meet us at the cemetery?" he asked between sobs.

"You ain't listenin' to me, kid," Zoot said patiently. "Greg has to lay low for a while. That means he can't go out in public. The cemetery is public. Greg can't go there." Zoot quickly said, "But he said for you not to cry, and that he's sorry he can't be there and that he's thinkin' about you. Okay?"

Ivan nodded as he put a clean handkerchief in the pocket of the new suit Gladys had bought him for the funeral.

"I'll drop you off and come back for you in an hour," Zoot told him. "Because, as you can see, I ain't exackly dressed for a funeral."

Zoot's nickname came from his penchant for wearing zoot suits, a fad of the day. The one he wore today was bright green and put Ivan in mind of a Christmas tree.

"By the way, kid, Greg sent you this twenny bucks to buy food and stuff, and thirty bucks more for the rent next month, in case he ain't back yet," Zoot said. "Fifty in all."

At the cemetery, a green canvas shade had been set up on the grass. Ivan could see people inside. He knew the man in the black suit with the white collar was the minister. The man sat in the front row with Gladys and Pearl, who had left the seat between them empty for Ivan. Sitting in the second row were Mrs. Holloway, the neighbor who had taken care of Mama and the lady from the corner drugstore where they bought Mama's medicine.

"Where's Greg?" asked Pearl.

"Had to work," Ivan lied as he took his seat between his two sisters. Gladys and Pearl exchanged disapproving glances.

The minister said a lot of nice things about Mama that were supposed to make everyone feel better, but they only made Ivan sadder, and he was glad when the minister finished talking. They lowered the coffin into the grave, and everyone threw flowers on top of it.

Pearl offered to drop Ivan off at home on her way to work, but Ivan told her that Zoot was coming to pick him up. Pearl gave him a look, but didn't say anything. She and Gladys gave him hugs and Pearl said she would call him on her break that afternoon to see how he was doing.

Ivan walked around, reading names on the gravestones for a while. He felt very alone. He saw Gladys and Pearl standing beside the canvas tent, talking, and made his way inside the tent, where he could hear what they were saying.

"We can't take him," Gladys was saying. "Tony agreed to pay for the funeral, and the suit, but he draws the line at having him live with us."

"Well, we can't take him," Pearl said. "There's hardly room for us in our closet of an apartment. Besides, I'm working two jobs and Erik's at the hospital all the time. He won't finish his internship for another year. I just hate to think of leaving him there with Greg. No telling what he could pick up from Greg's gangster friends. Maybe you could change Tony's mind?"

"That's out of the question," Gladys insisted. "We entertain Tony's business clients in our home, Pearl. We can't have him hanging around. It would be too embarrassing."

"Why would it be embarrassing?" asked Pearl. "He's well-behaved, and he's polite."

"But he's stupid," Gladys said.

"He is not stupid!" Pearl replied angrily. "He's a little slow, that's all, and he seems slower than he actually is because he looks like a grown man, but he's still a boy."

"He'll be sixteen next month," Gladys said. "You got married when you were sixteen, for God's sake. Maybe the Army would take him. That would take care of everything."

"I was almost seventeen when I got married. And the Army won't take him until he's seventeen."

Silent tears streamed down Ivan's cheeks. His sister thought he was stupid and was embarrassed to have him around. That made his heart hurt. He walked to the road to wait for Zoot.

CHAPTER 19

Los Angeles, California, 1951
(Forty-six years before the killings)

It had been two weeks since Mama's funeral, and Ivan hadn't heard from Greg. The day after Mama's funeral, he had ridden his bike to the grocery store to buy food and detective magazines. He spent almost ten of the twenty dollars Zoot had brought him on magazines, Scooter Pies, Mars Bars, Wonder Bread, baloney, and Nehi soda pop. Pearl always said to eat fruits and vegetables everyday so he wouldn't get sick, so he bought lettuce to put on his sandwiches, and apples.

Yesterday, there had been a knock on the door and Ivan thought Greg was home, but it was just Mrs. Delaney asking about the rent. He gave her the thirty dollars.

Since Mama's funeral, Ivan just ate and slept and listened to the radio and read his detective magazines and waited for Greg to come home. After two weeks, he needed to buy more groceries. As he carried the groceries into the apartment, he heard someone moving around in Greg's room.

"HANDS UP OR YOU'RE DEAD!"

Ivan dropped the groceries and pushed his hands into the air.

"Ivan?" asked the gunman. "Oh, thank God!"

"Greg?" Ivan asked timidly.

"Yeah, it's me," said Greg quietly, walking into the living room. "I'm sorry if I scared you."

Greg threw his arms around the terrified Ivan and hugged him for a long time.

"Why are you crying, Greg?" Ivan asked. "And why are you all dirty and stinky?"

Greg told him, "I'm crying because I'm so happy to see you again."

"Me too, Greg. Where have you been?"

"Here and there. Did Zoot give you the sixty bucks I sent?"

"He gave me fifty dollars. I paid Mrs. Delaney the rent."

"I missed you, Ivan." Greg said. "I'm sorry I couldn't go to your mama's funeral. And I'm afraid I'm going to have to go away again soon, maybe for a long time, and I have to tell you something very important. More important than anything else I've ever told you."

"Really? What?" Ivan's curiosity was aroused.

"Listen good, little brother," Greg began. He turned Ivan's face up until they were eye to eye.

"I just put something in your hiding place under the floorboards. I pushed it way back, so it may be hard to reach. I want you to leave it there until I come back, but if I'm not back in three weeks, I want you to have it. Okay?"

"Okay," Ivan agreed. "What is it?"

"I can't tell you now, but you may know soon enough."

"But why won't you come back?" asked Ivan, starting to cry.

"Don't cry, Ivan," Greg pleaded. "Please. I need you to be strong and I need you to promise me something."

"Okay, Greg," Ivan said, sniffing and wiping his eyes on his sleeve. "I promise. What is it?"

"Promise me that you won't ever tell anybody about what I put under the floorboards. Not ever. No matter what. Not Pearl or Gladys or Zoot or the cops or a minister or a judge or anyone. Ever. Even if they beg you or threaten you. It's important, Ivan. Really important."

"I promise, Greg," Ivan assured him. "I won't never tell nobody, no matter what."

"Good! Now, I need to take a bath and get some sleep. I'm really tired."

After his bath, Greg walked into the bedroom and began getting dressed.

"Are you going out?" Ivan asked, disappointed.

"No," answered Greg. "I'm going to bed, but I'm going to sleep in my clothes"

"Shoes too?" asked Ivan.

"Shoes too," confirmed Greg.

"That's funny," said Ivan, smiling. "Why?"

"I might have to leave in a hurry," Greg replied.

"Why?" asked Ivan.

"I really can't talk about it, Ivan," Greg said. "Sorry. Believe me, it's better for you not to know."

When he had finished dressing, Greg laid down on the sheets and pulled the covers over himself.

"Greg," said Ivan tentatively, "Can I lay down next to you for a while?"

"Sure." Greg said, scooting over.

"Greg?"

"Ivan," said Greg. "I really need to go sleep now. By the way, did you get that social security card like I told you to?"

"I forgot. Do you have a social security card, Greg?"

"No," said Greg. "You could say my jobs have all been for cash, money, but I don't want you to be like me, Ivan. I want you to have a regular job, like Papa did. Promise me you'll do that, Ivan."

"Okay," Ivan said. "But how do I get a regular job?"

"I want you to go to the post office tomorrow and fill out an application for a social security card, and mail it in right away. By the time you get your card, you'll be old enough to get a job, legally. Then I want you to go to the produce mart where Pearl works and tell Mr. Dunder you need a job. I think he'll hire you, because you're young and strong, and healthy young men are hard to find these days, with the war and all."

"How come you never went in the Army, Greg?" Ivan asked.

"That's a story for another day. I'm going to sleep now."

CHAPTER 20

Los Angeles, California, 1951
(Forty-six years before the killings)

Ivan hurried up the stairs. He wanted to tell Greg he got the social security form, and show him his new detective magazine. Ivan had begged to stay home with Greg that day, but Greg had made him go to the movies. Zoot was coming by to talk to Greg about some private business. After that, he said, he had to rest some more because he had to leave that night, which made Ivan sad. Ivan stopped suddenly at the top of the stairs. The door to the apartment was standing open and he could see that the living room was a mess. The radio and lamps lay in pieces on the floor. The sofa cushions were on the floor too, with the stuffing pulled out of them.

Ivan's heart pounded. Someone was in Mama's room.

"It's me, Greg," he called out. "Don't shoot!"

"Greg ain't here, Ivan," Zoot said as he walked out of Mama's room. He lowered the gun in his hand.

"Where did he go?" Ivan asked. "His car's out front."

"That's a good question, kid," Zoot said, tucking the gun into the shoulder holster under his purple jacket. "These real bad-lookin' guys come and took him away. I don't know where they took him, but they were really mad."

"Are they going to kill him?" Ivan asked somberly.

"Well, I ain't gonna lie to ya, kid," Zoot said. "These are really bad guys, and they're really mad at Greg, on accounta he took somethin' that belongs to one of them. So if they ain't killed him yet, they're gonna. Either way, he ain't never comin' back."

Ivan waited for the tears to come to his eyes, but none came. He just looked at Zoot.

"What are you doin' here, Zoot? Why are things tore up?"

"Well, Ivan," Zoot said. "Greg had somethin' that belonged to me too, and I want it back, so I'm tryin' to find it. It's probably in a paper bag, or an envelope, or somethin'. Did you see anythin' like that?"

"No," Ivan said, truthfully.

"Well, just the same," Zoot said. "I'm gonna look around some more, in case he hid it here somewhere. Okay, kid?"

"I guess so," Ivan said.

"Why don't you come an' help me look?" Zoot smiled, moving the gun inside his jacket. "Two can look bettern' one."

"Okay," Ivan agreed. He was sweating. A lot.

Zoot began tearing up the other two bedrooms, slashing the mattresses, breaking mirrors, and overturning the dresser drawers. He searched the pockets of all the clothes in Greg's closet then dumped the dirty clothes out of the laundry basket onto the closet floor and went through them. He opened the door to the hall closet, searched the coat pockets, and stuck his hand into the galoshes and rain boots. Ivan stood by helplessly, watching and holding his breath and sweating profusely. Finally, Zoot stopped searching and turned to him.

"Sorry about the mess, kid," he said, smiling. He wrote something down on a piece of paper.

"Lissen, kid," Zoot continued. "In case you do find a paper bag or a envelope or somethin' that you know ain't yer property, call this number and I'll come over and pick it up. Okay?"

"Okay," Ivan agreed.

After Zoot had gone Ivan locked the door, went to Greg's room and lay down on the pile of dirty laundry. He curled into a fetal position and began shaking and cried uncontrollably. He felt like he would never be able to stop.

CHAPTER 21

Los Angeles, California, 1951
(Forty-six years before the killings)

It was here! It was Ivan's sixteenth birthday, and he had the best present he could have gotten, except if Greg would come home. He tore open the envelope even before he opened the birthday cards from Gladys and Pearl. There, on the little white card, was printed his very own social security number. Also printed on the card was his new name: GREGOE ISAAC CRENSKI. It was Papa's name, and Greg's name, and now it was his name. He signed his new name with Papa's old ink pen, then went to Mama's bedroom, removed Greg's birth certificate from Mama's Bible, and put it into an envelope with the little card. He took the bus to the Department of Motor Vehicles. He'd been studying the book every day while he waited for his social security card to arrive. He filled out the form and, to his great relief, passed the written test. No one questioned that he was twenty years old. He was given a temporary permit, and told to come back within two weeks to take the driving test.

The next morning, Ivan removed a thousand dollars from the five thousand dollars Greg had left under the floorboards. Using his new identity, he bought a four-year-old Studebaker for three hundred dollars and spent two days driving it around town. He practiced hand signals, left turns, and parallel parking until they were almost automatic. He received his license in the mail a week later. He would use the license to open a bank account one day soon, and deposit the rest of Greg's money into it.

The day after his driver's license arrived, Ivan drove to the United States Army Selective Service Office and enlisted in the United States Army. He was given two weeks to report to Fort Ord, in northern California, for basic training.

On Memorial Day, 1951, sixteen-year-old Ivan Joseph Crenski, who was now twenty-year-old Gregoe Isaac Crenski, packed his clothes, his money, his brother's money, his mama's Bible, and his detective magazines into his Studebaker and headed for Fort Ord, where he was going to be a soldier, and wear a uniform, and shoot bad guys. Maybe he would be a hero.

CHAPTER 22

Fort Ord, California, 1951:
(Forty-six years before the killings)

Basic training at Fort Ord was difficult for sixteen-year-old Ivan, now twenty-year-old Gregoe Crenski, but he was determined to succeed so he could wear a uniform, carry a gun, shoot bad guys, and keep his country safe.

It took only a week for him to realize that he would be carrying a potato peeler and pushing a mop.

Ivan hated peeling potatoes and mopping floors, but he liked being a soldier. He had trimmed down a lot in basic training and thought he looked good in his uniform. He also liked being called "Crenski" and G.I., his new initials. He remained pretty much a loner, but was somewhat friendly with his Kitchen Police mate, Timmy Lawrence.

Timmy hated Sarge, but Ivan liked him, because he reminded him of his brother. When Ivan messed up, Sarge yelled at him and made him do things over and over again until he got them right, like Greg used to do. Ivan always remembered to thank him for it. Ivan especially liked it when Sarge called him a moron, like Greg did. Ivan would smile and Sarge would walk away shaking his head.

Ivan could tell Sarge liked him too, because he let him mop the floors and made Timmy wash the pots and pans. Once, Sarge caught Ivan telling Timmy how much he hated peeling potatoes and Timmy said Ivan was in trouble. But the next day, Sarge switched Ivan from peeling potatoes to making sandwiches. Ivan liked making sandwiches because he got to go in early in the morning and leave after lunch mess, and didn't have to mop. It was a lucky break for Ivan because having nights off led to a new and profitable sideline for him.

Every evening lots of guys played poker in the barracks. Others shot craps. They taught G.I., the name they all called Ivan, to play draw poker and shoot craps. He lost all of his pay the first two months and had to go to the bank and take five dollars out of the money he had deposited so he could buy stuff he needed at the base exchange.

On Ivan's second trip to the bank, Baldwin, his fellow sandwich maker, asked for a ride to the telegraph office to pick up some money his mother had wired him because his wallet had been stolen. On the way to town, he confided to G.I. that he had actually lost his money gambling. G.I. told him he didn't have to lie to his mother, that he would lend him a few dollars until the next payday.

Word spread quickly that G.I. Crenski had money for payday loans. Within two months he was lending out over three hundred dollars a month at 25 percent interest; within six months, it had grown to almost a thousand. He bought a notebook and had the men sign for the loans. On paydays, G.I. would sit on a folding chair outside the metal Quonset hut that served as the pay hall. The men were paid in cash, and as they left the pay hall, they would stop and settle their debts.

G.I. reenlisted twice, but when Sarge decided to retire, he decided not to reenlist again. At the end of his nine years, the five thousand dollars Ivan, now Greg, had put into his brother's account, including the money he had borrowed and repaid with interest, had grown to almost nine thousand dollars. The balance in his own account was almost thirty thousand dollars, a considerable sum at a time when a middle-class home sold for around twenty-five thousand. The day he was discharged, G.I. went to San Francisco and bought himself a used Rolex watch and traded his old Studebaker for a two-year-old powder-blue Cadillac.

Sarge had a friend who ran the kitchen at Folsom State Prison, not far from Fort Ord, who gave Greg a job in the kitchen there.

In the town of Folsom, Greg located a small card room where people played poker and a game called "Pan." Greg played five-card draw and lost steadily. After he lost his money each evening, he hung around and chatted with people who were waiting for a seat.

Roman Neal, the manager of the club, a handsome, middle-aged, black man, often carved out a little time to chat with Greg. Greg liked Roman, and on his days off he would go to the club early to help him set up. Roman had been everywhere. He told Greg that the best music and the best food in the world were in New Orleans, and that he should go there some day.

Roman had come to Folsom to be near his brother, who was serving a life sentence for murder. Roman was the only person Greg ever talked to about his own brother, saying his name was Isaac so he wouldn't have to explain why they had the same name.

"Greg, my friend," Roman said one day, "why do you continue to play poker day after day when you lose all the time?"

"I know I'm not a good player, but I like bein' around the people. Sometimes I forget which hand beats what."

"I notice you watch the door every time someone comes in. Are you hiding from someone?"

"No." Greg laughed. "You remember I told you about my brother Isaac? Well, I know it's stupid because he's probly dead, but they never found his body, and I keep thinkin' he might of got away somehow. He played poker a lot, and I keep thinkin' that someday I'll be sittin' in a card room somewhere and he'll walk in."

"But didn't you tell me that you grew up in LA?"

"Yeah."

"Then why are you looking for him here in Folsom?"

"Because Sarge got me a job here. I'm not good at fillin' out applications and talkin' about myself and stuff."

"I see," said Roman, and let it drop.

The next Saturday morning, when Greg arrived at the card room, Roman gave him coffee and asked him if he had ever considered playing lowball poker. Roman told him it was simpler than draw because there were fewer possible hands, and that he might find it less confusing.

The next day, Sunday, the card room was closed. Roman spent several hours teaching Greg the fundamentals of lowball poker, and they started practicing on Sunday afternoons. Roman drilled him on various betting strategies, and told him players were often wary of raising players with a lot of chips on the table, fearing they might raise back. It took several months and considerable losses before Greg started breaking even, but in less than a year, he was winning regularly. He never let his chips fall below fifty dollars, a substantial stack at the time.

Greg had been at Folsom for ten years when one Saturday morning, Roman showed him an ad he had circled in the San Francisco newspaper. The Carlisle Brewery of Denver, Colorado, was opening a new plant near Los Angeles, and they were going to hire a lot of people. Roman had underlined the words, "No Experience Needed."

"It's often human nature for people to go back to where they came from," Roman said. "Believe me, if it wasn't for my brother, I'd be back in New Orleans in a New York minute. How long has it been since your brother disappeared?"

Greg thought for a minute. "Nineteen years now." He hadn't realized it had been that long.

"How about if I send away for an application and help you fill it out?"

"I guess that would be all right. Thanks."

The night before Greg's departure, Roman took him out to a nice restaurant and gave him a small gold coin as a farewell gift. Touched, Greg took off his Rolex and gave it to Roman.

"I can't accept this," Roman insisted.

"Please. I want you to have it," Greg assured him. "You're my good friend. Besides, I'm going to buy a new one."

As Roman replaced his old watch with the Rolex, Greg commented that people at the other tables seemed to be staring at them.

"Don't you know why?" Roman asked. He explained that a lot of people didn't think black and white people should socialize together, especially not in public.

Greg mulled Roman's words over for a moment before commenting on the issue that, at the time, was splitting the entire country apart, causing riots, sit-ins, and varying degrees of turmoil. Greg was able to confine his opinion to four words.

"Well, that's pretty silly," he said.

Roman smiled.

Greg arrived in Los Angeles in his new mint-green Cadillac Coupe de Ville. He found an affordable one-bedroom apartment in Studio City and transferred his accounts to the local bank. His brother's account was now worth over seventeen thousand dollars, and his own was worth almost sixty thousand.

When it first opened, the Carlisle Brewery had few employee amenities. There was a lunchroom with tables, chairs, soda, and candy machines, but not much else. Greg made himself two sandwiches each night and put them in his lunch bucket in the refrigerator before he went to bed. The next morning, he added a package of cookies or cupcakes and some chips and an apple. The other guys started buying sandwiches from him, and soon he was bringing in dozens of sandwiches, apples, and extra packages of chips and desserts.

Eventually, the company installed a large refrigerator for him to keep the sandwiches in. He started having a local deli make them for him, hired one of the swing shift guys to sell them during second lunch, and was clearing a lot more money from the sandwiches than he was from his job as a bottler. By the time the company cafeteria opened three years later, Greg had accumulated a tidy sum.

One day, Phillip Greer, the company's financial officer, came in for his daily Coca-Cola. As he often did, Mr. Greer chatted with Greg about the company's plans for the future. He confided to Greg that he was going to put every cent he could get his hands on into Carlisle stock the next day.

Greg took three hours off the next morning and opened a brokerage account, investing everything he and his brother owned in Carlisle stock. The next day, the stock split four to one and he made a small fortune. He sold some shares and replaced the money he had taken from his brother's account plus a thousand dollars.

The stock split several times over the years and Greg became a relatively wealthy man. He continued to live frugally, his only luxuries being a new Cadillac every five years, a new Rolex every ten years, and some fancy jewelry.

On his nights off, he played poker at the casinos, eventually becoming quite competent at lowball. He usually rented a room at a motel near one of the casinos, slept until 1:00 a.m. and went to the casino when many players were drunk or half asleep, and it was easier to win their money.

He never stopped looking for his brother.

CHAPTER 23

Laughlin, Nevada, 1997
(Six days after the killings)

"SURPRISE!"

As Pree and Louie entered the community room, Pree was greeted with shouts, hugs, air kisses, and pats on the back from Laria and her children, May and the twins, Gage, Bob, Val and Freddie, the sisters, Barry, and even Mike and Annette.

Mary and Bart Baker arrived late, as usual.

"This time it's not my fault," Mary proclaimed before they even got inside. "Bart is building a block wall for another neighbor, and he forgot the time."

"Block walls are hard work," Louie said. "I did a lot of block work until last year, when my eyesight started going."

"He should have better sense," Mary said. "He's pushing seventy. I keep telling him to slow down before he has a heart attack or a stroke or something."

"Hard work keeps you strong." Bart smiled, flexing his impressive biceps and taking his wife's fussing with his usual good humor.

"That's true," Louie confirmed. "Be grateful you can still do it."

Bart had worn his hearing aids, and he and Louie spent most of the evening trading stories about construction, the Korean Conflict, and other topics of interest to their generation.

Pree wore a new sweater set and bracelet her daughter Staci and grandson Justin had sent from Tucson. Jimmy was on the road, but had left his usual card with money, and Lu sent regrets and a gift card. She and Crush were in Las Vegas.

After a game of musical chairs, they all enjoyed pizza, and topped it off with Marietta's buttermilk chocolate cake. By the time the cake was served, Louie and Bart were fast asleep and Dora was stretched out on the floor, snoring.

"Bart nods off earlier and earlier these days," Mary said.

"Louie too," Pree said. "Although he stayed awake until after 2:00 a.m. on New Year's Eve."

"Not Bart. He barely made it through dessert. He left the party and went home to bed before eight thirty. The rest of us stayed and played Blackjack until after two, though."

It was a fun evening. Bob poured plastic glasses of non-alcoholic champagne for everyone, and they toasted Pree. Mike, who had hardly said a word all evening, surprised them by making a toast as well, which was actually an announcement. He told them he had called Laria into the station that afternoon to give her some good news, and that he had given the same news to Bob by phone. Now he wanted to share it with the rest of them. He said that Laria's alibi had checked out, and the Las Vegas police had found insufficient evidence to bring charges against her. The official cause of death was, "Undetermined: suspected murder/suicide."

Everyone cheered and clicked their glasses together. Bob grabbed Laria and hugged her until he became aware that people were looking at them and quickly released her. To relieve the awkwardness, Pree grabbed Laria and also gave her a hug. Over Laria's shoulder, she could see Bob. He was beaming.

As Laria walked the guests to their cars, she and Pree agreed to talk the next day about arrangements for Greg's and Mape's remains.

Driving home, it occurred to Pree that Bart was strong enough to have toted Greg's satchel to her doorstep, and he apparently had no alibi for the time of the killings. But he also had no motive, not to mention he was one of the most docile men she had ever met. She immediately ruled him out and was ashamed of herself for entertaining such ugly thoughts about her dear friend.

CHAPTER 24

Bullhead City, Arizona, 1997
(Eight days after the killings)

Pree had naively hoped that 1997 might be the year in which she would seize control of her life again. Now she feared things would only get worse. She would have to go to Las Vegas to claim the remains of the man responsible for making her life a living hell for the past two years then arrange for some kind of a memorial service honoring the jackass because technically she was still his wife and he had no other living relatives and his only friend was dead.

Even worse, Cal Hall, her former boss, had sent her a letter offering her a dream job as his assistant at a movie studio in Los Angeles. Pree was flattered and excited.

The fly in the ointment was Louie. Dear Louie. Not that Pree was irreplaceable and, of course, Louie had known when he hired her she wasn't going to stay forever. She had six months to find someone suitable, so she was probably worrying for nothing.

Today's stressor was that poor Harry Handy was in the hospital and his wife said he might never be able to return to work. Pree had spent the morning emptying trash containers around the park and carrying the bags of trash to the dumpster. She couldn't locate a repairman to fix the broken dryer in the washhouse, and God only knew when the grass would get mowed.

At the moment, she was on a fifteen-foot ladder trying to remove the Christmas lights from the giant evergreen near the river. She was about four inches short of being able to reach the star on top of the tree, and was contemplating stepping onto the top rung of the ladder that had a tag on it stating, "Warning: Do Not Use as a Step." And just when she was sure her life couldn't get any worse, she heard the voice from hell.

"I know you consider yourself to be above us mere mortals, Pree, but this is ridiculous. What are you doing up there?"

"Clyde," Pree said. "How did you get in here?"

Pree slowly backed down the ladder hoping with all her heart that Clyde wasn't looking at her fat behind.

"Through the gate. I saw you enter the code when I brought you home the other morning. Twelve twenty-five. Christmas Day. Duh."

"And why are you here?" Pree asked, annoyed.

"I need a favor," he replied.

"Forget it, Clyde," Pree said. "I don't have any more money for you."

"I don't need money, I need advice," Clyde said. "Remember when I told you I can't figure out why my boss and coworkers don't like me? You said we would have to talk about it at another time, and I thought this might be a good time."

"Actually, Clyde," Pree told him. "There couldn't be a worse time. Our handyman has had a stroke, and I'm filling in for him. After I get the lights off of this tree, I have to find someone to fix a dryer that will no longer heat, and then I have to mow the grass. Maybe another time."

"I really need to talk to you today Pree," Clyde said. "Uncle Bob said you used to be a boss, and I really need an experienced opinion. I'm afraid I'm going to get fired if I can't turn things around soon. Maybe we could make a deal. If I take the lights down for you and mow the grass, could you spare a few minutes? It shouldn't take more than half an hour. I even made a list."

How could she refuse? Clyde was tall enough to reach the star. *Oh, crud!*

"All right, Clyde," she said. "It's a deal. But I'm not sure I'm the right person to ask for help. I've never worked in security."

"You're exactly the right person," he replied, scampering up the ladder. "Because you used to be a boss and you don't like me either. Believe me, nothing you say could make me feel any worse than I already do."

Pree took the star from Clyde and carried it over to the storage boxes she had laid on the concrete tables in the plaza. They fell into a routine and in a short while, all the lights had been removed from the tree and enclosed in the storage boxes.

Inside the storage room, as Clyde stacked the boxes neatly in the corner, his eye was drawn to some fishing gear in the corner.

"Wow!" Clyde exclaimed. "This is top of the line fishing equipment! Is it yours?"

"Heavens no!" Pree said. "It belongs to Louie, the owner. He's my boss. He's lost most of his eyesight so I manage the trailer park for him and look after him and Dora, his dog."

"Can he still fish?" asked Clyde. "It would be awful if he had to give up fishing."

"You're a fisherman?" Pree asked.

"Yeah," Clyde said. "Since I was a kid. Uncle Bob taught me. But I don't have any fishing gear out here."

Pree said, "Louie still fishes when he has someone to help him, usually my son or Barry or Jo, tenants who like to fish. Right now, they're all away, though."

"Where is Louie now?" asked Clyde.

"Taking his afternoon nap," Pree answered. "He'll be asleep for another hour or so, so I guess we should have that talk."

"First, let me take a crack at that dryer," Clyde said. "Do you have a screwdriver handy?"

In no time, the dryer was working perfectly.

"I seem to have a knack for fixing things," Clyde said.

As Clyde returned the screwdriver to the toolbox, a rollaway cot caught Pree's eye, reminding her of Clyde's living conditions. Tenants borrowed the cot occasionally when they had overnight guests.

"Are you still sleeping in that storage shed?" she asked Clyde.

"Yeah," Clyde replied, "It's not so bad, though. There's a mattress on the floor under my sleeping bag, and I used some of the money you loaned me to buy a heavy comforter at the thrift store, so I stay pretty warm, even when the wind blows."

"Well, let's go sit on the plaza and have that talk," Pree said.

"Okay, Clyde," she said after they were seated with drinks in front of them. "What seems to be the problem?"

"It's pretty simple, really. People just don't seem to like me, except for my family, and I don't know why."

"No comment," Pree said. "Let's talk about the things on your list."

One by one they examined Clyde's problems, with Pree playing devil's advocate. She led him through some role-playing and role-reversal exercises in an attempt to give him a different perspective, and was impressed with how quickly he was able to pinpoint the issues as they went through the process.

When they finished, Clyde said sheepishly, "Okay, I think I get how I've screwed up, but what's done is done. What can I do about it now?"

"Frankly, Clyde, I've wondered for some time now why you work so hard at being a jerk," Pree told him. "And now I find that when you drop the smart-ass attitude, you're a pretty likeable person."

He looked embarrassed. "It's hard to talk about."

"Suit yourself," said Pree, standing and picking up the empty glasses and cans from the table.

"No, wait, please," Clyde said. "I'm sorry. I really need to talk this out, Pree. I have to change things."

Reluctantly, Pree sat back down.

"The truth is," Clyde said. "I was a nerd in high school. Laugh if you like, but I was a Science and Chess Club, Coke-bottle glasses, pens in the pocket protector, took my mom to the prom, nerd. For graduation, my mom and grandmother paid for eye surgery and I got rid of the glasses. But there's no surgery to correct nerdiness, so I tried to correct it myself. In college, I watched the popular guys and tried to be cool like they were. But cool just doesn't seem to work for me. Sometimes I think maybe I should just give up and turn back into my nerdy self."

"What you apparently don't realize, Clyde, is that girls may go for the cool guys in high school and college, but when they grow up and get into the real world, the smart girls prefer guys that are stable, reliable, and motivated. In other words, guys like you."

"Yeah right," Clyde said. "You're just blowing smoke to make me feel better."

"Come on, Clyde," she half teased. "You know I would never try to make you feel better. But you do seem to be a pretty good guy when you lose the stupid remarks and the arrogant attitude, and you're good-looking. Just be yourself, and learn to look at things from the other person's point of view like you did today, and I think you'll do just fine."

"I hope you're right," he said hopefully. "Because there's a girl I'd really like to ask out, but I don't think she likes me."

"Oh?" said Pree, suddenly interested. "Come on, tell."

"Her name is Conni," Clyde said shyly. "Without the 'e'"

"And?"

"She takes applications at the Las Vegas Metro Police Department," he said. "I've applied for a job there, and I go in every week to remind her that I'm still interested, but she acts like she doesn't like me. You know, kind of like you do."

Pree laughed. "Tell me what you say to her," she said. "And please tell me you don't call her 'Sweet Cheeks.'"

Clyde rolled his eyes and grinned.

Louie saved Clyde from embarrassing himself further by stepping out onto his doorstep with Dora and saying, "Oh, you have company."

"Come, join us," Pree said. "Meet Clyde Snyder, Bob's nephew. Clyde, Louie here is my boss."

"That's debatable," Louie laughed as he worked his way down the steps and out to the plaza. Dora hurried to the dog run to poop. Louie was carrying a baggie and a paper towel. Pree took them from him and headed to the dog run.

"Here, let me," Clyde said, taking them from her and hurrying toward the already-waiting poop pile.

While Clyde washed his hands at the outdoor sink, Pree went into her trailer and made a pitcher of lemonade, Louie's favorite. By the time she got back to the table, Louie and Clyde had decided to go fishing. As they fished, she heard bursts of laughter coming from the dock. Louie was no doubt regaling Clyde with stories of his past, most of which Pree knew by heart.

Afternoon turned into evening, and the men remained on the dock, fishing, talking, and laughing. Pree invited Clyde to stay for dinner. She put some potatoes in the oven, lit some charcoals in a stone fire ring on the plaza then told the guys she was going to the store to get some steaks. She splurged on rib eyes, her favorite. Clyde took over the grilling duties while Pree made the salad. Louie contributed a bottle of wine.

When they finished eating, Clyde insisted on carrying the dishes into Pree's trailer, rinsing them, and putting them into the dishwasher.

Pree stayed on the plaza with Louie. She told him about Clyde's predicament and sleeping arrangements, and asked him if it would be all right if Clyde slept on the cot in the storage room for a while, until things got better.

"Of course not," Louie said, adamantly. "I'm surprised you would suggest such a thing, Pree."

Pree looked up to see Clyde walking toward them. She could tell by the look on his face that he had heard everything. She was devastated.

"We can't have this young man sleeping in the storage room," Louie continued. "When I have a perfectly fine bed in my guest room that hasn't been slept in for five years. He can sleep there for a while, until he gets on his feet."

"Are you sure?" asked Pree, looking apologetically at Clyde. "You just met him."

"And how long did I know you, young lady, when I put my life and my business into your hands and let you move into my parents' trailer?" he asked.

It was a truly awkward situation, but Clyde settled things by graciously declining Louie's offer, insisting that he was perfectly comfortable where he was. He took his keys out of his pocket and prepared to leave.

"Of course you're not comfortable there," Louie insisted. "It's a storage shed for crying out loud. Besides, it'll be nice to have someone else in the house with me for a while. We can fish every day. And Pree could use some extra help right now."

As Clyde turned to leave, Pree said, "Louie's right, Clyde. I could really use some help, and I know Louie would welcome your company, at least for a couple of weeks, until Barry gets back."

"It sounds great," Clyde told Louie. "But there's a slight problem. I usually get home from work between twelve thirty and one thirty in the morning. I'm pretty quiet, but I might wake you up."

"Don't worry," Louie assured him. "I sleep like a log."

"Okay then, if you're sure," Clyde said hesitatingly. "I'll be as helpful as I can."

At a few minutes after nine the next morning, Pree grabbed her glass of Diet Pepsi and walked over to Louie's trailer to check things out. The odor of cinnamon assailed her nostrils as she entered. Louie was sitting at the table eating breakfast and Clyde was refilling their coffee cups.

"Sit down and have some breakfast," Louie said, smiling. "Scrambled eggs and cinnamon toast. It's delicious!"

"Yes," Clyde said, setting the coffee cups on the table. "One egg or two?"

"No eggs, thanks," Pree said, grabbing a piece of cinnamon toast.

"Louie," she began. "After we take Dora out, I need to go to Laughlin to talk to my friend Laria about making arrangements for our husbands' remains," Pree said. "I'll pick you up a Subway sandwich on my way back, but lunch may be a little late."

"Dora's already been out," Louie said. "And I showed Clyde around the park."

Pree was impressed.

Clyde explained, "I'm a morning person."

"When do you sleep?" she asked.

"I slept a few hours when I got in this morning, and I'm planning to take a nap this afternoon, when Louie takes his," Clyde said. "And I'll make lunch, so there's no need to hurry back."

"We're going fishing after our naps," Louie said, obviously pleased at the prospect.

"Sounds great," Pree said. She explained Dora's lunchtime food and medication routine to Clyde.

When breakfast was over, Clyde jumped up, rinsed the dishes and put them in the dishwasher. "Now, I think I saw a lawn mower in the storage room," he said to Pree. "If you'll unlock the door for me, I'll get started on the lawn."

"Why don't you just give him the extra set of keys to the washhouse and storage room?" Louie asked. "He'll need them while he's here."

Pree hurried to her trailer to fetch them.

As she prepared to leave for Laughlin, Pree could see Clyde mowing the grass from her kitchen window. Louie was sitting in the plaza with Dora. A germ of an idea came into Pree's mind. Dared she hope that Clyde might be her potential replacement? Her ticket out of here?

CHAPTER 25

Bullhead City, Arizona, 1995
(Two years before the killings)

Greg was wearying of the whole plan. He had lost the list Mape had helped him make and feared Mape would be really upset when he found out.

Greg knew Pree was worried about him, and it made him feel bad to lie to her, but even that didn't make him feel as bad as having to cash in his stock and draw out all his money, especially since the market was gaining every day. He had just deposited a total of twenty thousand dollars in checks from his stock account into his players' banks at four of the Laughlin casinos. The people at the casinos knew him and didn't ask questions when he deposited checks, or even when he drew out cash, as long as he kept the amounts low. He was kind of proud that he had been able to work out a routine for getting the cash out of the stock market without making anyone suspicious. He hadn't even told Mape about it.

Just now, he had put almost ten thousand dollars in cash, adjusted by the money he had spent and the gains and losses from the poker games he had played to make the withdrawals seem legitimate, into the suitcase in the storage unit; the unit Pree didn't know about. He had held back a few hundreds. Greg liked to pay for things with hundreds. Like the jewelry he wore, it let people know he wasn't a loser. He had also pocketed a couple of tens for ice cream. He didn't like to flash hundreds in front of Maude, especially not when her grandson Nath was there. Nath scared him a little. Nath's friend Nico scared him a lot.

The suitcase was over half full now, and the satchel was already full. It would take several more weeks to finish converting the deposits into cash, though. He avoided making large cash withdrawals so as not to raise suspicion.

Mape had begun to complain about how long it was taking him to clear out the money, but that was because he didn't know how much stock Greg actually owned. If he knew, he'd be after Greg for even more money to lose at the Hold'em tables. He was already hinting around about needing a replacement for the old hatchback Greg had given him and Laria for a wedding present.

The important thing was that there would be no money in the stock account when he filed for the divorce. Mape said, otherwise the court would give half of it to Pree, like they gave half of everything he owned to Laria. Except for the ninety thousand dollars they'd had in their savings account that he had told Laria he lost gambling.

Greg trusted Mape to do what was best, of course, but sometimes Greg thought Mape was wrong about Pree, and maybe about Laria too. It was all making him really confused.

The only good thing about bringing his money to the storage locker was that it was on the same street as the gas station with the Yummy Cone Ice Cream Parlor. Greg loved ice cream. Good ice cream, not that low-fat, sugar-free stuff Pree was making him eat since the doctor told him he had to lose weight on account of his blood pressure. And he really liked talking to Maude, the woman who worked at the ice cream store. Poor Maude! She was sixty-seven years old, but still had to work because she'd been married to a no-good loafer who, to hear Maude tell it, had lain around drunk most of the time they were married. Maude had cleaned houses for cash to support herself and her daughter, Nita, and only qualified for a pittance in social security benefits. She couldn't clean houses anymore because of her bad back, so she worked for minimum wage at the Yummy Cone.

Greg drove out of the storage lot, bypassed Miracle Mile, and drove to the highway, where he made a right turn into the Yummy

Cone lot. He gassed up his Town Car at the pump, then parked and went in to the store.

"Turn the sign around," Maude called to him from behind the counter. "It's closin' time."

By the time Greg had taken a seat in the booth, Maude had set the biggest banana split he had ever seen in front of him.

"What have you been up to?" Greg asked as he swirled two cherries in the whipped cream and stuck them into his mouth.

"Same old, same old," she replied. "Ain't been too busy, 'cept Nath didn't show again today, so I had to do the cleanin' up. I'll have to hitch home too. He was my ride, an' I got no bus money."

Maude lived in a trailer park in Willow Valley, about twelve miles down the highway, too far to walk. Greg had taken her home a few times when her grandson had been a no-show.

"I can hang around and give you a ride," he offered.

It was the answer Maude was counting on.

Greg wasn't sure why he liked Maude. He didn't want to have sex with her or anything, although sometimes it seemed like maybe she wanted him to. It just felt good to be with her. She was grateful for the little things he did, like giving her a ride home or buying her a few groceries or a carton of cigarettes. It gave him the same good feeling it gave him to do nice things for Rowena and her kids. Pree said once she thought he had a Santa Claus complex. He just liked making people feel good. He liked making Pree and her kids feel good too, but it wasn't the same. They appreciated what he did for them and all, but they didn't really need anything. Not like Maude and Rowena did.

Jeanne Jessup came in and poured herself a cup of coffee from the fresh pot Maude had just made. Jeanne, a student at the local community college, came in after Maude closed each night and worked until 6:00 a.m. selling gas, cigarettes, candy, coffee, and sodas through a bulletproof glass window.

They said good night to Jeanne and left.

"Do you want to get some Mexican food at Casa Serena?" Greg asked, the banana split notwithstanding. Greg really liked the food there and Pree wouldn't be making dinner tonight. She had her Spanish class at the high school. She and Mary Baker always ate together at Carl's Jr. before they went to class.

"That would be a real treat!" Maude said enthusiastically.

Greg smiled. Maybe he did have a Santa Claus complex.

"Do you know why Nath didn't show up for work today?" Greg asked after they ordered and the server brought Maude a bottle of beer and him a Coke. He asked mostly to make conversation. Talking to people was Greg's favorite thing to do.

"Probably strung out again," Maude said, matter-of-factly, shoving the sliver of lime into the bottle and taking a sip of her Corona. "Nico, his old cellmate at the pen, showed up an' they been hangin' out. Nico plea-bargained to fifteen years for manslaughter after somebody paid him to kill a guy. Nico's real mean-looking. He does have a nice car, though. A Buick. I think he might of stole it. Most nights he picks Nath up after work and they give me a ride home. If Nath's parole officer finds out he's been seein' Nico, they could both go back in. I try to talk to him some, but he gets all fired up when he's high, so I shut my mouth. He even shoved me once. That's when Nita, his mom, moved in with me. I try to steer clear of him when he's drinkin' or usin'."

After dinner, Maude went to the powder room while Greg waited for the server to process his credit card. His heart jumped when a man leaving the restaurant smiled and waved at him. It was Bart Baker, Mary's husband. He was with his sister, Camilla, Mary's best friend. Greg was frantic. Had they seen Maude? This was bad. If Pree found out, it could ruin everything.

CHAPTER 26

Bullhead City, Arizona, 1995
(The year before the killings)

"Grandma?"

Pree struggled to shake off the slumber that consumed her.

"Justin? Come in, sweetheart."

She sat up in bed, pulling the covers around her.

"Grandma, there's a big truck in front of the house, like a moving van, with a car hooked to the back of it. A man just got out of it."

The doorbell rang.

"Maybe the driver's lost or something."

Pree looked at the digital clock on the nightstand. It was 4:48 a.m. She shook Greg.

The doorbell persisted, non-stop. They threw on their robes, hurried down the hall, peeked through the stained glass and opened the door.

"Good morning, everyone," said Mape, displaying his gap-toothed grin. "What's for breakfast?"

"Mape," Pree said groggily. "What are you doing here?"

"What does it look like?" he asked, walking into the house. "I'm visiting. Didn't Greg tell you?" Turning to Greg, he continued, "Didn't I tell you I'd stop by on my way to New Jersey to say goodbye to my best friends?"

"Oh," Greg said. "Was that today? I thought it was next week."

"So I'm a little early," Mape teased.

112

The door to the guestroom opened and Alma, Pree's mother, walked into the hallway.

"Is it time to get up?" she asked. She sometimes got confused, especially in unfamiliar surroundings.

"No, Mom," Pree said gently, escorting her mother back to the guest room. "Greg's friend just dropped by for a visit. Go back to sleep, now."

By the time Pree got her mother settled, Staci and Jimmy had come into the kitchen from the guest wing to see what the commotion was about.

"Oh," Mape said. "I didn't realize you had company."

"That's because you didn't call first," Pree said. "My family is visiting this week, for an early holiday celebration."

"Happy Thanksgiving, everyone," Mape said, flashing the comical grin again.

Jimmy, Staci, and Justin waved and returned to the guest wing.

"I'm afraid our beds are all filled until tomorrow night, Mape," Pree said. "But Greg can get you a room across the river for tonight. The kids will be leaving tomorrow, and you can move into the guest wing. I'm not sure what your schedule is, but we're leaving for California on Friday to take my mother home and to go Christmas shopping. You're welcome to stay until then."

"Hold on," Mape said. "You don't have to worry about me. I'm just dropping by. Don't worry about putting me up."

Pree exhaled and felt some of the tension leave her body.

"A sleeping bag in the corner is good enough for me," Mape continued. "I just wanted to see my best friends one last time before I move on to my new life in Jersey."

The tension returned.

Greg suggested, "How about the sofa in my office? Without the cushions it's like a twin bed. He could sleep there."

"Good idea, Greg," Pree agreed. "It's better than the floor, Mape. Tomorrow you can move into the guest wing."

"Sounds like a plan to me," Mape said. "I'll go get my stuff out of the truck in a minute. But first, how about that breakfast? I'm starved."

"Help yourself to anything you can find in the kitchen," Pree said as she headed back to the bedroom. "But don't overdo it. I'm making Belgian waffles around nine thirty."

"Is Mape always like this?" asked Staci. They were still at the breakfast table. Mape and Greg had gone to the casinos.

"Always," Pree said.

"I've only been around him once before," Jimmy said. "He was a jerk then too."

Pree said, "He doesn't seem to be able to help it. Mary thinks he's compensating for a gigantic inferiority complex."

"Is it considered a complex if someone really is inferior?" Staci asked.

Her remark broke the tension, and they all laughed.

"What I don't understand is why Greg tolerates Mape the way he does," Staci said. "Mape's abuse just seems to roll off of him."

"Nobody understands that. It's one of the great mysteries of the universe," Pree told them.

CHAPTER 27

Bullhead City, Arizona, 1995
(The year before the killings)

"What did you do to piss your neighbors off?" Mape asked Pree when she walked into the kitchen on Friday morning. Her kids had left the day before, and Greg and Mape were sitting at the table, drinking coffee.

"What neighbors is that?" she asked. There were vacant lots on each side of their property, and the only neighbors they knew were Warrner and Lydia Farrell, the neighbors in the house adjacent to the lot to the left of them.

"Well," Mape said, "someone has it in for you. All four of the outside tires on my truck got slashed to smithereens last night. And someone threw eggs onto the doors and the windshield."

"What?" Pree was alarmed. She'd never heard reports of any vandalism in the neighborhood. She realized immediately that Mape was the vandal. Greg sat wordlessly, not looking at her.

Mape said, "It's a mess. I'll call the rental company, but I doubt they'll be able to get anyone up here until Monday."

"That's okay," Pree said, refusing to get caught up in his game.

"Oh, wait," Mape said. "Weren't you guys going to leave for California today? I sure wouldn't want to keep you from your trip. Your mother probably needs to get home."

"That's okay, Mape," she repeated. "We can take Mother home next week. It's not like she has any place she has to be." Pree decided to run her own game for a while. She was pretty sure the tire-slashing

115

was a scheme to give Mape and Greg a chance to spend a few days together without her. She had known for some time now that something was going on between them, and although she was clueless as to what it might be, she knew it didn't bode well for her. Her trial balloon brought results.

"But you were going shopping," Mape whined. He had switched to his smarmy persona. "I wouldn't want you to miss out on that on my account. Maybe Greg could stay here with me, and you could take your mother home and shop with your friends."

Mape gave Greg a hard look.

"Oh," Greg said when Mape's message kicked in. "I can always go to Vegas and shop. Why don't you go ahead without me this time? Weren't you going to have lunch with Norina Owens?"

"Go without you? Don't be silly," Pree said as she went to the bedroom to shower, dress, and pack.

Mape glared at Greg, who shrugged. He'd done his best.

Pree let them sweat for another hour while she prepared herself and her mother for the trip home.

At the last minute, it occurred to Pree that she wouldn't be able to lock the dead bolt on the door of the closet in Greg's office. It was the closet in which they kept important papers and valuables, including the lockbox that contained their jewelry, emergency cash, and passports. They had replaced the wooden door of the closet with a steel one when they moved in, and they opened it only when they needed to get something from, or return something to it.

The problem today was that Mape had insisted on remaining in the office, sleeping on the couch, and now his clothes were hanging in the security closet, so Pree couldn't lock the door. She solved the problem by placing the lockbox in the trunk of her car.

CHAPTER 28

Bullhead City, Arizona, 1995
(The year before the killings)

As if Pree wasn't worried enough about Greg, Mary had just phoned to tell her about Bart and Camilla seeing Greg having dinner with the Yummy Cone woman. Could he have a girlfriend? Was that why he'd been acting so weird lately? Sometimes late at night she heard sounds coming from his bathroom, like he may be crying. And he'd gained an enormous amount of weight. She worried he may be having a breakdown of some kind. She suspected it was the large amount of medication he'd been taking. Vicodin, Demerol, and other stuff she'd never heard of. Mape picked up his prescriptions for him from some doctor in California. Every time she tried to get him to go to a local doctor, he got surly and wouldn't discuss it. During his last episode, she thought he might become violent, but he ended up crying like a baby. He apologized afterward and was his old self again for a couple of days.

That evening after dinner, Pree found Greg in his office and asked him if he wanted to take a walk. "I'm still kind of tired from my trip," Greg said. He had just returned from his farewell visit to Las Vegas with Mape.

"Okay, then," she said, "why don't you just sit there, and I'll help you clean off your desk. Taxes will be due soon and we haven't organized your papers since before Thanksgiving."

She picked up an unopened envelope and Greg immediately jumped up and grabbed it from her hand.

"Put that down," he insisted. "That's mine!"

"I know it's yours, Greg," she said, somewhat dumbfounded. "I always help you organize your desk. What's going on?"

"Nothing!" he said, his voice almost a shout.

"Nothing," he repeated, smiling, his voice softer and more controlled. "I just want to start doing it for myself. Okay?"

"Of course," she said, sitting down at the other end of the sofa. She sat quietly, giving him time to cool down and herself time to collect her thoughts.

"You do too much for me already," he said finally, smiling.

"Is this a good time to talk about the woman you've been seeing?" Pree tried to sound casual.

"Wh-wh-what woman?" He stammered, caught off guard by her question. "What are you talking about?"

"Greg," she said, trying hard to keep her voice even and unthreatening. "I'm sure you know which woman. The one you've been taking to dinner. Or maybe there's more than one?"

"No," he said, lowering his head. "There's just one."

"Are you having an affair with her?" Pree asked.

"No!" he said emphatically. "I wouldn't do that."

He turned to look at her.

"I love you, Pree, honest I do. She's just a woman I know. She has to work because she don't get enough social security money to live on. I just help her out, like I did with Rowena, but she's just a friend, honest."

"Okay, I'll believe that she's just your friend. For now, anyway."

"So what do you want me to do?"

"Well, I think I should meet her, don't you?"

"Yes," he replied, reluctantly. "I guess so."

"Why don't you find out what night she's free next week and invite her here to dinner? Nothing fancy. We can get acquainted."

"Here?" Greg asked. "You want me to invite her here?"

"Why not? Or if you prefer, we can take her to dinner at a restaurant. Who knows? Maybe she and I will become friends too."

Greg's heart was racing as he asked, "Can I think about it for a while?"

"Of course," Pree said. "I heard the dryer buzz. I'd better go take care of the laundry."

On her way out of the room, she turned back at the doorway.

"By the way, Greg, what's her name?"

"Amy," he lied. It was the first name that came to mind.

As soon as Pree left, Greg panicked. What had he gotten himself into? He couldn't introduce Maude to Pree. If Maude got a look at Pree's jewelry and clothes, especially her wedding ring, she'd be after him for more money in a flash. She was already hinting around for a new refrigerator. He sure couldn't let her see where they lived. And there was Nath. If Nath ever got wind he was well-off, there is no telling what he might do. Him and that killer friend of his.

Greg wished he could call Mape. He'd know what to do. But Mape didn't know about Maude and he'd think Greg was a super moron for getting himself into a situation like this. If Pree got mad and decided to divorce him, it would wreck their whole plan, and Mape might never speak to him again. He wouldn't be able to stand that.

Greg considered the situation and made a decision about Maude. He found Pree in her office recliner, reading.

"Pree," he said. "I've been thinking. I don't think you'd like Maude for a friend. To tell the truth, I don't like her too much, myself. I just feel sorry for her. I think I'll just stop seeing her. Is that okay?"

"It's okay with me," Pree said. "It's your decision."

So her name is Maude, not Amy. Why had he lied? Pree wondered. Something was going on, and she was pretty sure this wouldn't be the end of it.

Greg felt as if a heavy burden had been lifted from his shoulders. It had been easier than he had expected. He had told Maude his wife had found out he was seeing her and was jealous. She'd gotten a little upset at first, but when he handed her the envelope, and she saw the two hundred dollar bills, she settled down and said she understood. She kissed him on the cheek and gave him a free Yummy Cone. Now he wouldn't have to worry about Pree asking for a divorce, and Mape wouldn't be mad at him for messing up the plan. He sighed with relief.

CHAPTER 29

Bullhead City, Arizona, 1996
(The year of the killings)

Pree sat drinking a Diet Pepsi and watching *Letterman* on the family room TV, where she had retreated after being awakened by a collect call from New Jersey. Half an hour later, Greg walked into the room then over to the refrigerator to grab a soda for himself.

"Be sure to get a caffeine-free one," Pree cautioned, "so you can get back to sleep. We want to get an early start tomorrow."

"Oh yeah," Greg said. "We need to talk about that. Why do I have to go with you? I forgot."

"We're going to arrange for someone to do some repairs on Mother's house, remember?"

"Do I have to go? I think I'll stay home."

"You were looking forward to it yesterday. What changed your mind?"

"Nothin'," Greg replied curtly. "I just thought I'd stay here."

It was obvious Greg had taken more pills. His eyes were glassy and his speech was already starting to slur. She knew to proceed cautiously because lately he was becoming confrontational, especially during the first hour or so after taking the drugs.

"What did Mape want?' she asked, trying to sound casual.

"Not that it's any of your business," he snapped, "but he needs to borrow some money."

"Again?"

"What do you mean, again?" he asked. "You act like he's always askin' me for money."

"Greg, honey, he asks you for money all the time. I don't care, so don't get snippy with me. I was just curious, that's all. When I lend my kids money, you ask me what it's for and I tell you. What's going on?"

"If you must know, he wants me to invest twenty-five thousand dollars and be his partner in his antiques business."

"Really? Does he want you to move back to New Jersey and help run the business?"

Had that been the reason for all the scheming before Mape left?

"No. He says I'll be a silent partner. I'll just be half owner, and I'll get half of the profits."

"If there are any."

"What do you mean by that?" Greg asked, raising his voice a bit.

"Calm down. I didn't mean anything."

"Yes, you did," he said, accusingly. "And I am calm."

"Then why are you shouting?"

"Oh," he said, lowering his voice. "I didn't mean to yell. But what do you mean if there are any profits? Mape knows what he's doing."

"Fine," Pree replied, realizing she'd overstepped. Greg seemed even more animated than usual. She was pretty sure the quantity of pills he was taking had been escalating, and he was continuing to gain weight. Lately, she had begun to fear that he would overdose.

"It's none of my business, anyway. He's your friend, so do what you like."

"No," he said, calmer now. "I'm sorry. I know you're just looking out for me, and I want to know what you meant. Why don't you think I should go into business with him?"

"I think it's getting late, and I have to get up early. You can stay home tomorrow if you want. We can talk about this another time."

"No!" Greg shouted.

"I mean *no*," he said, placing a finger to his lips and lowering his voice. "He wants the money tomorrow, and I want to know now why you think he might not make any profits. Mape's not stupid, you know."

"I have never said he was stupid," she reminded him. "It's just that he's never owned a business before, so he doesn't have a track record. You might consider just giving him twenty-five thousand dollars, and not being his partner."

"You mean as a gift?" He asked, disbelieving. "Why would I do that?"

"Because he's your friend, he needs it, and you can afford it. That way, if the business fails, and if he runs up a lot of debts, his creditors can't come to you for payment."

"Oh, I see." He let the thought roll around in his brain for a while. "Well, that makes sense, I guess. But you still haven't said why you think his business might not be successful."

"For all I know, he'll be a huge success."

"You want him to fail, don't you? Admit it!"

"Why would I want him to fail?"

"Because you hate him! I know you hate him!"

Greg jumped to his feet and began pacing and waving his arms around. Frightened, Pree backed away from him, stepping into the hallway so she could reach the front door if necessary.

"I don't hate Mape, Greg," she said calmly. "I just don't like the way he talks down to you sometimes. He calls you a moron, for God's sake, and I resent that because I love you. Other than that, I don't have a problem with Mape."

She hoped God would forgive her for that one.

Greg fell onto the love seat, sobbing, and began beating himself in the face with his fists.

"Greg, what are you doing?" Pree said. "Please don't do that."

"I can't take it anymore," he said, continuing to sob and pulling on strands of his hair. "I just can't take it."

"Greg, honey, you're scaring me," Pree said. "Please, stop."

He calmed down instantly, wiped his eyes on the sleeve of his bathrobe, and grinned at her. He sat silently for several minutes, giggling occasionally. When he finally spoke, it was in a calm, quiet voice.

"Do you know what I'd like to do right now?" he asked, his head still bowed and his eyes still closed. "Go out to my car and get my gun and shoot you through the head, then blow my own brains out."

Pree felt shivers run down her spine. Keeping her voice as steady as possible she said, "I'm going to go to bed now, so we won't keep saying things we'll be sorry for later. I'll see you in the morning."

She backed slowly down the hall until she was out of his line of sight, then turned into the entryway, where she could open the door and activate the alarm if he went out to the garage. She could get to the Ferrell's house next door before he could get the gun and reach her. She stood in the entryway, still trembling, fighting back tears, for several minutes. The situation was finally defused when she heard the familiar snoring coming from the family room. He always slept hard when his drugs wore off. He would be out for several hours, so she went to bed in the guestroom.

Pree came awake instantly when the guestroom light came on and Greg said her name. Instinctively, she rolled onto the floor, putting the bed between herself and the door. She peeked over the edge of bed and saw that Greg had no gun.

"I'm sorry, Pree," he said. "I don't know what gets into me lately. I love you, honest I do. I just want to come to bed now, and I want to go with you to California tomorrow. We'll have a good time, I promise. Please forgive me."

"Okay, Greg," she said, crawling back into bed, thankful this episode was over. She had to make sure there wouldn't be another.

"Thank you, sweetheart," he said, putting his arms around her. "You're a good woman."

It was late the next morning when they awoke and they scurried about getting ready for their trip. At the last minute, Greg complained that his favorite shirt, the gray one with the silky finish, wasn't in his closet. To avoid an argument, Pree hurried to the laundry room, turned on the iron, and was fetching the shirt from the ironing basket when Greg walked through to the garage with his luggage. She heard the garage door opening as Greg popped in and said he had to make a quick trip to the store to get something, and would be right back.

"No, honey, please," she said. "We'll be late for our appointments with the painter and the plumber if we don't leave right now. We'll be pushing the speed limits as it is. Whatever you need, we can get in California."

"I'll be right back," Greg insisted, quickly closing the door.

He breathed a sigh of relief as he headed down the road. It wasn't until he was shaving that it had dawned on him that he hadn't taken any money for the trip out of the suitcase in the storage unit. He knew Pree hadn't believed the story about needing something from the store, but it was the only excuse he could think of to get out of the house without her. He needed money to gamble at the card clubs, and he liked to sit down at the table with a large wad of hundreds. Poker players respected a man with a lot of cash.

He would have to smooth things out with Pree when he got home. Maybe he would buy some flowers at the store. To take to her mother! That would be a great excuse.

Pree stood, bewildered, listening to Greg's car drive away. Obviously, something was going on. It was time to find out. She grabbed her keys and purse and hurried out the door.

When she didn't see his car in the Albertson's lot, she headed down Miracle Mile, toward the cross street that led to the ice cream store. Suddenly, she saw Greg's car coming toward her, dangerously fast. He zoomed past her, so absorbed he didn't notice it was her car. She made a U-turn and followed him back to the market. When he got out of his car, she honked her horn. His eyes opened wide as he recognized her, and he stood motionless for several seconds. She assumed he was trying to think of a plausible story, but she no longer cared. She went home.

It was almost half an hour later when Greg's car pulled into the garage. He walked in, carrying a large bouquet of yellow roses, her mother's favorite.

"Sorry I took so long," Greg smiled. "I thought your mother would like these. I wanted to surprise you."

"What surprised me, Greg, was when you zoomed past me on Miracle Mile. You were in such a hurry you didn't even notice my car. You were coming from the ice cream store, so it's obvious you're still seeing that woman."

"That's a lie!" he shouted. "I am not seeing her anymore!"

"Then what were you doing speeding away from the street where the ice cream store is? The only other business in that area is that new storage facility. Have you rented a space in that facility?"

"No!" he lied, shouting.

He was trapped. If he told her about the storage space, she would want a key, and the whole plan would be ruined. Mape would be finished with him for good. In desperation, he opened the door to get away. Pree grabbed his arm.

"Wait, Greg," she said angrily, grabbing his arm. "It's time for us to talk about this. I want to know what's going on."

Panicking, he pulled his arm back and shoved her away, hard. As he ran out the door Pree fell backward onto the tile floor, bumping her head on the wall, and knocking over the ironing board. The hot iron fell onto her arm and burned a small, pointed triangle into it. She lay, there listening to Greg's car pull away, stunned both by the blow to her head and by the fact that Greg had actually shoved her. Finally, she stood up. She was a bit light-headed, but was able to right the ironing board and unplug the iron.

As she rubbed salve on the burn and prepared an icepack for her head, she tried to decide what to do about the whole bizarre situation. For sure, it was time to end the marriage.

CHAPTER 30

Bullhead City, Arizona, 1996
(The year of the killings)

Pree figured Greg would be gone for a while. When they had argued in the past, he would usually spend a week or two in either Los Angeles or Las Vegas, "getting his head straight", a habit she prayed would continue. She needed time to figure out how to dissolve the marriage with as little animosity as possible, or such was her hope. He had been so unhappy lately he might welcome the chance to end things on an amicable basis. A divorce would leave him free to hang out with Mape. Mape would certainly have some influence on the way things worked out, especially the financial settlement, but she was hopeful that they could part on good terms in spite of that.

Time went by, her children visited and left, and February approached. Realizing she and Greg would have to file joint income tax returns one last time, Pree prepared her part of the tax information.

Reluctant to touch the mass of papers that had accumulated on top of Greg's desk after the fuss he had made about organizing them himself, she finally decided to collect only the tax-related documents and take them to Eileen Okazaki, their accountant, unopened, and let her sort it out. It would be one less thing for them to take care of when he got back.

She was pulling out bank statements when her eyes were drawn to a document that had "MORTGAGE APPLICATION" printed across the top. She was stunned. Greg was preparing to apply for a four-hundred-thousand-dollar mortgage on their home. He had penciled her name and initials in some of the spaces and signature lines. Further digging produced applications for loans on their cars and their boat, her name also penciled in.

Pree had known for some time that Greg and Mape had been up to something, but she wasn't prepared for this. Finally, overcome by the enormity of the situation, she gave in to the tears she'd been holding back all day.

A half hour later, her head pounding and her eyes swollen, she took two aspirin and walked back into Greg's office.

To hell with respecting his privacy. All's fair in love and war, and this now qualified as war. She pulled out the brokerage statements and discovered the balance was a little over sixty thousand dollars. The market had been strong for several months. By even the roughest of estimates, his stock should be worth well over a million dollars. She opened the earlier statements. It appeared Greg had been liquidating his stock at the rate of twenty thousand dollars a week since April. That was about the time Laria had filed for divorce from Mape.

Her next move was to make a thorough search of the desk, hoping to find something that would tell her what Greg and Mape were up to. In the top left drawer, she found the cards she had signed when they had first moved to Bullhead City, to put her name on his stock account. He hadn't mailed them. She made a mental note to call her retirement agency the next morning and remove Greg as her beneficiary, and to remove him from her life insurance policy. She was about to call it a night when a small, bright blue notebook, wedged in the back of the drawer, caught her eye. She removed the drawer and dislodged it. Before putting the notebook back, she absently flipped through the pages. There was a list of some kind on the first few pages. Again she recognized Greg's printing style, except for the E's. The first few were his usual squared-off letters, but later ones looked like backward 3s. Odd. The hair on the back of her neck stood on end and she shuddered.

The first two items on the list were numbered. The others were not.

1. RENT SAFE DEPOSIT BOX - VEGAS
2. PUT JEWELRY IN S/D BOX - VEGAS
   LIQUIDATE STOCK
   REMOVE ALL PAPERS FROM HOUSE
   REMOVE JEWELRY FROM HOUSE
   GET LOAN ON CHRYSLER
   RENT APT - VEGAS
   ARRANGE FOR LOAN ON HOUSE
   SELL BOAT
   SELL JEEP
   SET UP RESIDENCE - VEGAS
   GET ATTORNEY - DIVORCE
   GET P.O. BOX
   PROMISSORY NOTE - BLANKS
   START WEARING FAKE JEWELRY
   ARRANGE MAX LOAN ON HOUSE
   COURT- JEWELRY -INVESTMENT
   FUR COATS - INVESTMENT
   GET LOAN ON LINCOLN
   LEAVE NO PAPERWORK IN HOUSE
   GET ALL VALUABLES OUT OF HOUSE
   NOTE WHERE SHE HAS BANK ACCOUNTS

The next morning, Pree made an appointment with Robert Laub, Esq., a prominent divorce attorney in Kingman.

She arrived at Mr. Laub's office a few minutes early. The ground was covered with slush and melting snow. Not realizing how high the Kingman elevation was, she hadn't worn a coat and was grateful for the burst of warm air that greeted her as she opened the door. After announcing herself to Carolyn, the office manager, Pree walked over and sat on a chintz-covered chair near a beautiful sandstone fireplace that covered an entire wall and contained a roaring fire.

Pree saw a pretty blonde woman working at a computer in a backroom. A young red-headed woman, apparently a client, had handed Carolyn some money and the two of them chatted amiably about a man named "Shad." A tall, fiftyish, slightly balding man came into the office. He put down his worn leather briefcase and took off his overcoat. He wore a nicely tailored gray suit and rimless glasses. Pree thought him handsome in a distinguished, low-key way.

He joined in the conversation about Shad for a few minutes, then walked over to Pree and introduced himself. She followed him into his nicely appointed office. There was a smaller fireplace on the wall to the right of the desk, but there was no fire in it, and the room was a bit chilly.

"Why don't we start with you telling me why you're seeking a divorce," he said, his voice businesslike but not lacking in sympathy. He had obviously been at this for a long time.

He listened attentively as Pree gave him an overview of her relationship with Greg, ending with finding the notebook in his desk the night before. She opened her briefcase and handed him the statements, the loan applications, and the notebook. Months later, Mr. Laub would tell her that, as he reached across the desk to take the documents from her, he thought hers was one of the most forlorn faces he had ever seen.

When she told him about Greg shoving her, he asked if she would like for him to get her a restraining order.

After pondering it, she said sadly, "I guess I need one." She armed herself with tissues from a box on his desk and told him of Greg's remark about shooting her through the head.

"We'll try to obtain one by tomorrow," he told her.

Then came the bad news. He told her that this was an unusual case and was likely to become very messy. He said it could go on for an extended time, and he would need a five thousand-dollar retainer to represent her.

Pree gasped!

"But I have no money," she said. "I gave all my savings and the proceeds from the sale of both of my condos to Greg, as my contribution to the cost of our home, which he paid cash for."

"You gave him everything?" Mr. Laub asked.

"Yes," she said. "It was foolish, but I just didn't anticipate anything like this ever happening."

"I noticed that your name is on one of the bank accounts," he said. "What about that?"

"But that's Greg's money," she told him. "Each month I contribute seven hundred dollars to the cost of maintaining our household, and he contributes eight hundred. Once he was in Las Vegas and wasn't here to pay his share, so he put my name on this account and gave me a book of checks so I could write a check for his share if it ever happened again."

"And have you ever written a check on the account?"

"Yes, two, for eight hundred dollars each. When he was winning in Vegas and didn't want to come home."

"Well, Mrs. Crenski, I can tell you that if your name is on the account, it's your money too, but it's up to you if you want to use it to pay the retainer. I also notice that the list in the notebook makes reference to jewelry, and that's a very nice ring you're wearing. I might be willing to take jewelry if you aren't able to come up with the cash."

Pree had no idea what to do. "Can I think about it and let you know tomorrow?" she asked, getting up from her chair.

"Of course. Here's my card. Just call and let Carolyn or Donna Browne, our paralegal, know. We can start the restraining order process as soon as we hear from you."

Pree nodded. He walked her to the door and she left. He turned to Carolyn and said, "We won't see that one again."

CHAPTER 31

Bullhead City, Arizona, 1996
(The year of the killings)

"My god, woman, you look like hell!"

"Like I need you to tell me that?" Pree said. "Thanks for meeting me on such short notice."

Pree had called Mary before she left Kingman, and the two of them met at the local Arby's. Pree had no appetite, but drank a Diet Pepsi.

"So you went to Kingman to see an attorney about a divorce?" Mary said between bites of her sandwich. "I thought you were going to wait until the slime bag came home, and try to work something out."

Pree set the briefcase on the table, retrieved the stack of documents she had found on Greg's desk and handed them across to Mary.

"Holy crap!" was Mary's assessment of the situation, reiterated several times as she read the documents between bites of sandwich and sips of coffee.

"You knew the twits were up to something. But this?"

Pree told her about her meeting with Mr. Laub.

"What's the problem?" Mary asked. "Just go to the bank tomorrow and get that money for your lawyer, and get the restraining order."

"Mary! You know I can't take that money. I can't steal. Not even from Greg."

"Look. The way I see it, you've got everything you own invested in your house. That's worth what? Maybe half a mil?"

"Give or take."

"Then why can't you just go to the bank and 'borrow,' interest-free, of course, the money you need from Greg, then pay him back after the house is sold?"

Pree thought about it. It was probably her only way out.

*　　*　　*

"Mary? It's me," Pree said into the receiver. "I just got home."

"Did you take the money?"

"Borrowed," Pree reminded her.

"Okay, borrowed. How much?"

"Fifty-five thousand frickin' dollars!"

"You're kidding."

"I'm as serious as a root canal."

"Dear God! You finally grew a spine. Congratulations!"

"I knew you'd be proud. I took the five thousand to the attorney and got the restraining order. I've already taped copies of it to the front door with a note and Mr. Laub's card."

"Well, congratulations on your new backbone."

"Thanks. I expected to feel guilty, but I actually feel relieved."

"Enjoy it while you can, kiddo. You know all hell is going to break loose when the dirtbag gets home."

CHAPTER 32

**Kingman, Arizona, 1996
(The year of the killings)**

All hell did break loose when Greg returned, but after a Bullhead City Police Officer arrived on the scene and explained to him the consequences of violating the restraining order. He calmed down and left. He then filed a lawsuit to get back the money Pree had "borrowed," and to force her to evacuate "his" house. Pree and Mary were on their way to Kingman for the hearing. There were still patches of snow on the ground.

"Mape called me last night," Pree said.

"You have got to be kidding! What did he want?"

"Probably to find out what I was going to say in court today. He was smarmy, of course. He said he was sorry to hear we were splitting up, and told me Greg was heartbroken, then asked me what happened."

"What did you tell him?"

"That it was the woman. I said that Greg had promised to give her up, but that I caught him sneaking off to see her. He said he hadn't known about her, was sorry to hear it, and hung up. He was probably relieved that I didn't mention the notebook and the other things Mr. Laub is going to spring on him and Greg today,"

"Good girl!"

Inside the courthouse, a number of people were talking softly, mostly in groups of two or three, the suits and ties distinguishing the attorneys from the clients. Mr. Laub was sitting at one of two wooden tables in front of the low railing that separated the visitor seating from the official court area. There were two empty chairs to his left. Greg and Mape were sitting at the other table with a third man, also suited and tied, whom Pree took to be Greg's attorney. Pree introduced Mary to Mr. Laub and avoided looking at Greg and Mape as she took the seat next to him. Mary glared at them, then walked back into the visitor area and sat next to the aisle, near the back of the courtroom.

"Remember what we talked about yesterday," Mr. Laub reminded Pree, patting her hand. "You'll do just fine."

They all stood as Edward Conlan, the court clerk, announced the judge, and the Honorable Joseph Fabella took the bench and told them to be seated.

Mr. Laub asked that Mape be excused from the courtroom so that he could be called to testify later. The judge so ordered, and Mape stood and sauntered out of the courtroom, fuming.

Both attorneys gave short summations, and Greg's attorney, Chris Clarke, called Greg to the stand.

The entire morning consisted of Greg's testimony; Pree testified in the afternoon. Their testimony was totally conflicting, and it became obvious that one of them was lying, the fact that they were both under oath notwithstanding. But Pree was able to produce cancelled checks, receipts, and had even found copies of the deposit slips from the money she had paid to Greg as her share of the cost of buying their home, which belied Greg's testimony that he had paid for it all himself. He claimed she was a gold digger who made it a habit to marry and divorce men for their money, which she contradicted with documents proving that Greg was her second husband, and that she had been married to her first husband for twenty-seven years. Greg was completely shocked when Mr. Laub produced the notebook, which disproved his statements that he was happily married and had never wanted a divorce.

When questioned about the $1,120,243.29 that had been in his stock account the previous spring, Greg testified that he had lost it gambling. When asked about the sixty-one thousand dollars that had been in the account two months earlier, he grinned and stated that he had lost that gambling as well.

Still grinning, he stated, "I've got a real bad gamblin' problem. If I don't get back that money she stole from me, I'll be livin' in my car."

Before calling Mape to the stand, Mr. Laub said to Pree, "You've told me Mape is a jerk. Can you suggest something I could ask him to bring out his obnoxious qualities?"

"Just ask him his name," Pree smiled.

Mape did not disappoint. He began by refusing to be sworn in, which kept everyone waiting while the clerk retrieved the alternative affirmation statement.

Mape took the stand at a little after two thirty. Mr. Laub stood and began questioning him.

MR. LAUB: How long have you and Mr. Crenski been friends?

MAPE: Since 1979. You can do the math.

MR. LAUB: Would you say you are best friends?

MAPE: I guess so.

MR. LAUB: So would you say there's not much you wouldn't do for each other?

MAPE: "I wouldn't do anything illegal for him, if that's what you mean. If you're trying to trap me, you can give it up. I was a sheriff for over thirty years, so I know the ropes.

MR. LAUB: How do you feel about Greg's marriage to Mrs. Crenski?

MAPE: Pree? Fine. He was happy with her until she threw him out. She said he had a girlfriend, but he didn't. He just felt sorry for that woman and was helping her out. I'd like for them to get back together.

MR. LAUB: So you would never encourage him to get a divorce or to do anything to harm their relationship?

MAPE: No, I wouldn't! If she blames me for this, she's sadly mistaken. She's always been jealous of my friendship with Greg, which is stupid.

MR. LAUB, *introduces a red envelope into evidence then removes from it the semiapology card Mape had sent her after the Las Vegas fiasco, in which the E's are printed like backward threes. He hands the card to Mape.* Is this your handwriting on this card?

MAPE, *looks at the card.* You obviously don't know handwriting from printing. This is printing. The reason I sent this to Pree is…

MR. LAUB, *takes back the card.* Thank you. (*He hands Mape the notebook, and opens it to the first page of the list*). And is this also your handwriting? Excuse me, your printing?

MAPE *stares at the notebook, not speaking.*

MR. LAUB: Mr. Belata?

MAPE: Yes, it appears to be my printing.

MR. LAUB: Did you write—excuse me—print what appears to be a plan to break up the Crenski's marriage and defraud Mrs. Crenski of her share of their assets?

MAPE, *takes a few moments to think about the question.* I had to help Greg get rid of her. He never would have done it on his own, and she was bleeding him dry, buying carpet they didn't need and the like. He would have been broke in no time, the way she was spending his money. As his friend, I had to stop her, before he ended up penniless.

MR. LAUB: Mr. Belata, have you ever taken money from Mr. Crenski?

MAPE: What? If she's trying to say I've been bleeding Greg, she's lying. Yes, I have borrowed money from him over the years. I have a wife and three small kids, and I never allowed my wife to work, so sometimes things got tight. Emergencies and such. But we kept track, and when we sold our house, we paid him back every cent, twenty-five thousand dollars. If she tells you otherwise, she's a liar. Did she say we didn't?

MR. LAUB, *introduces three additional documents into evidence and hands one of them to Mape.* Mr. Belata, this is a copy of Mr. Crenski's federal income tax statement for 1995. This appears to be a promissory note for forty thousand dollars, signed by you, that Mr. Crenski wrote off as an uncollectible debt. (*He hands Mape the next document.*) And here, in his 1994 tax statement there appears to be another promissory note, for thirty thousand dollars, signed by you and written off as a bad debt by Mr. Crenski. (*He hands Mape the final document.*) And here, in 1993, is yet another one for twenty-two thousand dollars. Is it your testimony that you repaid Mr. Crenski all ninety-two thousand dollars? Because we can find no record that Mr. Crenski ever reported receiving the money from you, or ever paid the taxes on it.

Mape, stunned, said nothing.

Suddenly, Greg jumped out of his chair and shouted. "I OBJECT, YOUR HONOR. THAT IS IRREVERANT!"

Everyone in the room, including Mr. Laub and the judge, burst out laughing, except for Mape, who was unable to see the humor in anything at that moment.

The judge banged the gavel and called the room to order. "Mr. Crenski," he said as sternly as he was able, "I decide what is 'reverent' and 'irreverent' in this courtroom. However, we have gotten pretty far afield from the matter at hand. Mr. Laub and Mr. Clarke, I believe I have enough information to rule on the petition before me, unless you have something you would like to add?"

Neither attorney had anything to add, so Judge Fabela stated that he would issue his ruling within ten days and adjourned court.

Five days later, Pree was notified by Mr. Laub that she would be allowed to keep the money and to live in the house until it was sold.

"Thank you so much," she said. "I'd like to ask you a question. All my life I have heard that perjury is a very serious crime. It must have been obvious to the judge that Greg and Mape were lying, yet nothing was done about it."

"Would you rather have your husband in jail or the $50,000?" Mr. Laub asked. "Justice is meted out in many different ways."

Pree and Mary celebrated over lunch at Harrah's then went to the Riverside to see a movie.

CHAPTER 33

Laughlin, Nevada, 1997
(Nine days after the killings)

Pree's knock was answered by a striking young strawberry blonde woman.

"Come in," the woman said. "You must be Pree. I'm June. June Stapp."

"Auntie Pree!" Joey squealed, squeezing past June and hugging Pree. "This is Mrs. Stapp. She's our teacher, only she's not really our teacher. I forgot what she is, though."

"She's our tutor, dummy," Dani said from behind June.

"Oh yeah," Joey said. "Our tutor. That's the same as a teacher, except she comes to your house. She's real nice."

Coley and Dani were sitting on the sofa, each holding a sleeping baby. Pree recognized Dani's bundle as Lauryn.

"This is Jonny," Coley whispered, pulling back the blanket so Pree could see the baby she was holding. "He's six months old. He's really cute too. And he doesn't cry."

"They've never seen him when he's unhappy," June assured her. "He has a healthy set of lungs. Why don't you have a seat? Laria's not quite ready. Lauryn spit up on her and she had to change."

"I guess you've met June," Laria said coming out of the bedroom. She was wearing the same lavender sweatshirt she'd been wearing that dreadful day at the police station. Had it really been only nine days ago? Laria looked like a totally different person now. Relaxed, happy, and animated. She had done something different with her hair, and she was wearing makeup. She looked quite pretty.

In the car, Pree handed Laria an envelope containing five thousand dollars in hundreds from the shoebox.

"I've been dreading this for days," Pree said.

"Me too," Laria agreed. "I'm just glad we're doing it together. Bob and May, and even June, bless their hearts, have been wonderful. Bob's been great with the kids. It's sad that he wasn't able to have children with his wife, especially since it destroyed their marriage that way."

Bob couldn't have kids? It destroyed his marriage?

"Frankly, I'm a little concerned about the way the children have taken to Bob," Laria continued. "I'm afraid he may be filling the void left by their father's death."

"It's possible, I guess," Pree said.

"I'm worried about how they're going to react when we get back home and Bob isn't around anymore," Laria continued. "I'm sure they're going to miss him."

"I've been wondering the same thing about you," Pree said. "How are you going to feel when Bob isn't around anymore?"

"Pree! What are you suggesting?" Laria asked, her face flushing. "Bob and I aren't having an affair."

"I wasn't suggesting that you are," Pree said, turning to look at Laria. "But at the party it was obvious there's something going on between the two of you. There's some kind of chemistry there."

Laria was silent for several minutes.

"I'm not saying it will, but how would you feel if something did develop between Bob and me?" Laria asked.

"Truthfully?" Pree asked, pausing for a moment to think about it. "I'm sure I'd feel bad about not being able to spend as much time with Bob anymore. I'm already feeling that. But realistically, our relationship is never going to be more than friendship. So if there's a possibility that you two can find more than that with each other, you should go for it."

"Are you sure?" asked Laria. Her eyes were glassy. "Because I couldn't stand to hurt you again."

"I'm sure," Pree assured her. "Besides, I may not be hanging around here too much longer anyway. I've been thinking seriously about rejoining the rat race."

The rest of the drive was uneventful. The baby cooperated by staying asleep.

At the coroner's office, each woman was given a large plastic bag containing her husband's personal belongings. They stopped for a quick bite before tackling the next item on their list: arranging for pickup and disposal of the bodies.

While they waited for their salads, Pree said, "As you know, I plan to have Greg's remains cremated. I checked into having a small memorial service for him on the cruise ship operated by the Riverside Hotel, the Uss Riverside. Their ad said the ship can be chartered for weddings, but they assured me that chartering it for a memorial service would be no problem. They said any of the ministers on their list would be happy to perform the service."

"I spoke to Lance, the youngest of Mape's four sons from his first marriage. He volunteered to say a few words at his father's service. He said he was sure whatever I decided to do would be all right with the family and that he doubted that the rest of the family would be able make the trip from New Jersey. I told him to let me know if the family had any preferences. That was over a week ago, and I haven't heard from him, so I might as well go the cremation route for Mape too. We can have a joint service, if it's all right with you."

"That'll work out great," Pree said. "Pardon my lack of sentimentality, but we can get it over with all at once, and split the cost."

They made arrangements with a mortuary to have the bodies picked up and cremated, selected matching white porcelain urns for the ashes, and ordered a dozen death certificates each. The attendant didn't bat an eye when both women paid in cash. This was Vegas, after all.

They checked out Mape's apartment, which had been stripped of everything. Furniture, clothes, linens, medicines, food, dishes, papers; everything was gone. Marvin, the manager, was no help.

Laria said, "Mape could have shipped everything to Mexico, or put it into storage."

She looked at her watch. "We'd better go if we're going to check out Greg's place on the way back."

*   *   *

"It's just up ahead," Laria said as they approached Greg's cabin.

Laria turned onto a large, bare, expanse of dirt. Pree could see a stand of huge cottonwood trees about a hundred feet from the road and a small shed near the trees, but no house. They both gasped when they saw Mape's car. The hood was gone and the tires and hubcaps were missing. A crude, unpainted cabin came into view. The ground in front of the cabin had dried into a huge sandlot. Tire tracks, running helter-skelter, had formed ruts in the sand. Strips of yellow crime scene tape, stirred by a slight breeze, hung here and there from the porch and from the splintered boards that formed the outside of the cabin.

Laria parked a few yards from the porch steps and said quietly, "I'm going to wait for you here"

Pree got out of the van and slowly climbed the steps. Her feet felt like boulders and she had an even heavier feeling in the pit of her stomach.

The darkness and dankness of the enclosed porch gave her the creeps. The front door stood open. As her eyes adjusted, she noticed that the cabin had been emptied, but not neatly, like Mape's apartment had been. The furniture was gone, kitchen drawers were turned upside down on the floor, and the trash can had been emptied onto the cracked gray kitchen linoleum. A pair of Gregs's overalls lay on the floor by the bedroom closet. The light bulb over the bathroom sink was gone, and an empty toilet paper holder lay on the floor next to the toilet.

Pree had seen enough. She hurried back to the car. As soon as she was in the passenger seat, Laria started the engine, and drove away.

"They must have taken Greg's car too," Pree said.

"Possibly," Laria said. "But I didn't see it the morning I was here either. It should have been here then."

"What about that building over there?" Pree asked, pointing to a cinderblock structure across the street. "Maybe he rented it or something."

As Laria drove across the road, Pree opened the bag she had received at the coroner's office and took out two key rings. The second key she tried opened the padlock. As Pree lifted the door, Greg's white Lincoln Town Car slowly came into view. It took less than two minutes for Pree to find the new combination for the door lock in Greg's wallet.

Luckily, the car started right up, and they drove both cars back to Laughlin with the van in the lead. Laria drove directly to the Lazy River so Pree could leave Greg's car in the tenants' boat and RV parking area across the street from the trailer park. She got back into Laria's van and rode back to the condo to pick up her own car and go home.

CHAPTER 34

Las Vegas, Nevada, 1997
(Ten days after the killings)

"Oh no," Conni Turnock said. "For a minute, I thought I saw Creepy Guy drive into the parking lot in a white Chrysler Fifth Avenue. It's probably not him, though. There was an old man and a dog in the back seat."

"He rides that noisy motorcycle, doesn't he?" asked Kirstyn Ballard.

Conni nodded. She and Kirstyn occupied neighboring desks in the lobby of the Las Vegas Metropolitan Police Department administrative offices. Kirstyn was the department's receptionist, and Conni was the recruitment assistant. Both women cringed when Clyde Snyder walked past the row of windows toward the door.

"Time to make copies." Kirstyn said, jumping up and grabbing a stack of papers from the top of her desk. "I'll be in the workroom if you need me."

"Don't you dare leave me alone with him," Conni said in her most threatening voice.

"Sorry," Kirstyn called back as she hurried down the hallway. "I owe you."

Conni braced herself as the door opened and Clyde entered. He smiled as he walked across the large reception area toward her desk. He was carrying two vases of red carnations, each vase sporting a red bow.

"Good afternoon, Ms. Turnock," Clyde said formally setting a vase of flowers on each desk. "How are you this morning?"

"Fine, thank you, Mr. Snyder," she replied, continuing his formal politeness. "May I ask what brings you here today?"

"I received my grades from last semester's courses," he said, placing a piece of yellow paper on her desk. "And I'd like to have them attached to my application, with the others."

"I'd be happy to do that for you," she said.

"And where is Ms. Ballard today?"

"She's in the workroom making copies. Why?"

She braced herself for the first of his inane remarks, now well overdue.

"I was hoping to apologize to both of you. And to give you these flowers."

"Apologize? Give us flowers? For what?" she asked.

"For all the juvenile remarks I've subjected you to in the past, and to assure you that it won't happen again. I've joined AA."

"AA?" Her eyebrows raised in genuine surprise. "I didn't realize you were a drinking man."

"Not *that* AA." He said, smiling. "I'm now a charter member of Assholes Anonymous. You can't tell me you haven't noticed I'm an asshole."

That one got to her and a giggle escaped.

"See?" he said. "You have noticed. Apparently everyone has, except me."

"And what brought on this sudden desire to mend your ways?" she asked, somewhat interested. He seemed sincere, and she found it kind of endearing.

"I had a long talk with a friend of mine. At least I think she's my friend now. She didn't like me much before, though. So when I asked her for help, she had no problem telling me what a jerk I am. Was. I told her about you and Ms. Ballard, and about how much I want to be a policeman, and she gave me some advice. I'm here today to see if it works."

He stopped for a minute to formulate his next words.

"First, she said I should apologize to you ladies, which I hope I just did. To you, anyway.

"Secondly, she said I should tell you why I've been such a jerk, which is because I was trying to impress you, and to hide the fact that I'm a nerd. I was a nerd in high school, I was a nerd in college, I'm a nerd now, and I'll probably be a nerd until I die. I've tried to cover for it by saying the kinds of things the cool guys say, but it's time for me to admit that they don't work for me because I'm just not cool.

"My friend's third piece of advice was that one of the few times it's okay to exaggerate about yourself is when you're applying for a job. Since that's the main reason I'm here, I will now attempt to regale you. I'll try not to overdo it."

She smiled at him. She was so beautiful.

He took a few steps back and cleared his throat. "Why I want to be a policeman, by Clyde Snyder," he began, as if he were auditioning for a part in a school play.

She smiled again, so he continued.

"As you can see," he said, pointing at the paper on the desk. "Those are my grades from the two criminal justice classes I just completed at the Laughlin Annex of Clark County Community College. This makes four of the six required classes I've finished, and I got A's again. I'm actually pretty smart, and I come from a family of policemen, including my Uncle Bob who works for the LVMPD out of the Laughlin station. The point I'm trying to make is that ever since I can remember, I've wanted to be a policeman, and I'll be a good one. If not here, then somewhere else. I'm strong, I'm a hard worker, I'm loyal, and I'll be one of the most dedicated policemen on the force. The end."

He gave a mock bow to indicate he had finished reciting his piece.

He hesitated and cleared his throat before continuing. He knew his next remark would be stepping over the line.

"You will no doubt be relieved to know that I'm going to put an end to my frequent trips here to bug you. But – and I know I'm taking a big risk here – but I do intend to come back in a couple of weeks to ask you to have lunch with me, because you are one of the nicest and most beautiful women I have ever met in my entire life."

That said, he gave her an embarrassed salute, then turned and headed for the door. Her eyes followed him as he walked. She and Kirstyn always watched him leave. He had a nice butt, which he used to push the door open as he smiled and waved to her.

"Tuesdays at eleven work best for me," she called after him as the door was closing. His face flushed slightly as he gave her a thumbs up through the window.

"How did it go with the young lady?" Louie asked as Clyde got into Pree's car and started the engine.

"Pretty well, maybe," Clyde smiled. "I may have a date with her."

"Wow," Louie said. "You get to work your first full eight hour shift last night, and today you make a date with a pretty girl? Who knows what tomorrow will bring? Clyde, my boy, I think this is going to be your year."

"I hope you're right," Clyde said. "But right now, we'd better get over to the mortuary and pick up those ashes for Pree and her friend, then get home for our naps. I'm going to need a little more sleep before I go in tonight, in case I get to work another full shift."

"Did I miss anything?" Kirstyn asked when she returned. "What pearls did Mr. Wonderful bestow upon you today? And where did the flowers come from?"

"You're not going to believe what I'm about to tell you," Conni said.

CHAPTER 35

Bullhead City, Arizona, 1997
(Eleven days after the killings)

The day of the memorial service hadn't started out well. Laria had called to say that Mama Belata, Mape's sister Stella, and all four sons from his first marriage were coming to Mape's service, and she was afraid his crazy sister would create a scene.

Pree sighed. This was not good.

Laria's mother, Jessica, had driven in from California to take the children back to California after the service. She had brought Laria's black dress and a few other clothes. Jessica refused attend the service though. She felt it would be hypocritical to pay respects to a dead man she could hardly stomach when he was alive.

Pree was waiting for Jimmy to arrive. He was going to leave again right after the service, though. He was just passing through. Again. By now Pree was pretty certain he was avoiding her. Clyde was going to drive them and Louie over with the ashes, and Mary and Bart were going to be there too.

As Pree finished fastening a white carnation to the lapel of her black pantsuit—which, thanks to the magic of polyester, she could still more or less fit into, Jimmy walked in, carrying a small canvas bag. He kept his only suit in Pree's guestroom closet.

"Hi, Mom," he said, giving her a peck on the cheek. "I just need a quick shower and I'll be ready."

"And a shave," Pree said, rubbing her cheek. "Hurry. I want to get there a little early to place the urns and the photograph, and to have a last word with Reverend Sircole, the minister. Laria and I spent over an hour with him yesterday coming up with some positive things for him to say about Greg and Mape in their eulogies today."

"I could have told him everything good I know about both of those dickheads in about thirty seconds."

"It was a challenge," Pree admitted, smiling. "But he's dead now, so let's be charitable, okay?"

He gave a noncommittal grunt and headed for the shower.

They reached the boat a few minutes before the service was scheduled to begin. Pree hoped the dark clouds and the strong breeze weren't another bad omen. Jimmy carried the urns and Clyde helped Louie across the small gangplank into the boat, guided him to a polished oak bench in the third row, and sat next to him. The minister sat on a stool up front, reviewing his notes. He stood and smiled as they came aboard. Pree noticed a group of strangers, dressed mostly in black, sitting in the back of the boat, talking quietly. The Belata family. Pree recognized Lance.

Jimmy placed an urn at each end of the gold brocade cloth that covered a narrow, rectangular table that had been set up in the front of the boat then took a seat on the front bench. Pree put the photograph of Greg and Mape on an easel that stood in the middle of the table, between the urns. She'd had the picture, enlarged to poster size, and printed on card stock. She had taken it the day they took the kids fishing on Lake Mohave. The men were tanned and smiling, with their arms across each other's shoulders. It was the only picture she had of the two of them together, but it was a good one.

She checked out the five flower arrangements that had been placed in front of the table. There were two large ones, one from her family and the other from Laria's; an even larger one from Mape's family; and a white ceramic pot of azaleas, also white, from Rowena's family, with a nice message from Savannah. There was a small spray of red rosebuds for Greg from someone with the initials NH, saying the sender, he or she, would remember him always. Pree was trying to recall if Greg had ever mentioned anyone with those initials when she was distracted by the sound of children screaming.

"Grandma Belata!" Laria's children squealed as they ran toward the back of the boat. "Aunt Stella!"

Mape's family began hugging the children.

Laria and Bob stopped just inside the entryway to the boat, watching the scene unfold. Once again, Pree was struck by how beautiful Laria looked. Her fitted black dress, together with some small pearl earrings, made her look rather sophisticated. She was wearing a very stylish tan coat, an improvement over the navy windbreaker she'd been wearing since she'd arrived. Bob was holding the baby carrier. Pree watched as Stella glanced over at them, and saw Laria nod and raise her hand in a tentative wave. Stella lifted her head and turned away.

Laria and Bob walked to the front of the boat, stopping to shake hands and exchange a few words with Clyde and Louie. Bob took a seat in the front row, set the baby carrier on the bench next to him, and introduced himself to Jimmy, leaving space between them for the women. Laria reminded Reverend Sircole that Lance would be saying a few words on behalf of Mape's family when her children ran up to her, shouting. She held a finger to her lips to shush them.

"Mommy, Mommy, can we sit in the back with Grandma and Aunt Stella?" they asked, trying to whisper. "Please."

"Yes, of course," Laria said, forcing a smile.

The children shouted an enthusiastic, "Thanks!" then hurried back to rejoin the Belata entourage.

As the captain started to pull the gangplank and close the door, Bart and Mary hurried in. Pree walked over to welcome them.

"It was good of you to come," Pree said to the late arrivals.

"Extremely good of us, if you ask me," Mary said, not bothering to keep her voice down. "Considering we couldn't stand the bastards when they were alive."

Pree hurried them to the bench in the third row, where Bart and Louie immediately became engaged in conversation.

"If everyone's here, we'd better get started," Reverend Sircole announced. "Captain Courtney just informed me there's a storm headed this way. We'll begin by observing a few minutes of quiet meditation in memory of the departed as the boat carries us down the river, away from the casinos, to more serene and appropriate surrounding."

The boat pulled away from the dock.

Lance, the youngest son from Mape's first family, walked up and sat behind Laria, tapping her on the shoulder. He whispered, "Could I speak with you for a minute, please?"

Laria nodded and stood.

"First," Lance said, his voice low. "Thanks for letting the kids sit with us during the service."

"Certainly," Laria said. "I hope they'll always have a connection to Mape's family."

"Thank you," Lance said. "That makes this next question a little easier. Grandma and Aunt Stella want to know if we can take the kids for the day. With Dad gone, who knows when they'll get to see them again? I promise to have them back to you by bedtime."

Laria didn't respond for a few moments.

"It would mean a lot to us," Lance prodded.

"Sure," Laria said reluctantly. "I guess that'll be okay. Where are you staying?"

"At the Ramada Express."

"Good. The kids love the arcade there, and the hamburgers, and they like to ride the train."

"How about if I pick them up in the registration parking area in front of the hotel at eight o'clock this evening?"

"Great! And thanks again. I have your number in case I need to call you. And there's one more thing."

"Yes?" Laria said warily.

"What are you planning to do with Dad's ashes?"

"Scatter them in the river, with Greg's. Why?"

"Aunt Stella is not happy about the cremation. I forgot to mention that little detail to them, and apparently they wanted to bury Dad in the family plot back home. I didn't even know we had a family plot. Anyway, they'd like to take the ashes back to New Jersey for burial."

"Of course. I'll let the minister know."

"Thanks, Laria. And I apologize again for my family's behavior."

She waved him off. "It's a difficult situation for all of us."

As they turned around to return to their respective seats, the boat suddenly lurched. The water had become choppy and the boat started to rock.

"Sorry folks, but the storm is coming in faster than expected," Captain Courtney announced over the loud speaker. "We've just encountered some strong winds, and we're going to have to turn back."

Reverend Sircole, working to keep his balance, started the service immediately. He had done a commendable job of formulating Pree's and Laria's information from the previous day into proper eulogies, making Greg and Mape sound like fine, caring people. He spoke as fast as respect for the departed would allow. Lance's comments about Mape were also hurried, but heartfelt. Their remarks were interrupted from time to time by the sharp movement of the boat.

The boat's rocking became only slightly less pronounced as they rounded the bend and the casinos came back into view. The minister announced that Mape's family would inter his ashes in the family plot in New Jersey. He also announced that, due to the strong winds, Greg's family would not be able to scatter his ashes in the river, as planned, and would have to wait for another time, when conditions were more favorable. Pree gave Jimmy a disheartened look.

"I don't think I'm ever going to be rid of that man," she whispered.

"Yes, Mom, you are," Jimmy assured her as he stood up, picked up the urn containing Greg's ashes, steadied himself, opened a window, and unceremoniously hurled it into the river.

"Goodbye, Greg." He said through the window. "Rot in hell."

"Mission accomplished," he said, closing the window. "Sorry, Reverend." He was smiling as he sat back down.

Pree knew the Belata family must be horrified. Clyde quietly explained to Louie what had happened. Louie clapped his hands together and burst out laughing. He was quickly joined by Clyde, then Bart, Mary, and Jimmy. Their laughter echoed through the boat.

"I can't believe you did that," Pree said shaking her head in disbelief, stifling a smile.

"Sorry, Mom," Jimmy said, his laugh belying the sincerity of his words. "But at least you're rid of him now. For good."

"Son, there could be a problem," Pree whispered. "Are you sure those were Greg's ashes? What if they were Mape's? The urns are identical"

"Oops!" He said. "I'm pretty sure I put Greg's urn on this end of the table, but I'll check, just to be sure."

"If those are Greg's ashes on the table, pull the name label off the bottom oo Mape's family won't know," Pree said. It was an unconscionable thing to do, she realized, but the alternative would surely cause heartbreak to Mape's family and might very well incite a riot on the boat.

Jimmy stood, walked over and picked up the remaining urn, checking to be sure it contained Mape's ashes.

"NOOOO!" came a shout from the back of the boat.

Everyone turned to see Stella hurrying down the center aisle, screaming, crying, and bracing herself on the backs of the oak benches to keep her balance as she fought the motion of the boat.

"Give me that!" she yelled, grabbing the urn out of Jimmy's hands. "You'll throw my brother's ashes into the river over my dead body! We're taking him home for a proper burial!"

Jimmy let go of the urn and sat back down next to his mother.

"It's Mape," he assured her under his breath.

Pree exhaled in relief then heard a thud, followed by a crash. She turned to see Stella lying flat on her stomach in the aisle. The fourth row bench had been knocked over and the urn lay on the floor in front of the prone woman. Thankfully, it hadn't broken, but the lid had been knocked off, and the urn had rolled down the aisle. Mape's ashes made a gray, grainy streak across the hardwood floor of the boat.

"Don't touch me!" Stella shouted at Jimmy as he attempted to help her up. Lance appeared to assist her. When she was as upright as the rolling of the boat allowed, the hysterical Stella fell to her knees and began scooping up the coarse, gray ashes with her gloved hands, pouring them back into the urn. Lance tried to help, but she pushed him away.

"Let me do it!" she sobbed. "I told Mama we shouldn't come here, but no, she wouldn't listen to me, of course. She's never listened to me, so why would she start now?"

She continued sobbing and railing and scraping up the piles of ashes, but her efforts to pick up the finer dust were to no avail.

"I need a dustpan or something flat to scrape them onto," she screeched. "Somebody get me something. Now!"

Captain Courtney hurried up with a whisk broom in his hand.

"I found this in the storage closet," he said, "but no dust pan."

"Here, use this," Pree said, handing her the large cardboard photograph of Mape and Greg.

Stella glared at her then grabbed the picture out of her hands. Working carefully so as not to lose her balance, and trying not to get ashes on Mape's side of the photograph, she managed to sweep up most of her brother's remains and poured them into the urn, which Lance held in place to prevent the motion of the boat from knocking it over again.

Just when it seemed the situation was under control, Joey called from the back of the boat, "Mommy, I feel sick." All eyes were on the boy as he made his way to his mother, holding on to the backs of the benches to balance himself. The color had drained from his face.

Laria hurried to her son. Using the side aisle, since Stella and Lance were blocking the center, she braced herself between the benches and the outside wall, moving as quickly as possible. She was still several feet away from Joey, and could only watch in horror as he vomited on the floor in the spot where the center aisle intersected with the aisle that lead to the exit door, a spot that everyone would have to pass to exit the boat. By the time she reached her son, Laria had removed a wad of tissues from her coat pocket. Struggling against the movement of the boat, she sat her hysterical son down on the nearest bench and cleaned him up as best she could.

"I'm sorry, Joey," she said, hugging him and trying to soothe him. "Mommy didn't bring any Dramamine. Just sit very still. We're almost back to the dock. I'm going to go clean up the mess."

"No, Mommy. Don't leave. I might barf again."

"Here you go, Ma'am," Captain Courtney said, handing her a small plastic bag. "Take this, just in case."

He placed a larger black plastic bag over the mess and placed an orange plastic traffic cone on each side of the bag. The cones fell over immediately and rolled back and forth in arcs. "This will take care of it until we dock and the maintenance crew comes aboard. They'll clean it up."

"I'm so sorry," Laria apologized.

"Don't be." He smiled reassuringly. "It happens more often than you might think."

The passengers, except for Stella, breathed a collective sigh of relief when they felt the boat hit the dock. Captain Courtney quickly opened the door and pushed the small gangplank into place. Lance and his brother Leon lifted the sobbing Stella from the floor.

"Come on Aunt Stella," Lance said in a placating tone. "We have to go now."

To everyone's relief, the distraught Stella allowed them to lead her down the aisle, around the barf barrier, and off the boat. Laria slid herself and Joey across to the far side of the bench on which they were sitting, out of harm's way, as Stella passed.

The entire Belata entourage exited the boat as quickly as possible. Nicole and Danelle blew Laria a kiss. Mape's other two sons helped their grandmother. Leon carried the urn. All at once, Joey began screaming and trying to pull free of his mother's grasp.

"Wait for me," he shouted. "I'm coming too."

"I'm sorry, sweetheart," Laria said, tightening her grip on his arm. "You can't go with Grandma when you're sick."

"But I'm not sick anymore!" Joey screamed. He tried unsuccessfully to pull away from his mother, and had to settle for stomping his feet and throwing himself on the bench, kicking, and crying and shouting, "That's not fair! I want to go too!"

Bob grabbed the baby carrier and hurried up the center aisle to the bench where Joey was becoming more and more hysterical. He handed the carrier to Laria and picked up the screaming boy, saying, "If Mommy said you're okay, we'll go to the arcade later."

"No!" Joey screamed. "I don't want to go to the arcade; I want to go with Grandma and Aunt Stella!"

At the front of the boat, Pree looked on in amazement. She'd never seen any of Laria's kids act out like this before. The more Bob tried to soothe Joey, the louder the child screamed and tried to break free. Laria looked on, frustrated, embarrassed, and helpless. Her son would not be consoled.

Pree looked around, conducting a visual survey of the boat. The overturned bench still lay on its back. A thin layer of Mape's ashes still remained on the floor, a significant portion of them forming a line of gray footprints, running down the aisle and around the plastic-covered pile of vomit and the two orange cones rolling around next to it. The poster of the two departed friends stuck out of a trashcan by the door, where they smiled through a coat of Mape's ashes. Joey continued kicking, trying to free himself from Bob's grip, and wailing loudly. His screams had awakened Lauryn, who had now joined her brother in a high-decibel duet.

"Well," Pree commented as she observed the destruction and chaos. "That went pretty well, don't you think?"

Even the good reverend had to chuckle at that one.

Their laughter was interrupted by Lance, who walked back onto the boat and over to Laria.

"I apologize for Aunt Stella," he said. "As you know, she tends to take the hysterical approach to things."

"Its fine," Laria assured him. "It was an emotional situation."

"Thanks," he said. "But what I really came back for, is to see if Jo Jo is well enough to go with us."

"Probably," Laria said. "I think he just had a little motion sickness. He gets it in the car sometimes, usually when we're driving on winding roads"

Joey, who had silenced himself mid-tantrum when he saw Lance walk back onto the boat, insisted, "I feel good now, Mommy. I really, really do."

Laria looked at the eager boy, who was wiping his face with the remaining tissues

"See? Look at me," he said, smiling as Bob put him back down on the floor.

A quick inspection assured Laria that his color had returned, and he wasn't feverish, so she reluctantly gave permission for him to go, extracting a promise from Lance that he would call her if any symptoms returned. Lance and his little brother left the boat hand in hand.

"Remember I told you that I'm not Jo Jo anymore?" They heard Joey say to his big brother as they walked away. "I'm Joey now."

"Well, is everyone up for the buffet here at the Riverside?" Pree asked after Lance and Joey were out of earshot.

"Sounds good to me," Jimmy said. "All this fun and games has given me an appetite. Then I'll have to change and be on my way."

The others chimed in their acceptances.

"I'm afraid I'm not going to be able to join the party," Laria said. "I have to go home and let my mother know she can spend the afternoon at the casino playing the slots. She'll be pleased."

"I'll see you home," Bob said. "I need to get some sleep. I go on duty at ten."

Lauryn had stopped crying and resumed napping. Laria put her back into her carrier and covered her with the blanket then handed the carrier to Bob. Laria walked to the front of the boat and grabbed the diaper bag from under the bench. As they started to leave, she turned back to Pree.

"The rent on the condo is paid through Sunday, so I'll be staying over to tie up a few loose ends. I'll call you." She grabbed Bob's hand and they walked off the boat.

"Those two have gotten pretty chummy," Mary commented indignantly as soon as the couple was out of hearing range. "I guess we all know whose loose ends she's planning to tie up."

More laughter.

Pree thanked Reverend Sircole and handed him two envelopes, from Laria and herself. She took fifty dollars out of her purse and gave it to Captain Courtney. He protested a bit, but she insisted it was for service beyond the call of duty.

As they walked through the casino on the way to the restaurant, Mary pulled Pree aside.

"Did you know about the thing between Laria and Bob?" she asked.

"Yes, I did. Laria and I talked about it on our trip to Las Vegas last week, and I told her to go for it. I think it's a good match."

Lunch turned out to be a lot of fun. In retrospect, Pree had to admit that the day she had dreaded so fiercely had turned out to be a real hoot. Who'd have guessed?

At the end of the day, Laria's exhausted but happy children fell asleep in their beds, clad in their new pajamas that Grandma Belata had bought them, hugging the Barbies and the Batman action figure that had been a gift from Aunt Stella. Most of Mape's earthly remains sat in an urn on a dresser at the Ramada Express, awaiting transportation across the country, and burial in the family plot. A small portion of Mape had gotten sucked up into a vacuum cleaner by the Uss Riverside maintenance crew and poured into a plastic garbage bag that currently sat in a dumpster awaiting transportation to the Clark County landfill. The remaining traces of Mape had been mopped up by the same maintenance crew and now resided in the Laughlin sewer system. Ivan Josef Crenski, thought to be Gregoe Isaac Crenski, finally realized one of his boyhood fantasies: He was sleeping with the fishes at the bottom of the Colorado River.

CHAPTER 36

Bullhead City, Arizona, 1996
(The year of the killings)

"Mape! Please don't hang up on me again. I'm really, really sorry. Please."

"You're sorry? Explain to me how sorry is going to keep me out of prison, you moron!" Mape shouted. "Don't you realize what you've done? Tax fraud is a federal offense! Al Capone served eight years for tax evasion!"

"I can fix it. I promise. I'll pay the money back to the goverment. I'll say I signed your name. You can say you didn't know nuthin' about it."

"That's a great idea, you idiot. Then I'll have a perjury charge against me too. I should have my head examined for getting involved with someone as stupid as you!"

"I'm sorry, Mape. I didn't think about Pree finding out."

"You got that right, Greg, you don't think. Because you're an idiot! As soon as she snitches to the IRS, we can kiss our freedom goodbye. Why didn't you put the papers in storage? Can you at least tell me that?"

"I must have forgot."

"You must have forgot," Mape's voice became so soft and controlled it frightened Greg a little. "I'm through babysitting you, Greg. I want you to stop calling me."

Greg became very quiet. It was true. He'd been a terrible burden on Mape from the start.

"Okay, Mape, if that's what you really want. I'm going to leave you alone. I'll have our accountant, Ms. Okazaki, find out how much it will cost me to clear my record. I hope it won't take all my money to make things right again, but even if it does, it'll be worth it if you'll talk to me again."

"There you go, talking like an idiot again. Why would you give away your money when all you have to do is quiet that witch so she can't turn us in and destroy her copies of the tax papers."

"You know I can't go near her or the house," Greg said. "She'll have me arrested. And how can I quiet her? I can't gag her can I?"

"Forget it then. I'm through doing your thinking for you. You can call me again when she's out of the picture. Otherwise, you can forget you ever knew me."

"But Mape, I don't know what you mean by when she's out of the pitcher. How can I get her out of the pitcher? Tell me. Please. I'll do whatever you say!"

"Figure it out, Greg."

Greg listened to the dial tone for a few seconds. He had never felt so alone in his life. He called Mape at least a dozen times over the following two days, but when he said Pree still wasn't out of the picture, Mape hung up on him. He had to get Pree out of the picture and get rid of the tax papers. Mape had said it would be simple, but Mape was smart, and he was a moron. But somehow he'd find a way.

CHAPTER 37

**Bullhead City, Arizona, 1996
(The year of the killings)**

The tall young man with the shaved head took a quick look around the lobby of the Bullhead City Police Station. He was sweating profusely.

"I want to talk to someone about a deal," he said.

The policewoman at the desk picked up her phone, punched in a four-digit extension, and explained the situation to someone inside.

Almost instantly a brown-haired, midthirty-ish uniformed policeman came through the door behind the receptionist's desk. He introduced himself as Sergeant Harry Winston.

"I understand you're inquiring about a deal?"

"Yeah. For Nico Rojo."

"Your name?"

"Nathaniel Hammer. Nath."

When they were settled in an interview room, Sergeant Winston asked Nath to explain what he would like for the police to do for him.

"Not for me," Nath said, avoiding eye contact. "For my friend, Nico Rojo. He was arrested last night for possession with intent to distribute. Maybe we can do a trade or something."

"Why don't you start by telling me what it is you have to trade."

"Well, there's this old guy, a friend of my grandma's. He's looking for somebody to off his old lady and burn down this house."

"Do you know why?"

"Not for sure. I think he wants his wife offed because they're getting a divorce, and he doesn't want to pay her any money. I don't know about the house. His wife lives in it right now. Maybe he has insurance on it or something."

"How did you get this information?"

"He asked us about doing it for him. My grandma probably told him that Nico did time for manslaughter in Carson City. Anyway, he just showed up at this bar called the Chug-A-Lug one night, where me and Nico hang out sometimes, and bought us some beer and said he wanted to talk to us. I recognized him from the ice cream store where I work as a janitor. Well, free beer is free beer, so we said okay and sat down at a table with him in the back of the bar and started talking. After a bit, kind of out of the blue, he asked us how much it costs to have somebody killed in this town. He said a friend of his wanted his wife killed and his house burned down, but after a while, we figured out it was him. Nico said he would do it for two grand, and the guy agreed. He gave us ten bills up-front and said he'd give us the other half when the job was done. He said he'd already paid another guy a grand up-front, and he'd skipped town without doing the job, but that he knows where to find me if we try to stiff him. He gave us the directions to get to the house where his wife lives, and he drew us a layout of the place."

Nath removed two folded cocktail napkins from the pocket of his jacket and handed them across the table to Sergeant Winston. The map was on one of the napkins, the layout on the other, with the address and the guy's phone number.

"So why are you here?" the sergeant asked.

"Well, we never intended to actually do the job. Nico was going to use the thousand to set himself back up in the drug business. He figured in a week he could make enough money to give the guy back his thousand and tell him that he changed his mind about doing the job. Only, he got busted, and the drugs got confiscated before he got things set up. I figured maybe if we gave you this guy, you might make a deal."

"What kind of deal did you have in mind?"

"Maybe drop the charge against Nico? Or at least drop it to simple possession."

"Let me see what I can do, and I'll get back to you. Is there a number where I can reach you?"

"No, not really. The cops took Nico's cell phone, but I could come back here tomorrow."

"Okay. I should have some information for you by two o'clock tomorrow afternoon."

Nath left the police station and went to work, deciding he shouldn't get high while he was trying to make a deal with the police. After work, he took his grandma home, then went back to the room and slept for a while. At midnight, he got up and drove across the river. He had heard his grandma tell Jeanne one time that the old guy, Greg, liked to play poker at the casinos early in the morning, when a lot of the players were drunk. He spotted Greg's car in a handicapped space at the Flamingo, so he parked the Buick and waited.

It was just after 3:00 a.m. when Greg came out of the casino and drove away. The streets were almost deserted, so it was easy for Nath to tail him. Greg pulled into a parking lot at Hancock Haven, a small apartment complex on Hancock Street. Nath passed the apartment complex, turned around, and drove back just in time to see Greg enter apartment seven.

When Nath entered the police station at exactly two o'clock the next afternoon, the receptionist motioned to him to have a seat. Several minutes later, Sergeant Winston opened the side door and told to him to come in.

"Good news," Sergeant Winston said. "If you help us get this guy, the D.A. has agreed to one year in the county lockup for your friend. No prison time."

It wasn't as good as he had hoped for, but it could have been a lot worse, so Nath agreed.

When he left the police station, Nath called Greg and made arrangements to meet with him. Driving to the Hancock Arms, he repeated over and over what the officer had told him to say.

"Is she dead?" were the first words out of Greg's mouth when he opened the door and saw Nath standing there.

"Not yet. I need to talk to you."

"If you're here to tell me you can't do the job, give me back the money and leave."

"I just need to talk to you. Can I come in?"

Greg stood back and let the young man enter. Nath followed Greg through a path that had been cleared through the stacks of newspapers, piles of dirty clothes, and other clutter, including mouse droppings in one corner. The kitchen was piled with dirty dishes, and an unpleasant stench permeated the entire apartment.

"Excuse the mess," Greg apologized. "I'm not much of a housekeeper."

"You know, my mom is a housekeeper at the Golden Nugget, and she cleans houses on the side. Maybe it would be worth a few bucks to hire her to help you."

Greg didn't respond. He motioned Nath to an easy chair and took a seat on a small sofa.

"Okay, what's goin' on?" Greg asked after they were seated.

Nath explained to Greg about Nico's arrest and the confiscated drugs.

"So what you're saying is that I'm out a thousand dollars for nothin'? That ain't goin' to happen. You got forty-eight hours to get me my money, or a friend of mine will be payin' you a visit, if you know what I mean."

"I didn't say you won't get your money back," Nath said. "And you can probably get the job done too."

Greg calmed back down.

"First off, I'm going to pay back the money. It'll take a while, but you'll get back every penny. And Nico gave me the name of a guy he met inside who just got out of prison. He did seven years for arson. He lives in Kingman, and Nico is sure he'll do the job, because he needs money and he really likes to set fires. He should be able to get your wife too, if he does it the way you talked about. I can have the guy call you if you're interested."

Greg considered the matter for several minutes before answering.

"I want interest. A hundred and ten a month for ten months. Tell the guy to call me. What's his name?"

"Harry. I don't know his last name," Nath said as he stood to leave.

Greg followed him to the door. He felt a sudden let down as Nath walked away. It had been a long time since he'd had anyone to talk to. Mape still wouldn't answer his calls. On impulse, he called out, "You can have your mom call me. I'm sick of this mess."

CHAPTER 38

Bullhead City, Arizona, 1997
(Two months after the killings)

P ree's spirits were high when she got the news that the job as Cal
Hall's assistant was hers, beginning July 1. Her life seemed to be
coming together at last.

A potential conflict arose while they waited for Louie in the
doctor's office. When Clyde told her excitedly that he had gotten
accepted into the Las Vegas Metro Police Academy, Pree saw her
chance to leave fly out the window. But Clyde came up with a seemingly workable plan.

"If you do get the job, could you put them off until the middle
of August?" Clyde asked.

"Possibly. Why?"

"Uncle Bob is planning to retire soon. He's been offered a security job in California. Lieutenant Keebler said he can probably put
me on night patrol when I graduate, to train under Sergeant Ceja.
That way, I could live here and still look after Louie and the park. I'm
sure the sisters and Barry would help out in a bind."

"But you can't continue to do all the maintenance work," Pree
said.

"Already taken care of," Clyde smiled. "Claudia Price, the weekend dispatcher at the Laughlin station, has four cousins that own a
maintenance company. Robert, Court, Jeff, and Steven. They call
themselves 'the Price Cousins.' They have a good reputation and
Claudia is sure they would take on the Lazy River as a client."

After the doctor's visit, they stopped for Mexican food at Aguilez' restaurant, one of Louie's favorites. Dora played with the Aruilez's Chihuahua, Amigo, and with their granddaughter, Katrina, in their yard behind the restaurant. While they ate, Clyde and Pree laid out the plan for Louie in as much detail as possible. He was agreeable to it, and just like that it was settled. Pree was free to take the job in California.

Pree drove to Los Angeles for her interview by way of Las Vegas to sell Greg's coin collection. She browsed while a man in the back of the shop appraised the heavy case of coins. When a clerk told her he could recommend some good investment coins that she might consider adding to her collection, she declined. The appraiser offered her thirty-seven thousand dollars for the coins which she readily accepted. Waiting for the check to be prepared, Pree walked around the shop pretending to look at coins while she mulled over an idea that was forming in her brain.

"About those good values you mentioned before," Pree said as she put the check into her handbag. "I hit a six-thousand-dollar jackpot last night at the Mirage," she lied. "And I was planning to invest it in a CD, along with this check, but now, I'm wondering if I wouldn't be better off to invest the six thousand in coins."

"I believe you would," the man said, smiling.

"Why don't you pick out six thousand dollars' worth of your best coins while I go get the money?" she said, leaving the shop.

Pree had found a black leather pouch containing six thousand dollars in hundreds in the trunk of Greg's Lincoln. She carried it into the store and used it to purchase the coins. She visited four other coin dealers that morning and, using some of the satchel money, left Las Vegas with twenty-six thousand dollars in gold coins. For the next three and a half years, each time she visited a city of any size, she either bought or sold coins, buying them with cash and later receiving and depositing checks from the sales. Two and a half years later, she had converted all the money from the satchel and had made a modest profit on the coins, which she reported to the IRS.

CHAPTER 39

Bullhead City, Arizona, 1997
(The year of the killings)

Sergeant Harry Winston couldn't believe his good fortune. Detective Roger Teugh was expected to put in his retirement papers within the next year and both Harry and Ron Weyer were in line to fill Teugh's spot. Weyer's wife Linda, had given birth to a baby boy, and Ron was out on paternity leave the day Nath Hammer came in to ask for a deal. Detective Teugh and his wife Millie were on Maui at the time, so the case had fallen into Harry's lap. Harry intended to take the case through to conviction without a mistake, making him a shoo-in for the detective spot.

It was just after two in the afternoon and Harry was sitting in his dad's old Ford Fairlane in the parking lot at Colianno's Italian Restaurant. He wore grubby jeans, a faded flannel shirt, and a worn denim jacket. He was concerned when he saw no Town Car in the lot, and was relieved when an obesely overweight guy, medium height, sixty-something, knocked on the passenger window.

"You Harry?"

"Yeah. You Greg?"

"You want to go inside and get a pizza and a beer while we talk?"

Greg was elated at the prospect of having someone to talk to. Lately the guys in the poker rooms at the casinos had been getting a little testy when he tried to carry on a conversation at the tables.

"Okay. But I don't want no beer. I'll have coffee."

"Me too. I lay off the booze when I'm doing a job. Can't take a chance on slipping up."

The place was empty, except for a guy making pizza dough and another in a cowboy hat at the jukebox. They chose a booth in the back that offered privacy.

"Pepperoni okay with you?" Harry asked when a waiter appeared to take their order.

"Sure. Anything. And coffee."

"And iced tea for me," Harry said.

Harry had been on the force long enough to recognize that the guy was high on something. He didn't smell booze, so he figured drugs, kind of unusual for a guy his age. But it might make it easier to get him to incriminate himself on the wire.

"So, I understand you're in the market for someone to make things hot for a certain party," Harry said to get things started.

Greg grinned and nodded. "If the price is right."

"Two grand is my standard fee. Can you handle that?"

"I guess so." Greg agreed.

This time, Greg had prepared for the encounter in advance. After the waiter brought their drinks, Greg looked around the room to assure no one was watching them then took a folded piece of paper out of his shirt pocket. He felt like an actor in an old Edward G. Robinson picture.

"Here's the address and a map of how to get there. That's my phone number. That's the layout of the house." He pointed to a spot on the paper.

"That *X* there's the bedroom. There's a window across from the bed where my wife sleeps. You need to throw something through the window that will land on the bed and explode. You have to be sure the bedroom catches on fire too, and that it spreads to the rest of the house."

Harry picked up the paper and pretended to study it. "Are there blinds or curtains covering the window?"

"Blinds."

"That complicates things a bit."

Greg hadn't thought of that. He wondered if Nico would have thought of it or if he would have screwed the whole thing up. He shot Harry a worried look.

"No problem, my friend," Harry said. "I'll just use a flare gun, like the ones we used in 'Nam. They'll rip through anything."

Greg smiled. The man knew his business.

Harry searched his brain for a way to get the guy to say on the record that he wanted to have his wife killed.

"You looking to collect on an insurance policy?" Harry asked.

Greg stiffened and Harry regretted the question immediately.

"I apologize, pal. I was just making conversation. I've been locked up for so long it's good to have someone to talk to, that's all. Forget I asked."

"That's okay. I know how that feels. My best friend ain't speakin' to me right now on account of I screwed up really bad. But if you do your job right, all that should be over."

As they ate their pizza, Harry talked about life in prison, and how his ex-wife had taken his kid and all his money and run off with his best friend. Greg felt sorry for Harry and opened up to him like they were old friends. Harry was able keep Greg talking, but try as he might, he couldn't get him to say anything definite about having his wife killed.

Finally, as people started filtering into the restaurant, Harry picked up the check and said, "Look at the time! We've been talking for over two hours. I'd better get going."

When they got outside, Harry said, "Well, what do you think?"

Greg reached under his shirt and pulled an envelope from his waistband and handed it to Harry, who lifted up the flap and looked inside. He gave Greg a puzzled look. Inside the envelope was a stack of hundred dollar bills that had been cut in half.

"What's this?"

"No offense," Greg assured Harry. "But I already paid two guys a thousand bucks each to have this job done, and they ripped me off both times. I'll give you the other half of the bills when the job's done. Okay?"

"I guess so. Sure. You've got yourself a deal. I'll call you when it's done and tell you where to meet me for the payoff. Maybe we can get together for pizza or something afterwards."

Greg's lips spread into a wide grin. "I'd really like that," he said.

As Harry opened the door of the jalopy, he decided to try one more time to cinch a murder conspiracy conviction. He turned to Greg.

"There is one thing," he said. "Torching your house is no problem. And hopefully your old lady will be in the bed. But in case she isn't, I can take care of her anyway, if you want me to. I can hang around for a while with the flare gun, and get her if she tries to escape. But I'd be taking some extra risk, and it'd cost you a little extra. I'm sure you understand. It's just business."

"How much?"

"Another grand."

Greg mulled the idea over. He didn't want to alienate the guy, because he liked him, but a deal was a deal. If the guy shot a flare onto the bed while Pree was sleeping on it, she shouldn't be able to escape. It wasn't right that the guy was trying to jack him up for more money now.

"If you burn down the house there shouldn't be no problem."

"No problem," said Harry. "I just thought you might want to be sure you don't have to go through all this again."

Greg wavered for a couple of minutes but decided it would be stupid to pay the extra thousand if he didn't have to.

"No," he said. "I'm not ready to go that far yet."

"Mape?" Greg said hopefully as he picked up the receiver. He looked at the clock. It was almost three-fifteen in the morning.

"Who's Mape? This is Harry."

"Harry?" Greg was confused for a moment. "Oh yeah, Harry. What do you want?"

"What do I want? What else would I be calling you about? The job is done! She's burning as we speak."

"You did it already?"

"I decided there was no point in waiting around. I was already here in Bullhead City, and I had everything I needed in my truck.

Besides, I'm broke. That was my last twenty I used to pay for the pizza. I was counting on the advance from you, but those half bills you gave me won't spend, so I went ahead and did the job. Meet me in the lot behind the old movie theater at the end of Hancock. I'm already here. Nobody ever comes here after the last movie lets out. Bring the other halves of the bills, and some scotch tape if you have it. Maybe we can go to the Riverside afterward, and have ourselves a drink on me, to celebrate."

Greg sat for a minute, letting everything register.

"Okay," Greg said. "I'll get dressed and come meet you."

When Greg pulled into the lot behind the theater, Harry's truck was parked next to the building, and Harry was sitting on the delivery dock of the theater building, his jacket collar pulled up around his neck to ward off the cold. Greg parked his car and walked over to the dock and sat next to Harry. He was carrying an envelope.

"Are you sure the house burned?" he asked. "I got the answerin' machine when I called her number."

"I'm positive. Take it from a fire expert, those insulated phone and electrical lines they use nowadays can withstand a lot of heat. I've heard about cases where the whole building burns down, but the phones still work."

Harry paused to see if Greg would buy his story.

"Really? I never heard of that. But you're the expert. How did it go?"

"Great! I did exactly what you told me. I shot the flare in exactly half an hour after the bedroom light went out. I dumped gasoline around the outside of the bedroom wall before I shot the flare, and the place went up like kindling wood. I loaded another flare into the gun and waited around for a few minutes in case your wife got out. At no extra charge, by the way."

Greg smiled. He liked this guy.

Darn! Harry was hoping the guy would at least thank him for making the extra effort to get his wife. That would have been something anyway. Harry pointed at the envelope in Greg's hand.

"Is that for me?" he asked.

"Oh yeah. Do you have the bills I gave you earlier? The ones I cut?"

"Sure do," Harry said. He reached behind him and pulled the folded envelope out of his back pocket.

Greg took it from him, and handed Harry the envelope he had brought with him.

"I brought you new bills."

Harry removed the bills from the envelope and counted them.

"It's all here," he said. "I guess that means our business is done."

As they stood to leave, two uniformed officers ran out from behind a nearby dumpster.

"Freeze!" shouted one officer, pointing a gun at Greg. The other officer grabbed him and cuffed his hands behind him.

Harry read Greg his rights as the uniforms put him into the back seat of a marked patrol car that materialized from behind the church next door to the theater.

Harry felt great! He had made his first undercover collar, and it had gone without a hitch. He hoped he had enough on the tape for murder conspiracy.

CHAPTER 40

Bullhead City, Arizona, 1996
(The year of the killings)

L ooking around the apartment, Nita wondered if she had bitten off more than she wanted to chew. Greg apologized for the mess.

"We'd better get the business part over with so I can get started," she said. "I charge fifteen dollars an hour, cash. Thirty minutes or more counts as a full hour."

Greg agreed. He had been anxiously awaiting Nita's visit. Since Mape had stopped taking his calls, he'd been desperate for someone to talk to.

Nita spent the day sorting through the debris and getting things organized. Greg followed her around for the rest of the day talking nonstop, primarily about his wife who was bleeding him dry and a guy named Mape who, apparently, was a frickin' genius.

"I'm going to stop now," Nita said, finally. "The place looks pretty good. I've put in seven hours. That's a hundred and five dollars, but I'll settle for a hundred. I've sorted your laundry and put it into piles so it's ready to take to the laundry room. I didn't have time to actually clean, but I didn't see any cleaning supplies, anyway, or a broom or a mop or vacuum cleaner."

She handed him a piece of paper. "I made a list of things you'll need if you want me to come back next week and clean."

"Thank you. The place looks a thousand percent better," Greg said, handing her a hundred and a twenty. "The twenty's a tip."

Desperate not to be deprived of her companionship so soon, he said, "Listen, if I bought the stuff, would you come back tomorrow and do the laundry and clean?"

Nita refused politely.

"I'll give you a nice bonus," he coaxed. "And I'll pay you double. Thirty bucks an hour."

"All right," Nita conceded. "Just this once. I'll bring my mom's vacuum cleaner, and if you'll have all the things on the list here by eight o'clock in the morning, I'll put in four hours for a hundred dollars."

"Thank you," Greg said, beaming. He took another hundred out of his wallet and handed it to her, offering that if she would pick up the things on the list for him, she could keep the change.

A quick calculation told Nita she could get everything on the list for less than fifty bucks, possibly less than forty. She took the hundred and the list and left.

Nita picked up the supplies on her way home and drove through the bank to deposit the money Greg had paid her so Maude couldn't talk her out of it and Nath couldn't steal it.

"You look awfully pretty today," Greg said as Nita walked in with cleaning supplies and a vacuum cleaner the next morning.

Once again, Greg followed her around, talking and watching her clean, and ended up asking her if he could take her out for a nice dinner sometime.

"I guess so, if it's just as friends," she said. "I have to go now, but I'll be back in two weeks to clean again, if you want me to."

"Can't you come every week?" he asked. "You saw how messy I am, and I like talkin' to you."

He extracted the last two hundred-dollar bills from his wallet and handed them to her. He'd have to go to the storage locker today and get some more money.

"You've been too generous already," she said, returning one of the bills. "I'll see you next Tuesday."

CHAPTER 41

Bullhead City, Arizona, 1996
(The year of the killings)

Nath Hammer was broke and desperately in need of a fix, or at least a few beers. Being broke sucked! He had even driven to the Yummy Cone earlier to see if he could get his old job back, but there was some old geezer in there cleaning up and talking to his grandma. He had searched the room several times in hopes Nico had stashed some of the money before the cops came, but all he found was a switchblade knife stuck in the hem of one of the curtains. He was thinking hard about how Nico would get money under these circumstances when it came to him.

Nath's first stop was the Chug-A-Lug where Jackson, the owner, let him clean the bathrooms and mop the kitchen in exchange for a dime bag and a couple of beers, to get up his nerve.

Greg was apprehensive when he saw Nath at the door, afraid Nita had sent him to say she wasn't going to come back.

"What's up?" Greg asked as Nath walked past him into the living room and sat down.

"I saw in the paper that that guy, Harry, was an undercover cop. I just came by to tell you that I didn't know anything about that. Your place looks a lot better, by the way."

"I thought you said Nico knew the guy from prison."

"That's what he told me, hand to God."

Greg didn't say anything.

"You heard anything new from the police?"

"Yeah, they're charging me with arson conspiracy."

"I know. That was in the paper too. But you were trying to have your wife whacked. How come they're not charging you with murder conspiracy?"

Greg smiled.

"I've got this new lawyer, Marie Mifflin. She's real sharp. She got them to let me plead to the arson thing because when the cop tried to get me to pay extra to be sure he got my wife, I said I wasn't ready to go that far. I meant I wasn't ready to pay no more money, but Ms. Mifflin says it can be interpreted to mean that I didn't want her killed. So I may get off with a fine and probation and house arrest, and not have to do no prison time. I'd have to see a shrink, though. For five years." Greg smiled smugly. "Lucky, huh?"

Nath stood, walked over to the sofa and sat next to Greg.

"You know what else is lucky?" he asked. "It's lucky that me and Nico haven't told the cops about how you told us you were looking for someone to off your old lady."

Greg moved away from Nath, trying not to look upset. "So? The word of an ex-con ain't going to carry much weight."

"Maybe not, but how about the testimony of two ex-cons, a cop, and a bartender? The bartender at the Chug-A-Lug is Nico's business partner, and he'll say anything Nico tells him to say. So I guess it's up to you to decide if you want to take that kind of chance or not."

"Decide how?"

"Me and Nico might be persuaded to forget about the whole thing if you were to forget about the thousand you gave us before and come up with another thousand."

"I'm not giving you another cent!" Greg shouted. "This is blackmail!"

He stood and moved away from the sofa.

"I gave your mother all the money I have except for a hundred bucks, anyway" he said, opening his wallet and showing Nath the hundred.

"Well, then, here's what we'll do. Remember how I was supposed to pay you a hundred and ten dollars every month?"

Greg nodded.

"Well, that's all changed now. I'll take the hundred today, but now you're going to pay me a hundred and ten dollars every week."

Greg realized that he would most likely be paying for the rest of his life. There had to be a way out of this. But what?

Suddenly, Nath grabbed Greg by the front of his shirt and leaned over until their faces were inches apart. With his free hand he pulled something out of his pocket. Greg heard a click as Nath pointed a knife blade at his neck. His voice became low and menacing.

"I know you're not going to do something stupid, old man, like calling the cops, because that would get you locked up for a long time. And in case you're thinking about having me and Nico whacked or something, that didn't work out too well for you the last time you tried it, did it? And remember, two can play that game. You got that, old man?"

Greg nodded and Nath let go of his shirt. He fell to the floor on his knees and put his head on the carpet. He was shaking violently and sobbing so hard he didn't hear Nath leave.

Finally able to speak again, Greg dialed the familiar number, desperately hoping that Mape would tell him what to do. But each time he called, he got the beep and left a message. It took four messages to tell Mape about trying to have Pree killed, getting arrested, the arson charge, his new attorney, Nath and Nico, and the blackmail. When Mape still didn't pick up, Greg knew that he had truly been abandoned.

Then suddenly, he remembered that he had another friend. She had said so that very day. A friend that might be able to convince Nath to leave him alone.

Nita was irritated at being awakened by Greg's call, but calmed down when she saw it was only 8:15 p.m. and she'd fallen asleep in the recliner in front of the TV.

Haltingly, Greg reviewed the events of the evening with her. The hardest part was admitting to her that he actually had paid Nath and Nico to kill his wife, explaining that he had been hyped up on prescription drugs at the time; otherwise he would never have done such a terrible thing. Nita was stunned, not only by Greg's confession about his wife, but about Nath's blackmail scheme. This was a new low for her son.

When Greg had finished, Nita said, "I'm sorry my son is blackmailing you, Greg, but I hope you don't think I can stop him. I lost any control I had over that boy the day he discovered cocaine. I'm not sure why you called me."

"I'm not sure either," Greg admitted. "I guess I just hoped that being Nath's mother and all, you might be able to come up with something. I'm sorry I bothered you."

"If I come up with anything, I'll let you know. Do you still want me to clean for you next Tuesday?"

"Sure. You might as well."

"I'll see you then," she said, and the dial tone kicked in.

Greg was still in his pajamas the next morning when a knock on the door startled him. Fearing it was Nath he turned off the television and walked quietly to the door.

There was another knock and Nita's voice said, "Greg, open up. It's me. I think I may have a solution to your problem."

CHAPTER 42

Las Vegas, Nevada, 1997
(The year after the killings)

The auditorium was bustling with activity as Pree and Louie took their seats beside Laria and Conni, Clyde's girlfriend. Laria was still sporting the tan she had picked up on her Hawaiian honeymoon with Bob the previous month. Pree had been her matron of honor.

Pree and Louie were hosting a luncheon for Clyde at the Shooting Starr Hotel after the ceremony. Crush and Lu's friend, Sammy Starr, owned the hotel and casino and Lu had made arrangements for a first-rate affair in the Starrlight Room on the roof of Sammy's hotel, one of most elegant restaurants in town. The restaurant didn't open until 7:00 p.m., so they would have the place to themselves for the afternoon.

"Where's Bob?" Pree asked.

"Backstage. He's going to pin Clyde's badge on him. His mother was going to do it, but his grandmother is ill and they couldn't make the trip."

"I hope his friends can make it to the luncheon."

"Oh yes," Conni assured her. "We're all excited about it. He invited some friends from the academy. You'll like them. Steve Thomas and his wife, Sandy, and Bonnie Hall and her mysterious boyfriend, JR."

"Why mysterious?"

"Because she's been dating him for months and none of us have met him yet. We only know him as JR. Clyde met him yesterday.

179

I don't know why it's such a big secret. He's going to pin Bonnie's badge on her."

Forty-three uniformed new peace officers walked onto the stage to an outbreak of applause, took their seats, and the ceremony began. After the obligatory speeches by local dignitaries, the rookies were called, one by one, to step forward to receive handshakes, certificates, and the long-waited badges, which were pinned on them by spouses, family members, or friends who had been chosen for the honor.

"Officer Bonnie Hall," the announcer said, and a pretty auburn-haired woman rose from her seat and walked across the stage. "Officer Hall's badge will be pinned by her friend, James Olindo."

Startled, Pree looked up to see her son walk across the stage, pin a badge on the young officer, and kiss her cheek.

"Pree, isn't that your Jim?" Laria asked.

"You're JR's mother?" Conni asked.

"Yes, and he has some serious explaining to do," Pree said, the rage rising up inside of her again. Lately, almost everything Jimmy said or did seemed to anger her, and she knew it was because of the satchel, the money, and the lies. No matter how much she assured herself her son couldn't have had anything to do with the murders, the anger persisted. She was already dreading asking him why he was pinning that woman's badge on her. His answer was sure to piss her off.

After the ceremony, Clyde introduced Pree and Louie to his friends. Introducing Jim, he said, "Surprise!" and grinned sheepishly. It was to be the first of many surprises that day.

Pree was gracious, all the while trying to size the young woman up. She arranged for Clyde and Conni to escort the woman, Bonnie, and Louie to the hotel so that she and Jimmy could discuss a few things on the way.

"I guess this explains why I haven't seen much of you lately," Pree said after the others had left.

"Mom, everything's okay," Jimmy assured her. "Better than okay. Great! Just let me tell you what's going on."

"That would be a refreshing change."

They sat on opposite ends of a small bench. Jim had expected his mother to be hurt that he hadn't told her about Bonnie, but he didn't think it warranted such anger. Mothers could be a gigantic pain in the ass sometimes.

"Remember last Thanksgiving when I called and told you I was stuck on the road and couldn't be at your place until dinner time?"

Pree nodded.

"Well, I actually got to Bullhead City the night before. I was tired and I knew Staci and Justin would be sleeping on the couch and the futon and I would have to sleep in my truck anyway, so I decided to go over to the Riverside for a couple of beers and call it a night. The Loser's Lounge was full, so I was standing in the doorway listening to the music and drinking my beer when an attractive woman who was sitting at a table by herself asked me to join her."

"How kind of her," Pree said sarcastically.

"It was Sandy Thomas," Jimmy continued. "The woman you just met. She was waiting for Steve, her husband, to join her after his class at the college. I had hardly sat down when her husband and this beautiful woman walked in and Sandy introduced us. Of course, I realized it was a setup, and you know how much I hate to be fixed up with blind dates."

Pree nodded.

"I stood to leave, but when she said hello and smiled at me, I sat back down and bought her a drink. I'm still not sure what came over me."

"They're called hormones, son. I've seen the girl, remember?"

Ignoring his mother's barb, Jimmy continued.

"Anyway, I knew I wanted to see her again. It turned out she was a bartender at the Searchlight Nugget Casino and had to be there for the midnight shift. I followed her there in my truck and had a couple more beers then slept until eight o'clock, when her shift ended, had breakfast with her and came back to Bullhead City. The reason I left right after Thanksgiving dinner was to get back to Searchlight, and that's where I spent Christmas Eve and New Year's Eve and every other chance I've had to be with her."

"And you couldn't tell me about this woman until now because…?"

"Because I didn't want to get your hopes up until I was sure it was serious. Remember how disappointed you were when Becky and I broke off our engagement? It was by mutual agreement, but still you hardly spoke to me for weeks. Also, there are some things in her past that she's not proud of and didn't want me to tell you about until we were sure we were in it for the long haul."

"What kind of things?"

"Unsavory things. Like her mom was a drug addict and prostitute who died on the streets and she, herself, has been a cocktail waitress in a topless strip club. Luckily, she got her life together. She went to school and became a bartender then got her GED, and as of today she's a police officer. I'm proud of her, Mom."

"And you're telling me all this now because…?"

"Because Bonnie doesn't want you to find out later and feel like we deceived you. She insisted that I tell you everything before she would marry me."

"Marry you?" Pree asked, incredulous. "You're going to marry her?"

He pulled a ring box from his pocket and opened it, revealing a solitaire that looked to be well over a karat in size, and a band with several smaller diamonds in it. "That's an expensive set of rings," Pree commented, working hard to contain her anger. "And isn't that a new suit? What did you do, rob a bank?"

"Don't worry about it Mom, everything's under control. Clyde and I are going to propose to Conni and Bonnie at the luncheon. It's a surprise."

"Good heavens!" Pree exclaimed, jumping up from the bench. "The luncheon! We have to go. You can leave your truck here and ride with me."

"I sold my truck."

"What? Why would you do that?"

"I quit my job a week ago, Mom. Bonnie's been assigned to the Henderson precinct, so we rented a condo there."

"You quit your job then go out and buy a set of expensive diamond rings, a fancy new suit, and rent a condo?" Pree asked. She was exasperated. "Has this woman charmed the last bit of sense out of you?"

"I told you everything is under control," Jimmy assured her.

"I'll be right back, I have to pee," Pree said.

Inside the restroom, Pree hurriedly called Lu to say she and Jimmy would be a bit late, then quickly vented about her son's lunacy, including the engagement ring, and his being unemployed. Lu was able to calm her down a little, assuring her that everything could be worked out.

In the car Jimmy asked Pree if she was upset at him about something besides the business with Bonnie.

"Why would you ask me a question like that?" she asked.

"Because lately it seems like you're always ready to snap my head off."

"Maybe I'm going through the change!" she retorted.

"Come on, Mom, you're fifty-seven years old. That ship has sailed."

"I'm fifty-six, and you're just imagining things."

Jimmy turned on the radio.

Pree's mood elevated when she walked into the restaurant. The table was elegantly set, with a beautiful centerpiece and exquisite china and crystal. The graduates had changed into casual clothes. Jimmy's face brightened the minute he saw Bonnie. He gave her a kiss on the cheek and informed her that the deed had been done, and that his mother was steamed.

Pree gave Bonnie a quick nod then turned to Bob, who looked great. He had retired two months earlier, put his condo up for sale and moved to California, married Laria, and started a job as chief of security at the Six Flags Magic Mountain theme park near Los Angeles.

Everyone was in high spirits throughout lunch, after which both Clyde and Jimmy simultaneously got down on one knee and proposed to Conni and Bonnie. Their proposals were accepted enthusiastically. After that, Laria's mother brought the children in for Baked Alaska.

The party finally wound down and the guests chatted over cups of coffee.

Before they left, Lu told Jimmy there was a job available to him at the casino warehouse, which he gratefully accepted.

"I was disappointed in you today, my friend," Lu said to Pree after following her into the restroom. "You were awful to that girl and to your son too."

"I know," she agreed. "And I'm sorry. I get angry at him a lot lately, and I don't know why."

Okay, so that part wasn't entirely true.

"Is there something else going on between you and Jim?" Lu asked, catching Pree off guard. For a fleeting moment, she was tempted to unburden herself and confide in Lu about the satchel and money and her fears, but the moment passed and she assured her friend it was nothing.

"Well, he does seem to be crazy about the girl, and he's a good son, and that's all I'm going to say about that."

Pree spotted Jimmy and Bonnie in the corner and ambled over to them. Jimmy turned to leave, but Pree said, "It's okay, son. The witch is gone. Your mother is back."

Jimmy halted but didn't speak.

"It looks like I'm going to be your mother too, Bonnie, if you think you can put up with me. I came over to welcome you into our crazy family."

Bonnie, relieved, gave Pree a big smile, but Jimmy remained unmoved.

"And?" he asked.

"Oh, okay. I'm very sorry for being such a jerk. I should have been more understanding about your… "

"You don't have to grovel, Mom. You had me at 'I'm very sorry.'"

The tension broke and the three of them laughed.

"I know you just got engaged, but have you made any wedding plans yet?" Pree asked.

"Conni and I talked a little over dessert. We're thinking about a double wedding on Valentine's Day next year."

"Be sure to let me know when you set the date and I'll come to Vegas for a few days so we can shop for a gown and all the other bridal stuff."

"That would be wonderful, Mrs.... er... Pree."

Pree gave the girl a hug and said, "You'll have to start calling me Mom in a few months, anyway. You might as well start now."

That got her a hug from her son.

CHAPTER 43

Cottonwood Cove, Nevada, 1996
(The year of the killings)

The minute he saw the cabin, Greg knew it was perfect. It was almost invisible in the trees. Nita parked the Town Car in front of it.

As they climbed the steps, Nita explained, "I inherited this place from my stepdad. Mom and Nath don't know I have it. I'd actually like to live here, but it's too far to commute to work and back, so I just come here whenever I can. It's quiet and peaceful."

Nita undid the lock and propped the door open with a large rock. Greg followed her into the cabin.

"The electricity and water are already on. There's an old dial phone on the wall over there, but I've never had it connected."

Greg made no comment.

"If you decide to take the place," Nita continued hopefully. "You could leave the utilities in my name. The phone too, if you wanted. I could have the bills mailed to me here, and you could pay them. That way, there wouldn't be a record of you living at this address."

That got a nod from Greg, who was slowly making his way through the house.

"If I'd known I'd be showing you the house today I would have cleaned it up better."

"It looks fine," Greg said, finally speaking. "What about the furniture? Would you leave it here?"

"Sure. It kind of goes with the place, huh? It was my stepdad's too."

"The main drawback is that the house isn't insulated, and it gets real cold in the winter, as you can tell, and real hot in the summer. That stove over there in the corner burns wood. They sell it at the marina, but I've already bought enough to last the rest of the winter. There's more in the shed. There's a plug-in electric heater in the bathroom. There aren't any washer and dryer hookups though, so you'd have to have some installed or go to the Laundromat in Searchlight."

Greg looked the kitchen, bedroom, and bathroom over then opened the back door.

"All this land is yours too?" he asked.

"Yep," Nita replied proudly. "Eighty acres. They say property around here'll be worth a fortune someday, so near the lake and all. I hope so."

"Well, I like the place, but I don't see a garage. I don't like to leave the Lincoln out in the open, with all the sand that blows around."

Nita's heart sank. This could be a deal-breaker.

"Well, you'd be welcome to build one, of course, but it would be expensive."

Greg nodded. His attention was drawn to a cinderblock building across the road, with two heavy, rusted, iron doors hanging off their hinges. It stood in front of a three-story house. Both buildings appeared to be abandoned.

"What's that over there?" he asked.

"That? That place used to be a farm. I think the guy parked his tractor in the shed. After he died, his kids must have sold the tractor and just left the building there."

"Do you know where the owners live?"

"France, I think, or maybe Germany. Someplace far away like that. The place has been abandoned for years. Kids party there sometimes, mostly at spring break and New Year's Eve."

"What do you think would happen if I had a lift-up door put on the building and parked my car in it?"

"Probably nothing. People here pretty much mind their own business and leave each other alone."

They ate lunch at the Searchlight Nugget Casino restaurant and came to terms on the rental agreement.

Nita reluctantly said, "I hate to bring up unpleasant things, Greg, but what if your wife doesn't agree to the house arrest? What if you move here then have to go to jail?"

"My wife is supposed to meet with the district attorney this afternoon, and he's gonna ask her if she's gonna object to the house arrest or not. I should know by tomorrow."

CHAPTER 44

Kingman, Arizona, 1996
(The year of the killings)

Sergeant Winston, the Bullhead City police officer who arrested Greg, had just filled Pree in on the details of the arrest. They were waiting for Monty Cohn, the Mohave County District Attorney to join them.

It was difficult for Pree to believe that Greg wanted her dead, but it was also difficult for her to believe he wanted their lovely home burned down, and he had agreed to plead guilty to the arson charge.

"If he paid you to kill me, why are you only charging him with arson?" Pree asked the sergeant. "Why not conspiracy to commit murder?"

"You'll have to ask the district attorney about that, ma'am. I don't make those decisions."

It took less than five minutes for Monty Cohn, the district attorney, to explain that, since Greg's attorney could very likely use Greg's comment that he "wasn't ready to go that far yet," to convince a jury that he had changed his mind about having his wife killed. It was to everyone's advantage to let Greg plead to conspiracy to commit arson of an occupied structure. Otherwise, if they went for murder conspiracy, Greg could very likely leave the courtroom a free man, and there would be no consequences for his actions.

Pree suddenly realized that calling her here today had merely been window dressing. A deal had already been made.

Mr. Cohn went on to explain that Greg had agreed to plead guilty to the arson conspiracy charge and accept six months' incarceration and five years' probation with psychiatric intervention, which was, "not as severe as any of us would have liked, but it's a sure thing."

"So the victim has no say in the matter?" Pree asked.

"Intended victim," Mr. Cohn reminded her.

Angrily, Pree stood up to leave.

"There is one more matter, Mrs. Crenski," the district attorney said.

Here it comes, Pree thought. *This is the real reason they called me here.*

"If you're going to tell me that Greg has asked for house arrest instead of jail time, save your breath. Mr. Laub already told me, but I thought it was a joke. The man tried to have me killed, and he deserves to be locked up."

When Mr. Cohn finished explaining that Ms. Mifflin had lined up a doctor to testify that Greg was very ill and might not be able to withstand incarceration and that the guards at the local jail would testify that the night he was arrested, he became so hysterical that they had to remove him from the cell and handcuff him to a table all night. Then, when you added in the drug usage and his advanced age, there was a very good chance the judge would grant the request anyway.

"However, you are free to appear at the hearing and state your position if you wish to do so," he added.

"Yeah right." Pree turned to leave.

So much for justice, she thought as she stormed out of the courthouse.

CHAPTER 45

Cottonwood Cove, Nevada, 1996
(The year of the killings)

At the beep, Greg began his message.

"Mape, it's me again. I just want to tell you that I'm sorry for everything and I won't be callin' you no more. I think everything's going to be okay now. Ms. Mifflin, my new attorney, says Pree's not going to object to the house arrest, and I have this new friend—" *Beep.*

"It's me again. Like I said, my new friend, Nita, is helping me. Nath, the guy that's trying to blackmail me, is her son. Anyway, I'm rentin' a cabin from her, close to the Cottonwood Cove Marina. We even walked to the lake today. The cabin sits back off the road in some big trees, and you can't hardly see it unless you know it's there, so Nath won't be able to find me." *Beep.*

"It's me again. Nita's going with me to my hearing on March 26, to tell the judge I'm livin' in her cabin for free, so I can say I can't afford to pay rent, and maybe they'll let me stay there in Nevada. Ms. Mifflin said sometimes they do that in hardship cases. Well, that's it. I won't be callin' you no more." He hesitated for a moment then said, "Love, Greg."

*   *   *

Nita spent the afternoon soaking, shampooing, creaming, and perfuming literally every part of her body. The black chiffon dress she bought in Vegas with two hundred dollars from Greg's first rent payment was elegant, and it fit her like a glove. The heels on her new ninety-dollar shoes, on sale for half off, were four inches high, making her look taller and therefore, thinner.

This was her first real date with Greg, and she was going to spend the night at the cabin with him for the first time. She had splurged on a new lace nightgown and negligee set, also black.

Greg was looking quite handsome in his new suit, his recent weight gain notwithstanding. He welcomed Nita with a big smile. This special night out was to thank her for all she had done to help him get settled in his new home. They were also celebrating the fact that he would not be going to prison after all. His arson sentencing was scheduled for the next morning at 9:00 a.m., so this was probably the last chance they would have to get together outside of the cabin for at least six months. She was going to court with him to declare that she was letting him live in her cabin rent free. Nita didn't understand why, exactly, but Ms. Mifflin said that if she did that, Greg might not have to stay in Mohave County. It was the least she could do after everything Greg had done for her.

After dinner, Greg removed a small, velvet ring box from the inside pocket of his jacket and set it on the table. Nita panicked. Even if it wasn't an engagement ring, any ring would imply commitment, and Nita avoided personal commitments. They rarely seemed to end well for her.

Nita relaxed when she saw two keys stuck into the slot where the rings were supposed to fit. Pulling them out, she asked, "Aren't these the keys to your Lincoln?"

"Yes," Greg smiled. "As long as you're going to be driving me around, I figured it would be easier if you had your own keys." He pointed to two rows of numbers that he had written on the satin lining of the box. "The top number is the computer code that opens the driver's door, and the other one is the alarm code."

On two occasions, Greg had gotten a bit perturbed when he had to leave his poker game to open the trunk of his car so Nita could retrieve her jacket. Now, she would be able to do it for herself.

"That's very thoughtful of you, Greg," Nita told him. "Thanks."

Walking to the cabin, they held hands and laughed, recalling some hilarious bits from the ventriloquist's show they had seen after dinner. The moon was partially hidden by the clouds, so they could barely make out the cabin in the darkness. Greg gallantly went up the steps first, then turned and took Nita's hand to help her. She had just stepped onto the porch when a man's voice, coming from inside the walled portion of the porch, scared the bejesus out of her.

"What took you so long?" the strange voice demanded.

Nita screamed and threw her arms around Greg's neck. For a split-second she thought Nath might have found the cabin, but realized it was a more mature voice.

Greg didn't seem to be upset by the voice. Calmly, he asked, "Mape?"

"Of course it's Mape, you moron. Who else would show up to save you from screwing up your life?" Mape asked.

Greg managed to get the door open and turn on a light. As soon as they stepped inside Greg grabbed Mape and hugged him so hard and so long that Mape finally pushed him away. Nita excused herself, carried her overnight bag into the bedroom and closed the door.

So that's Mape, she thought. She was having trouble reconciling the bald-headed, gap-toothed, unshaven rooster of a man in the living room with the image of the great, all-knowing Mape she had formed from Greg's descriptions. No matter. Weariness settled over Nita, reminding her of the late hour. She supposed Mape would be staying the night.

"Here. Sit, sit," Greg said, ushering Mape to the sofa. Greg sat next to him. "I knew you would show up," Greg beamed.

"Don't I always?" Mape responded, ruffling Greg's hair. "That's what friends do. What time do we have to leave for court in the morning?"

"About eight o'clock," Greg told him.

"Hey, look at you in the fancy suit," Mape said. "You look like a movie star!"

Greg smiled, and blushed.

"And what's up with you and Godzilla girl?"

Greg's head came up with a start. "You shouldn't call Nita names, Mape. She's my friend. She's helping me."

"Sure, she's helping you," Mape said. "Like she helped her son set you up so she could rent you this dump. How much is she soaking you for rent, anyway?"

Greg heard the bedroom door open, and placed his finger over his lips to quiet Mape.

Resentment under control, Nita put on her happy face and greeted Mape with a smile.

"It's wonderful that you've come to give Greg your support tomorrow," she said.

"Well, I've been taking care of Greg for a long time," Mape said, laying his arm across Greg's shoulder and giving him a squeeze. "It gets to be a habit after a while."

Nita looked at Greg. He was smiling, and there was a radiance about him she hadn't seen before.

"Listen, it's late and it looks like you guys have plans for tonight," Mape said, winking at Greg. "So if you'll excuse me, I'll go out to my car and get some sleep."

"Your car? No, no. You can't sleep in your car. Sleep here," Greg insisted, patting the couch.

"No, no," Mape insisted, "the car's plenty good enough for me. I have my sleeping bag and pillow with me, and I've been sleeping in rest stops for the last three nights, so I'm used to it. If you don't mind, though, I would like to use your bathroom in the morning. You can probably tell it's been a while since I showered and shaved."

Mape finally let himself be persuaded to sleep on the couch. Nita brought out clean sheets, a pillow, and two blankets and began making up a bed for him.

"Well, if I'm going to be sleeping on clean sheets, I guess I'll have to take that shower tonight."

Nita informed Mape that the cabin had a bathtub but no shower. After forty-five minutes in the bathroom, Mape came out to find Nita asleep in the bed and Greg asleep in a chair.

Nita slept in one of Greg's pajama tops that night. No point in wasting an eighty-dollar nightie.

CHAPTER 46

**Willow Valley, Arizona, 1996
(The year of the killings)**

Nita Hammer's life sucked big-time since that little twit Mape had come to town. The day of Greg's arson hearing, she'd had to ride in the back seat while Mape drove the Lincoln and Greg sat up front with him.

Greg hadn't objected when Mape cut back on her cleaning schedule either. Mape told Greg that the cabin didn't need to be cleaned every week, that every two weeks would be enough. On most cleaning days after that, Mape took Greg to the casino in Searchlight to play cards while she worked. She wasn't sure how a guy under house arrest could do that, but that wasn't her business. She was forced to stop at the casino and pull Greg from the poker table and humiliatingly collect her money in front of the other casino patrons. Each time, Mape left his table and watched as Greg counted out the money, making sure he only paid her the sixty dollars he owed her, instead of the hundred he had always paid before.

On only two Tuesdays that entire summer was Greg at the cabin without Mape when she went to clean. It felt good to have him following her around again, talking to her as she worked. But Greg had changed. It wasn't just the fifty or sixty additional pounds he had gained. It was like his brain and body were moving in slow motion; something wasn't right. However, on both occasions, Greg had pressed a hundred-dollar bill into her hand when she left.

Nita assumed she would see more of Greg after he got off of house arrest, but Mape continued to occupy his time. At least she was getting the rent, and that alone had enhanced her little nest egg considerably. Soon, she would have enough money saved to move back to Vegas and enroll in dealer's school. The housekeeping job was beginning to take its toll on her body, and she wanted to learn to deal poker. The money was pretty good when you added in the tips, and poker dealers got to sit down.

When Nath hadn't shown up for Thanksgiving dinner, Nita figured he was either in jail again, or had moved away for good. But he walked into the trailer just as she and Maude were putting Christmas dinner on the table. He seemed to be sober, though, if you didn't count the odor of beer and pot that emanated from his pores. He said he'd been bussing tables and working as a janitor at a bar out on the highway and living in a rented room. Nita hastily stuck two twenties into a leftover Christmas card and wrote Nath's name on it.

They actually enjoyed a nice family day together. Nita treated them all to a movie after dinner, and Nath insisted on driving them in the Buick, which was filthy and reeked of pot, but it was a nice gesture, nonetheless. The fun came to an abrupt end that evening, however, as they were gathered around the table eating leftovers and Nath informed them he had been fired from his job at the bar the night before, on Christmas Eve, because there had been some money missing from the register and his boss had accused him of taking it. Nath swore to them he hadn't taken the money, and told them he had slept in the car the night before. He needed a place to stay, but just for a few days. His friend Nico was supposed to get out of jail before New Year's. They were knocking time off of his sentence for good behavior. He said he and Nico were going to Reno to live when he got out. He just needed a place to crash for three or four nights.

* * *

It was eleven o'clock the morning after Christmas, and Nita was sitting in the employee's dining room at the Golden Nugget when her friend Kaley said, "There's a man here to see you."

"Me?" Nita asked, surprised.

"Yeah," Kaylie said. "He said his name is Greg."

"Hello, Greg," Nita said cautiously when she walked into the casino. "What brings you here?"

"I don't have nuthin' to do today and thought you might like to go out for a movie and a nice dinner."

He's his old self again, Nita thought hopefully, *except for the extra weight.* Then she caught herself.

"Where's Mape?" she asked.

"Oh, he's doin' family stuff with his kids today."

"Why didn't you go with them?"

"I wasn't feelin' too good this mornin', but I threw up and I'm all better now."

The day was fun, the movie was good, and the dinner excellent. That night they stayed at the Riverside.

CHAPTER 47

Laughlin, Nevada, 1996
(The year of the killings)

Nita and the other maids were sharing guests-from-hell stories over lunch when Cristine, one of the blackjack dealers called out, "There's someone her to see Nita!"

Nita hurried down the back hallway and through the exit door. "Greg?" she asked excitedly.

It was Mape.

"Has something happened to Greg?" she asked.

"No, Greg's fine," Mape assured her. "I just need to talk to you."

Nita changed and met Mape in the lobby.

"Greg sent me here to tell you that he's moving to New Jersey. I'm sure he's told you about the successful antiques business he and I own back there."

"No, he's never mentioned it," she said, fighting tears.

"Really? That's where he gets most of his money. My sister's husband has been running the store for us while we've been out here waiting for Greg to get off of house arrest, but he's had a mild stroke and can't do it anymore, so we have to get back there right away."

Nita asked, "Why didn't Greg come here and tell me himself?"

"He tried to," Mape said. "Yesterday. But he just couldn't bring himself to do it."

"That's why he came here yesterday? To tell me goodbye?"

"Yes. But he couldn't go through with it. You know what a soft heart he has, and he cares a great deal about you. We're leaving tonight. My sons are helping him pack right now. I believe the furniture in the cabin belongs to you?"

She nodded. "Except for the washer and dryer, and the television and the microwave. Greg bought those."

"Yes. He said to tell you he wants you to have them."

"That's nice of him."

"He asked me to give you this too," he said, handing her a square, bright-green envelope with a black magic marker smudge on the front. "It's a thousand dollars, to help out until you can find a new tenant and another cleaning job."

She was touched.

Mape smiled and stood to leave. "He'll send you his new address as soon as he gets settled. Maybe you can visit sometime."

"That would be nice," she said.

"Oh, I almost forgot," he said. "Greg asked me to get his car keys back from you. We'll leave his house keys in the cabin."

Nita removed the two car keys from a zippered side pocket of her wallet and handed them to him.

As soon as Mape left, Nita locked herself in a stall in the ladies' room and let the tears flow. When she was finished, she felt more depressed than ever.

On her way home, Nita stopped at the Safeway in Bullhead City and bought half a gallon of Dreyer's Rocky Road ice cream and a bottle of Stoly. She drove through the ATM at her bank and deposited the rest of the money Mape had given her then went to the trailer to tie one on.

"Mom?" Nath said, trying to shake Nita awake. She finally got one of her eyes open a crack.

"Nath?" she said. She could tell she was slurring. "What time is it?"

"After midnight," he said.

Nita cracked the other eye enough to see that she was in the recliner in her mother's trailer. The hard thing she felt in her hand turned out to be the bottle of vodka. She took a swig. Nath removed the nearly empty bottle from her hand, took a quick swig, and gave it back. "Why are you drinking?"

"Because I've been dumped," she said sadly, trying to hold her head still. "By a no-good, rotten rat bastard that likes his scumbag jerk of a friend more than he likes me."

"You mean that Greg guy?" Nath asked, suddenly interested.

"No, I mean that Greg son of a bitch," she corrected, her chin falling forward onto her chest.

"I thought he moved away," Nath said, trying to sound disinterested. "He's not at his apartment anymore."

"I know," she said, raising her head back up and attempting to put her finger against her lips. "It was a secret, but I guess it doesn't matter now."

"What was a secret?" Nath asked.

"That he's been living in a cabin down by the marina. It's hidden by trees. So nobody could find him," she giggled.

"Oh, Katherine's Landing." Nath prompted, still trying to sound nonchalant.

"No," she giggled. "Not Katherine. Cottonwood… " Nita's shoulders slumped. Her head fell to one side, and she let go of the bottle. She was out again.

Nath grabbed the bottle and finished off the trickle of vodka that was left, thinking about what his mother had just said. *So he's hiding out in Cottonwood Cove, huh? Near the marina. In a cabin, hidden by trees.*

Nico would be very interested in that piece of information.

CHAPTER 48

Los Angeles, California, 1979
(Seventeen years before the killings)

Greg's heart did a flip-flop when the man walked into the Bicycle Club. Good. He was going to play again tonight.

Greg had seen the man before on Saturday nights, last week and the week before. Both times, it had taken all his willpower not to say something. But what if it wasn't his brother? He had to be sure.

Greg followed the man into the restaurant and sat at the counter, chatting with the waitress. He could see the guy in the mirror, eating the restaurant's three-dollar special, the same as he had done the week before. Once again, the man ate with his left hand, the same as Greg's brother had. The same as Greg did. And Papa had. The man had the same large ears that stuck out from his head, like his brother, and the same space between his two front teeth. His hair was turning gray and his hairline was receding too.

Like Papa's, Greg remembered.

It all fit. The hair, the teeth, the ears, the way he walked, the chin, the nose. Greg was both excited and frightened at what he was about to do. If the man had blue eyes, Greg would be sure it was his brother, and he would say something to him tonight.

Suddenly, the loud speaker in the restaurant announced, "MB, your ten/twenty stud seat is ready." The man quickly stood and hurried to the register, where he left his money and check. Greg noticed he had forgotten to leave a tip, so he walked over and put a dollar on the table.

Greg went back to the poker room and sat where he could continue watching the man, who only bought sixty dollars' worth of chips, not really a good stack for a ten/twenty game. With that kind of stack, the guy should be playing at a three/six table, or even a two/four. The guy pushed all his chips in on the third hand and lost everything. He got up from the table and walked toward the exit.

Greg hurried along behind him, summoned his courage, and called out, "Excuse me, sir."

The man turned around and glared at Greg, who figured he was probably in a bad mood because he lost his money so fast. When Greg saw the blue eyes glaring at him, he could contain himself no longer. It was his brother!

"Excuse me, but is your name Greg?" Ivan asked excitedly. "Gregoe Crenski?"

The man continued to glare. "Maybe. Who's asking?"

"Greg, it's me, Ivan!" Ivan shouted, tears gathering in his eyes. He thrust out his arms to hug his brother. "It's Ivan, your brother!"

The man stepped back, confused, and stared at Ivan in disbelief for several seconds. When he finally spoke, his voice was soft. "Ivan? Is it really you? I wouldn't have recognized you."

"That because it's been twenty-eight years since those men took you away," Ivan said, putting his arms back down to his sides. "I was only sixteen, remember? I'm grown-up now."

"So you are," Greg said, shaking his head. "I guess I still think of you as a kid."

"You've changed too, Greg. A lot. You seem shorter."

"That's because you're taller," Greg laughed.

"Come on," Greg said. "Let's have that hug now."

Ivan grabbed his brother and held him for so long that Greg finally pushed him away.

"We need to go somewhere and talk," Greg said.

Ivan said, "I have a motel room just a few blocks from here. We can talk there. I'll drive if you want."

"You'll have to," Greg said. "My pickup's twelve years old, and it started heating up on the way over here today."

"Wow," Greg said when he saw the Cadillac. "It looks like my little brother hit a jackpot or two somewhere along the way."

"Not really," Ivan said modestly, blushing. "But I have had some good luck."

"Remember what you used to call me when we were little?" Ivan asked as he removed two Dr. Peppers from the motel fridge.

Greg thought for a minute then said, "No, I guess I've forgotten."

"You called me a moron all the time when I said something stupid."

"I do remember," Greg said. "But I promise not to do it anymore."

"It's okay," Ivan said. "It was kinda like a special nickname or somethin'. You can still call me that if you want to."

"We'll see," Greg told him. "But right now, I want to hear about the family, and what's happened to you since I left."

"Well," Ivan started, "of course, Papa died a few years before you left, and you remember my mama died right before you left, and my sisters, Pearl and Gladys, got married and left before you did."

"That's right. It's coming back now," Greg said. "How are your sisters these days? Still married? Any kids?"

"I don't know," Ivan said, sadly. "I haven't seen them since I left home. They're not listed in the phone book. I went down to the produce district about a year ago to see if anybody knew what happened to Pearl, but nobody remembered her."

For the next two hours, Greg talked nonstop, first telling his brother about Zoot being at the house when he got home that day.

"I think he was looking for the money you hid, but he didn't find it. I found it after he left and I saved it for you. Anyhow, Zoot's the one that told me that the bad guys took you, and that I wasn't never going to see you again."

Greg said. "I always suspected it was Zoot who led them to me."

"I think Zoot stole your car too," Ivan said, "that Buick you had, because it was out in front of our building when I came home that day, and that night it was gone."

Greg nodded, and Ivan kept talking. He went on to tell Greg about how he took his identity, about the army and Sarge, Folsom

Prison and Roman, the Carlisle Brewery, Rowena and the kids, and every major event of his life that he could think of.

"It sounds like my baby brother's been pretty busy," Greg told Ivan when he finally stopped talking. "I'm impressed."

Ivan beamed at the praise from his brother. "How about you?" he asked. "What have you been doin' all these years? I always knew you'd get away from those bad guys. How'd you do it?"

"That's a pretty long story," Greg said, "and it's late. Maybe we should save it for another time."

"Tell me now, please. I can't wait."

"Okay, then. Let me use the bathroom first."

Ivan was all ears when Greg returned and began his story.

"What happened was I had won some money playing poker from a guy that was mobbed up. It was quite a lot of money."

"Was it the five thousand bucks you hid under the floor at the apartment?"

"Yes. That plus another thousand I put under the seat of the Buick for my getaway. I knew they'd be coming after me eventually. I'm glad you found the money, Ivan. I figured you would need it with me gone."

"I sure did," Ivan assured him. "But I only borrowed it. I put it in the bank and saved it for you."

"That's great," Greg said, smiling. "Believe me, I can use it. But getting back to what happened, the money actually belonged to the boss of the guy I won it from who was an enforcer for the mob, and he wanted it back. As I said, I'm sure Zoot told them where to find me. Anyway, just as I was leaving the apartment to get away, they grabbed me. They pistol-whipped me to try to get me to tell them where the money was. When that didn't work, they gagged me and tied me up, then threw me in the trunk of a car. I must have passed out because the next thing I knew it was dark and we were in a deserted parking lot next to a warehouse, near the ocean. I was on the ground. As soon as they saw I was awake, one of them started working me over with a tire iron. I was sure I was a goner when all of a sudden, a car drove into the lot, and they jumped into their car and took off, leaving me there on the ground, bleeding.

"The guy in the car was the night watchman, coming by to make his rounds. He took me into his office, where he untied me and cleaned me up and wrapped a towel around my head. He gave me some water and some aspirin. He offered to call the cops, but I think he was relieved when I told him not to. I said I just wanted to get out of town as fast as I could. I only had thirty bucks in my pocket, so I lay on a cot and rested for a couple of hours while the guy made his rounds, then he took me to the railroad yard and boosted me into a boxcar. Lots of guys rode the rails during those years. It was safe then, not like now. The railroad cops didn't hassle you much as long as you didn't cause any trouble. I met some nice fellows on the trains and in the hobo villages too."

While Greg was talking, Ivan took two more bottles of Dr. Pepper from the little fridge and opened them, handing one to Greg.

"Thanks," Greg said, taking a healthy slug of the cold soda before continuing. "Anyway, they had beaten me so badly that all I could do the next few days was sleep on some straw in a boxcar while the train moved across the country. Some brothers named Joe and Tom saw I was hurt and brought me water and some beans or jerky every day until I could do for myself."

"You were really a hobo? Like in the pitchers?" Ivan asked, amused.

Greg nodded, smiling.

"The thing that happened next is the part you'll find hard to believe. One morning, the train stopped in a place called Slickstone, New Jersey, and I decided to walk into the little town and buy some shoelaces. When I walked into the store, I nodded good morning to a couple of sort of pretty women who were trying on gloves. Would you believe, all of a sudden one of the women looked at me and screamed and ran over and grabbed me and started yelling 'Mape! Mape! I knew you'd come back to us someday.' I had no idea what she was talking about, and I tried to push her away."

"Mape? That's a funny thing for someone to yell," Ivan said. "Did you ever find out what it meant?"

"Oh yes," Greg said. "It was the name of the woman's little brother who everyone thought had drowned when he was four years old, even though they never found the body. His name was Maple, which was his mother's family name, but they called him Mape. The woman, Stella, thought I was him. It was weird."

"Why did she think that?" Ivan asked.

"Because, believe it or not, I was a dead ringer for her father, and her brother, the real Mape, had looked a lot like him when he was little."

Greg pulled out a worn black-and-white picture of a man and woman and handed it to Ivan.

"See? That's the father and mother when they were young. He passed away about ten years ago, may he rest in peace."

"You really do look like him," Ivan agreed, looking from Greg to the photograph, amazed at the resemblance. "He looks a lot like you did when we still lived at home."

"I know," Greg agreed. "That's what's so amazing. I was almost the son's age too. It was uncanny."

"So what did you do next?" Ivan asked, excited. This was better than watching a picture show.

"Well, it was like it was fate. I had already been trying to think of a way to get a new identity, and there it was, like a gift. So I became their long-lost son, Maple Avril Belata. That's been my name for almost thirty years now, but everyone calls me Mape. The hysterical woman, who's my sister Stella now, took me home and her parents hugged me and kissed me and cried over me and everything. The next day, they had a big barbeque in the backyard and a bunch of relatives came over to see me and welcome me back."

"Wow!" Ivan said. "Did they ask you where you'd been for all those years?"

"Oh, sure," he said. "They took me to see a doctor and everything. The local sheriff, who turned out to be my dad's cousin, even talked to me, trying to find out what happened since that day at the river. I told them I didn't remember anything. I said sometimes I thought I remembered playing by a river when I was a kid, but the only thing I remembered for sure was waking up in a boxcar on a moving train, a grown man, recovering from a bad beating. These days, with lie detectors and DNA and everything, I couldn't have gotten away with it, but back then nobody knew much about amnesia, especially in a small town like that. Besides, I looked so much like the father, and they all wanted so desperately for me to be Mape, they didn't investigate too much. They said it was God's hand that had led me back home to them. I know it sounds pretty far-fetched, but it's the honest-to-goodness truth."

"Mape," Ivan laughed. "Is that what I should call you now?"

"Yes," Mape said, suddenly growing serious. "That's very important, Ivan. If my mother and sister ever found out I'm an imposter it would break their hearts, and they'd probably have nothing to do with me anymore. I might even get kicked off the force."

"The force?" Ivan asked. "What force?"

"I'm a sheriff," Mape told him. "A deputy with the Los Angeles County Sheriff's Department."

"A sheriff?" Ivan asked, excitedly. "With a gun and a badge and everything?"

"That's right," Mape said.

"Do you shoot bad guys?" Ivan asked. "Like in the pitchers?"

"I used to, in New Jersey, but now I'm a bailiff in a courtroom in Santa Monica."

Greg just sat smiling at his brother. A sheriff. A hero. This was turning out better than he had ever hoped.

"I was married for a long time to the cousin of my friend, Caden Logan. I have four sons. Lawson, Lawrence, we call him Larry, Leon, and Lance. Lawson, the oldest just turned twenty-five, and Lance, the youngest will be eighteen next month. Thank goodness, no more child support.

"My uncle's buddy helped me get the bailiff's job out here so I came to California last year to get away from Angela, my ex. She has money, a trust fund, but she's trying to make me pay through the nose for divorcing her. Right now, she's after me for tuition money for Lawson. She's a real witch."

Ivan smiled, but didn't comment.

"Well, kid, that's about it. Thanks to you, here we are. Pretty amazing, huh?"

Ivan agreed.

"Say, kid, I know, it's late, but I was hoping to play a little more poker tonight before I went broke. How about if we go back to the casino while the games are still going? Maybe you could advance me a hundred or two from the five thousand you're holding for me? Then maybe we can get together for dinner tomorrow and talk some more. My treat if I win."

"That sounds good," Ivan said. "But there's one more thing."

He asked if he could keep on being Greg, seeing as how Greg's name was Mape now.

"Of course you can, little brother," Mape told him. "I'd be honored."

Ivan, now officially Greg, smiled.

As they prepared to leave the room, Mape turned to Greg, a serious look on his face. "Listen, little brother, I have to ask a favor of you. A very important one."

"Sure," Greg said, assuming it was about the money. "Anything you want."

"You have to be very careful never to call me Greg. Even when we're alone, you must always call me Mape. And you can never tell anyone we're brothers. If word got out that I'm not who I say I am I could be in serious trouble. I could lose my family, and even my job. So if you ever call me Greg or mention that we're brothers, even when it's just the two of us, you'll never see me again. And I mean not ever. Do you understand?"

Greg nodded somberly and zipped his lips with his fingers.

On the way back to the casino, Greg insisted that Mape drive the Caddie. Greg's eyesight wasn't too great anymore. In the car, Greg told Mape that he would go to the cashier's window and withdraw two thousand dollars from his players bank and give it to him so he could send his son his tuition and get his car fixed. That done, he left Mape at the Bicycle Club after first arranging to meet him at six o'clock that evening for dinner. He was beside himself with joy. He was really Greg now, forever, and he had a lawman for a brother, and he was an uncle. He had a real family!

That evening at dinner, the brothers filled in the details of some of the things they had shared the night before.

Over dessert, Mape confessed to Greg that he'd run into some bad luck and had lost the entire two thousand dollars at the poker table that morning, and was in need of more money to get his truck repaired. Greg, who had never in his life risked more than two hundred dollars at the tables in a single night, was surprised that Mape had risked so much, especially since he seemed to need money so badly.

"Why don't I get you another thousand tonight to fix your truck and get you by this week and next week, we can come back and I'll bring you the other two thousand."

"That'll be great," Mape said. He hesitated then said, "By the way, today while I was waiting for you, I started thinking about how you said that you had invested my five thousand, and I was wondering if it's been drawing interest all these years."

"Yes," Greg smiled. "Around 5 percent most years."

"That's what I thought," Mape said. "The way I figured, at 5 percent each year times twenty-eight years, that's about seven thousand dollars. That means I should have about twelve thousand dollars coming to me. Right?"

Greg opened his mouth to explain about how the interest had compounded, and about the investments he had made, and was about to tell him he actually had over forty-two thousand dollars, but thought better of it. Based upon the events of the last twenty-four hours, Greg suspected he might be called upon to help his newfound brother out financially again in the future and figured he might as well do it with Mape's own money.

"That sounds about right," Greg said, smiling.

CHAPTER 49

Los Angeles, California, 1988
(Eight years before the killings)

Life as Mape's brother had its ups and downs, but to Greg, the ups were worth the downs many times over. They took trips to Las Vegas, Reno, Laughlin, and lots of other places. They even went to New Orleans once, and Greg got to meet two of Roman Neal's brothers and listen to them play music in a jazz club.

Greg's prediction about his brother's finances turned out to be on target. Wherever they went and whatever they did, he ended up paying for everything, sometimes even Mape's gambling. But he kept track and reimbursed himself for his brother's share of the expenses from Mape's secret account.

Greg was always careful to think of Mape only as his friend. He would rather die than lose his brother again.

Over the years, Greg continued his monthly visits to Rowena and her family. Jay dropped out of school after the eighth grade, but Savannah turned out to be bright and motivated. Greg paid her college tuition and bought her a brand-new Dodge Dart to drive. The old VW Beetle he had bought years before for Rowena had finally worn out. Mape, however, with his expertise at keeping worn out cars running, had plans for it.

"Something amusing happened in court this week," Mape said over burgers and fries one day.

Greg smiled. He knew it would be a story about someone getting away with a scam. Those were Mape's favorite cases. Mape was a con artist at heart.

"This guy in an old VW Beetle, like yours, was driving down the street and jammed on his brakes suddenly in front of this big, brand-new Oldsmobile that was following too fast behind him. He said it was to avoid hitting a cat. Well, the VW got rear-ended, totaled, and the guy ended up in the hospital with fractures and contusions, according to his doctor. And guess who his doctor is?"

"Dr. Foxx?" Greg asked. On most of his days off, he bought sandwiches and met Mape for lunch at the courthouse, usually going early so he could watch the trials. He had watched Dr. Theron Foxx testify a number of times in bodily injury cases, usually when Ferrell Masticha was representing the injured party.

"Yeah." Mape laughed between chews on his hamburger. "He and Ferrell Masticha make a good team, if you get what I mean. I'll tell you, if I ever decided to pull off a scam like that, I'd want those two to represent me. Can you believe it? The Oldsmobile owner's insurance company had to pay all the guy's medical expenses, plus the cost of his car, plus three hundred thousand for pain and suffering."

"That's a lot of money."

"Yes it is. Maybe you should think about pulling something like that. You've already got the VW."

Greg laughed.

"I'm serious, man," Mape said. "You might as well put the VW to good use when I get it running."

"I couldn't," Greg said, still not sure if Mape was kidding or not. "I'd get too flustered on the witness stand and trip myself up."

"No, you wouldn't," Mape assured him. "All you'd have to do is fall out onto the road as soon as the car hits you, then say you were knocked unconscious and don't remember anything until you woke up in the hospital. It would be a piece of cake. I know I could get Mr. Masticha to represent you, and Dr. Foxx to treat you."

"Nah," Greg said. "I might get hurt real bad or something."

"That wouldn't be a problem either," Mape persisted. "As soon as you step on the brake, you just have to take a deep breath and relax. I could help you practice that. Believe me, if I didn't have a family, I'd do it in a minute."

Over the next several days, Greg mulled over Mape's suggestion. When he'd finally gotten up the nerve to do it, it hadn't been as hard as he had feared. The insurance company offered to settle the case for two hundred thousand dollars over hospital and other expenses, and Greg didn't have to go to court at all. He just had to give a deposition. He adamantly maintained that he had been knocked unconscious and didn't remember anything between the time the dog ran in front of his car and when he woke up in the hospital emergency room. It took over a year to settle but all told, Greg collected $120,000, tax-free, after Mr. Masticha deducted his fee. He paid Dr. Foxx twenty thousand, and gave Mape ten thousand for his help.

Greg's auto insurance company paid off a small amount on the VW, but he couldn't get insurance on it any longer, even though Mape replaced the damaged door and fender and got it running again. This angered Mape, because he wanted Greg to use it in another accident. Greg was relieved though. He didn't want to do another accident. The back injury he had suffered from the first accident hurt constantly. The headaches from the concussion he suffered were becoming more and more severe, and he kept having to increase the amount of the pain meds Dr. Foxx had prescribed for him. Luckily, he had signed over limited power of attorney to Mape, so even after he moved to Bullhead City, Mape could continue to pick up his prescriptions from Dr. Foxx.

CHAPTER 50

Los Angeles, California, 1995
(The year before the killings)

Lately, Mape had begun to regret ever getting mixed up with Greg. After years of cleaning up Greg's messes, he had nothing to show for it but crumbs while Greg wore the fancy jewelry and drove the new cars and had God only knew how much money stashed away. It wasn't fair!

At times, Mape wished he had just walked away that night at the Bicycle Club. But he had been flat broke, and Angela was screaming her head off on the phone every day for money.

Steam had been pouring from under the hood of Mape's pickup when he pulled into the Bicycle Club parking lot that afternoon. His only hope for the money to patch up his radiator was to get lucky at the tables, but he lost his last sixty dollars in five minutes in a stud game and was on his way out of the casino to take one last try at the radiator, then to hitchhike home. He was at one of the lowest points of his life that evening, when out of nowhere stepped this strange man claiming to be his long-lost brother.

Mape's first inclination had been to deck him, but when the guy's arms shot out of his sleeves for a hug Mape spied the gold Rolex on his wrist and realized he was looking at some serious money, so he played along.

In all honesty, the money wasn't the only thing that hooked Mape that night. He was a natural-born con artist, instincts he'd had to struggle hard to curtail since he'd gotten into law enforcement.

So when this out of the blue rich ding-dong walked into his life and mistook him for his brother, Mape went for it.

Conning Greg had been a stroll in the park. He'd been so desperate to find his brother that all Mape had to do was sit back and let him lay it out for him. Then, after he had spilled his life history, it was pathetically easy for Mape to improvise and play along, something he'd been doing all his life.

The clincher, though, had been when Greg told him about finding the money his brother had hidden, and about keeping it for him. Mape had become an instant big brother.

Truth be told, the two of them had had a lot of fun together over the years. Mape got to call the shots and Greg provided the money. They had lived the good life for several years, until Laria entered the picture.

Marrying Laria had been one of the major screw ups of his life, second only to marrying Angela. It was the scam thing again. She'd been beautiful, innocent, naïve, and, at twenty-five, less than half his age. A real challenge. Like Greg, Laria was shy, naïve, and gullible.

The law office where she worked at the time was in a large complex of buildings that included the courthouse in which Mape was a bailiff. At lunch every day, Mape noticed this very pretty blonde girl who ate at the same table with her brunette friend. One day, the friend didn't show up and Laria was sitting alone. Mape quickly put on Greg's Rolex and diamond pinkie ring and they sat down at her table. Mape regaled her with silly jokes and magic tricks and by the time they went back to work she was laughing. It took only two weeks of turning on the charm and crying on Laria's shoulder about being lonely to convince Laria to go out to dinner with him. Three months later, she was pregnant and, at her father's insistence, they were engaged. Greg was thrilled. He got to be the best man at their wedding and wear a tuxedo. He loaned Mape his Caddie for the wedding trip and paid for the honeymoon. For a wedding gift, he gave them a nearly new blue Chevy Chevette hatchback, a nice family car. He didn't reimburse himself from Mape's account for any of the wedding-related expenses, or for the hatchback.

"It'll be a good family car," Greg explained.

Laria was delighted and gave Greg a big hug and a kiss on the cheek. Mape was less than thrilled.

Mape's marriage had presented the first obstacle in his relationship with Greg. A few months after the wedding, upon returning from a trip to New Jersey where Mape introduced his bride to his family, Laria hung up a collage of pictures from Mape's past that his mother had given her; his first communion, high school graduation, spelling bee championship, and others. Mape exploded when he saw it. He grabbed it and threw it in the trash, breaking the glass inside the frame.

"Don't ever do that again," he shouted. "Don't ever put out pictures or any other reminders of my childhood, and don't ever speak of it to me or to anyone else. It was a horrible time. I'm obligated to visit my family and pretend that everything was okay, but I refuse to be reminded of those times in my own home."

"I'm sorry," Laria said, puzzled, fighting back tears. "I had no idea. The way your mother and Stella talked—"

"They're both in total denial about what was going on, but it was a nightmare for me and I don't want it dredged up by you or anyone else."

"I'm sorry," Laria said again, touching her swelling belly. "Is there anything I can do to help?"

"The way you can help," Mape said. "Is never to bring it up again to me or to Greg or to your family or to any of your friends at work!"

Mape actually felt terrible about doing that to his wife, but he'd had no choice. As much as he joked about Greg being a moron, he knew that Greg was actually pretty bright about most things, especially numbers and financial stuff. He was just slow sometimes. It might take him a while to catch on to some of the things people did or said, but he eventually figured things out.

If Greg were to see Mape's boyhood pictures, or if Laria were to tell him one of Stella's stories about when he was a kid, it would just be a matter of time before he figured out that Mape had been blowing smoke at him with the disappearance and amnesia story that night at the motel. That would most likely end their friendship, along with the financial help. If Lance came to California to live, as he'd been talking about doing, Mape would just have to find a way to keep Greg away from him.

But to Mape's relief, Lance, being the youngest son, apparently either hadn't been subjected to Grandma's and Aunt Stella's stories about his father's boyhood, or had forgotten them.

Greg was a frequent visitor to the Belata home. He proved to be a good friend as well as good source of money when the babies were born, or the cars needed repairs, or when they were short on the down payment for their house.

Mape never worried much about not putting away money for the kids' college, or for his old age. With Greg's increasing health problems, especially after the accident, Mape figured he would out-live him, and Greg had no one else to leave his money to. He never really knew the extent of Greg's assets, because it was the one subject he couldn't get Greg to talk about, but he was sure it would be a sizable sum.

Until that woman came along and screwed everything up.

For the first few years after Greg married Pree, he and Mape didn't see much of each other. Greg moved into that ridiculous mansion in Arizona with Pree and Mape started working as much overtime as he could to buy the farm in New Jersey. The farm and antiques store were his dream. That's when everything went to hell in a handbasket, as the saying goes.

Out of the blue, Laria started questioning Mape's judgment, and arguing with him, things she had never done before. Then, just before the escrow on the sale of their house closed, Mape came home from work one night to find divorce papers and a note on the table from Laria, telling him she had decided not to move to New Jersey with him and that she'd taken the kids and moved in with her mother, now a widow, in Pasadena. Mape was furious. When he went to Pasadena to try to talk some sense into Laria, his mother-in-law called the cops. Laria talked her mother out of pressing charges if Mape agreed to leave peacefully and he had no choice but to comply. He still had a couple of months to go before his retirement kicked in, and he couldn't afford to blow it.

It wasn't hard to figure out what caused Laria to change like that. He would bet his overtime checks that Pree had put those ideas into her head. Laria would never have come up with such nonsense on her own.

The witch would pay!

CHAPTER 51

Bullhead City, Arizona, 1995
(The year before the killings)

"You've got to convince her to go to California without you," Mape insisted. He had stopped off in Bullhead City on his way to New Jersey. "This is our last chance to finalize our plan. How many of the things have you finished so far?"

"Uh, well, let's see," Greg said. "I've started cashing in the stock and putting the money in the new storage locker."

"What else?" Mape asked.

Greg hesitated, not wanting to upset Mape. "Not much," he said apologetically. "I think it's these pills. I can't seem to remember too good anymore."

"That's okay," Mape said. "I'll write it all down for you tomorrow after Pree leaves. We can take the jewelry to the storage locker while she's gone, and claim it was stolen."

It had taken four slashed tires on the U-Haul and eggs on the windshield the next morning, but in the end, Mape prevailed. He stayed over the weekend in Bullhead City with Greg, and Pree took her mother back to California alone. To Mape's chagrin, she took the lockbox with the jewelry to California with her.

Even after he arrived in New Jersey, Mape made Greg's life a nightmare, calling nearly every day for an update on how he was doing with the plan. Greg was in a panic because he couldn't find the notebook Mape had written the list in. He continued to cash in the stock and put the money into the storage locker, but he couldn't remember anything else that was on the list. He worried constantly that Pree would find out about the plan and divorce him before he had time to carry it out. Mape would really be mad if that happened. Greg started feeling afraid all the time, afraid of upsetting Mape and afraid of upsetting Pree. He knew that soon he would have to choose between them, and he didn't want to choose. But Mape kept reminding him that blood was thicker than water. Mape was right, of course; he really had no choice. He kept taking more and more of the painkillers and tranquilizers and antidepressants to keep down the panic. Sometimes, he told Pree he was going across the river to play cards, but most days he wasn't able to focus his brain on the cards, so he got a room comped at one of the hotels and crawled into bed and ate cookies and candy bars and cried until he fell asleep.

CHAPTER 52

**Slickstone, New Jersey, 1996
(The year of the killings)**

"God bless Capri Crenski!" If she had been in the room, Mape would have kissed her full on the lips. She had managed to do for him in one day what he'd been unable to do for himself in almost seventeen years.

By the time Mape reached Slickstone, New Jersey, by way of Atlantic City, his nest egg had dwindled to the ninety thousand Laria's father had left her, plus a few hundred dollars. Within thirty days, he had rented two acres of farmland with a small, two-bedroom house near the road, and opened his antiques store, been forced to sell his best pieces at a loss and dump the others, and was out of business.

It was from these dire straits that Pree had inadvertently rescued him. She had finally done exactly what Mape had predicted she would do; she had kicked Greg out of the house, cleaned out one of his bank accounts, filed for divorce, and taken out a restraining order against him.

Mape, in his role as Greg's friend, kept him stirred up as much as he could by long distance and convinced him to sue Pree for the money and the house. They agreed that as soon as the court date was set, Greg would send Mape money for a plane ticket. Happily, that day came sooner than expected, due to a court cancellation.

Three days before the hearing, Greg picked Mape up at the airport in Las Vegas. Their first stop was a Big and Tall Shop so Greg could buy some new clothes for his ever-expanding girth.

They stayed downtown at the Horseshoe, played poker all night, slept in, and had a great time together, just like when they were single, and Greg began to see the positive side of life without Pree.

Mape got a mobile phone, an expensive one, with a Nevada number. That way, Mape told Greg, even when he was in New Jersey, their calls back and forth would be charged as local Nevada calls, and they'd save lots of money. Delighted, Greg insisted on paying for the phone.

On the appointed day, they drove to Kingman for the hearing, buoyed by the idea of kicking Pree out of the house and getting Greg's money back. As Mape drove, they were almost giddy with anticipation. The witch would learn not to mess with them!

"I have never been so humiliated in my life!" Mape shouted at Greg. His hands shook as he drove the Lincoln back to Las Vegas after the hearing. "Do you know what this means?" he shouted, pounding on the steering wheel. "It means that when she turns us in to the IRS, we're both going to prison."

"I'm sorry," Greg apologized, his eyes downcast.

"Sorry doesn't help!" Mape said, pounding his hand against the steering wheel again. "How did she get her hands on those tax returns in the first place?"

"They were in the house," Greg said apologetically, working hard to hold back tears. Mape hadn't let him take any pain pills before they left for court that morning, and his head and back were killing him.

They were quiet for a while.

"I'm sorry," Greg finally said. "I'll make it up to you."

"Yes, you will," Mape agreed, still seething. "And you can start right now by not talking to me anymore. And anymore means never."

"Not ever?" Greg said, disbelieving. Tears spilled onto his cheeks.

"Not until Pree is out of the picture and the tax papers are destroyed."

At the airport, Mape grabbed his bags from the car and entered the terminal without speaking another word.

Let him stew, he thought. It would teach him a lesson, and would allow Mape to return to New Jersey and do what he had to do in peace, without being distracted by the obnoxious little twerp.

CHAPTER 53

Slickstone, New Jersey, 1996
(The year of the killings)

Mape's long exile in California had softened his recollection of his sister Stella's dramatic histrionics and constant bickering with his mother, but it soon came flooding back in vivid detail. His ex-wife continuously needled him and his relationship with his three older sons was cordial at best. It was time to move on.

Mape coped by reminding himself there was a small fortune in cash waiting for him in a storage facility in Bullhead City, Arizona. He just had to figure out how to get his hands on it. He had no idea how much was there, but it was sure to be a considerable amount. It had taken Greg several months to cash in the stock, so Mape estimated it could be as much as three or four hundred thousand dollars, possibly more. It was definitely time to cut his losses here in Jersey and get back to Nevada.

Mape had bought the mobile phone in anticipation of this moment. With the Nevada number, Greg would assume he was still in New Jersey while he was living in Las Vegas, waiting to make his move. He would be only two hours from Bullhead City by car; far enough from Greg that he wasn't likely to run into him, yet not too far from the money.

Fortunately, Greg had come through with the twenty-five thousand dollar buy-in into his antiques business.

So on a very cold day in February, he bid his mother and Stella farewell, telephoned goodbyes to his sons, and set out for Las Vegas after making a twenty-thousand-dollar, two-day stopover in Atlantic City.

In Las Vegas, Mape found a one-bedroom apartment on the outskirts of town and rented enough furniture to get by. The day after he moved in, he met his neighbor from the apartment above his, Mirabelle something or other. She was a petite brunette in her early forties. Except for a slightly crooked nose and bit of a belly, she wasn't bad looking. Mape took her to the buffet at the Tropicana one evening and they hit it off pretty well. She had a job as a computer operator for the city, so she wasn't looking for a sugar daddy, and the sex wasn't bad either. Mape didn't expect to be in the apartment too long anyway; only until his ship came in, so to speak. He longed for the day he could get rid of the embarrassing hatchback and replace it with some respectable wheels.

Greg was taking an assortment of pills regularly which, although impeding conversation with him, made him easier for Mape to manipulate.

Mape's scheme was quite simple. All he had to do was convince Greg to do something that would get him locked up for a while. He would have no choice but to trust his brother and best friend Mape with the keys to his storage facility to get the money to bail him out. Mape could be over the border to Mexico before Greg figured out what was happening. He already had his passport.

Mape could taste prosperity when, once again, Greg jerked it out from under him. He shook with rage after being humiliated in court. He knew the bitch would turn them in to the IRS for the reward. Why wouldn't she? Tax fraud was a serious crime. Angrily, Mape refused to answer Greg's calls until Pree was out of the picture and the tax papers were destroyed. But even as he spoke the words, he knew it was a futile gesture. He was in a real fix this time. Getting his hands on Greg's money and heading over the border was now the only hope he had of staying out of prison.

Greg's next act of lunacy, according to his phone messages, was to get himself arrested for hiring someone to kill Pree. It was a cop, of course. On top of that, he was being blackmailed. Mape felt like he was trapped in a soap opera. He needed to find a way to extract himself from this mess.

Then it occurred to Mape that if Greg got convicted of murder conspiracy he'd be sent up for a long time. It was the break he had been waiting for. He would let Greg stew for a few more days then, just when things were the bleakest, he would rush in and be the supportive friend; a friend Greg could trust with his life, as well as the key to his storage locker. Mape was on pins and needles as he waited to spring the trap. But when Greg called two days later he said everything was okay now, that he had moved to a new place, and met a woman who was going to help him through everything.

Over my dead body, Mape thought. *Find your own patsy, lady. This one's already spoken for.*

CHAPTER 54

**Las Vegas, Nevada, 1996
(The year of the killings)**

Mape had to admire this Nita woman's style. Greg was paying rent to live in her cabin, sleeping with her, and was even paying her to clean her own cabin. It was a sweet deal, but she was no match for a pro like Mape, who had invested seventeen years of his life into this con and wasn't about to let her and her son move in on it.

Greg was so grateful to have his old friend back, he hardly batted an eye at the news that helping him through this disaster was going to mean abandoning his family and his farm and his antiques shop and moving into the local area so he could be available any time Greg needed him. He pointed out to Greg that he himself stood to lose the twenty-five thousand he had recently invested in the business.

Greg didn't care. His extreme joy and relief at having his old friend back, and at having someone he could trust to guide him through the trouble he was in, was worth whatever it cost. He assured Mape that he would cover any and all costs they incurred. The next morning, Mape left for his apartment in Las Vegas with another twenty-five hundred dollars of Greg's money, with which he was to set himself up in an apartment in Las Vegas. When used properly, lying and laying on guilt could be a profitable commodity.

Pree apparently hadn't reported them to the IRS, but things took one bad turn after another anyway, driving Mape's frustration level close to the breaking point. No matter what he did to knock

Greg down, the imbecile bounced back up again. Things seemed to roll off of the lucky little creep like he was coated with Teflon. The amazing thing was that most of the time Greg was so zonked out on meds he hardly knew what was going on, not to mention he had the IQ of a crouton. It just wasn't right.

When Greg hired the cop to kill his wife, but was too cheap to pay extra to be sure the job got done right, he lucked out with house arrest and probation.

Next, Mape convinced Greg to change his psychiatrist and doctor's appointments to every other Tuesday and spend the hours of the canceled appointments at the Searchlight casino on Tuesdays while Nita cleaned his cabin. He also changed his doctor appointments and spent every other Friday in the poker room at the Riverside. His ankle alarm should have alerted someone that he had left home without authorization, yet nothing came of it. If the system had worked properly, Greg would have had to do some jail time in Kingman and would have been forced to entrust Mape with the keys to his storage locker so he could pay his bills for him. But once again, nothing happened.

Mape thought his break had finally come the morning he walked out of the men's room at the Riverside and saw Pree waiting for the elevator to the movie theater. He hurried to the poker room and motioned Greg away from the lowball table.

"Here's your chance to nail her," Mape told him excitedly. "Get up there and let that witch know she'd better give you back the money she stole!"

Hyped up on meds and sugar, Greg bolted to the escalator. But Pree had gotten rescued by some off-duty cop who took Greg to the local police station then turned him in to his probation officer. For anybody else, jail time for sure. All Greg got was a two-month extension of his house arrest and his every other Friday release time canceled. They didn't even check to see if he was still seeing his psychiatrist every Tuesday, so he still had a free morning every other week. Mape was appalled at the inadequacy of the justice system.

Frustrated and out of ideas, Mape curtailed his efforts to get his hands on the money until Greg's house arrest ended. They celebrated the occasion by spending a week at Mape's apartment in Las Vegas, eating, playing poker, and seeing some shows Mirabelle had been after Mape to take her to.

It was Mirabelle who first noticed that Greg's physical condition seemed to be deteriorating, and Mape was somewhat shocked when he finally took notice. Greg had gained at least sixty more pounds over the summer, and now tipped the scales at well over three hundred. His skin was sallow, with a bluish tint. His face had puffed up to the point that his eyes had become slits, and the whites had a yellowish tint. Mape wondered if the meds might be damaging Greg's liver. Mirabelle asked Mape if he thought Greg could be dying.

Mape assured Mirabelle that Greg was fine, but her question stuck in his mind. What if Greg did die? The question kept surfacing in Mape's brain, but he dismissed it each time. Sure, Greg was a giant pain in the ass, but he was still Mape's friend. A little jail time was one thing, but death was not an option. Those thoughts, however, didn't stop Mape from continuing to keep Greg's three-pill caddies full; one bunch of pills after breakfast, another after lunch, and a third at bedtime.

CHAPTER 55

Los Angeles, California, 1996
(Nine days before the killings)

Christmas was approaching and it was Mape's year to have the kids for the holidays. Mape loved his kids, but the idea of spending an entire week with them made him nervous. To his enormous relief, Lance called and said he and Leon wanted to meet in Las Vegas the day after Christmas to spend a few days with him and their younger sibs. The older boys could entertain the younger ones, freeing Mape to concentrate on Greg and the money. Two days before Christmas, Mape and Greg drove to California in the Lincoln. Greg waited in the car while Mape made a quick run to Dr. Foxx's clinic to pick up some refills. He told the doctor's assistant that Greg was having trouble sleeping and got some sleeping pills as well. They checked into a motel within walking distance of the Bicycle Club. Greg said he wasn't feeling well and was going to stay in the room and take a nap.

"I think I may have caught a flu bug or somethin'," Greg said.

Mape sat in a chair and turned on the television.

"Aren't you going to play today?" Greg asked, surprised.

"Can't," Mape replied. "Lost all my money."

Greg was quiet for a minute, the said, "Oh, what the heck! It's Christmas Eve. Take the keys out of my pocket and look in the trunk. I brought a little money along. It's in a black leather pouch. Go ahead and take three hundred. Merry Christmas!"

The pouch contained the last sixty-six hundred dollars of Mape's money. Greg had closed out the account and supposed he would soon be subsidizing Mape from his own funds.

Mape thanked him and went outside with the keys, grateful that he wasn't going to have to play with his own money after all. He unzipped the pouch and saw that it was full of hundreds. He removed only three of them, in case Greg was keeping track, and was zipping the pouch back up when he noticed a white file box with "Schwab Statements" written on the label in black marking pen. Curiosity got the better of him and he lifted the lid off the box. Inside was a hodgepodge of envelopes from Greg's brokerage firm. He sifted through the pile until he found an envelope dated the previous April, just about the time Greg had started cashing out the stock. At last he would know how much cash awaited him in the storage unit.

He was about to open the envelope when Greg called, "Can you find it?" from the doorway of the motel.

"Yeah," Mape replied. "Got it right here."

He quickly dropped the envelope, adjusted the lid back onto the box and closed the trunk. He returned the keys to Greg and began the short hike to the casino. It was a frequent source of irritation to Mape that Greg had given Nita keys to both the door and the trunk of his car, but had only seen fit to give Mape a door key. There was a button inside the glove box that was supposed to open the trunk, but Greg had it disabled when he bought the car so that if anyone ever broke into the car they wouldn't be able to get into the trunk, where he stowed cash and jewelry when he traveled.

At precisely one o'clock on Christmas Day, Mape drove the Lincoln into Laria's mother's driveway. The kids came running out. Mape got out of the car, hugged the girls, and swung Joey into the air. Laria came out and walked over to the passenger side of the car.

"Greg, what happened?" she asked. "You look terrible! Are you sick?"

"I was, but I'm better now," Greg said, patting his stomach. "I think it was somethin' I ate."

She handed him a square, bright green envelope with 'Uncle Greg' printed on the front in black marking pen. "Here's a little something from the kids," she said.

"Thanks," he said. "I've got somethin' for the kids back at the cabin, but I didn't get you nuthin'."

"That's good," she smiled, "because I didn't get you anything either. This is just from the kids." She kissed him on the cheek. His skin was clammy, but he wasn't feverish.

Mape backed out of the driveway. Laria waved until they were out of sight.

At the cabin, Mape carried the sleeping children inside, put them into Greg's bed, then made up the couch for Greg. He unloaded the Lincoln, and Greg parked it across the street in the garage. As soon as Greg started snoring, Mape crept into the kitchen, poured nearly half the sleeping pills onto a paper towel, and crushed them into powder with the bottom of a glass. He wrapped the powder inside one of the towels, put it and the other towel into a plastic baggie, placed the bottle in the kitchen drawer with the other pill bottles, and then stuck the glass into his suitcase. Exhausted, he climbed into bed with his children and immediately fell into a deep slumber.

The next morning, Greg didn't seem to notice anything unusual about his oatmeal. Mape was loading up the hatchback when Greg came out of the bathroom complaining of feeling dizzy.

"That's because you haven't taken your pills," Mape scolded. "Here, I'll get them for you."

"Thanks," Greg said. He filled a glass with water and took the pills.

Greg went into the bedroom and returned with three small Christmas stockings and the square green envelope Laria's card had been in. He had obliterated his name with a black marking pen.

Handing each child a small stocking containing a hundred-dollar bill, he said, "Merry Christmas, and thank you for the Sears gift certificate."

"You're welcome," the children replied.

"This is for your other boys," Greg said, handing Mape the green envelope. "It's a thousand dollars for them to split, so they can have a little fun while they're here."

"Thanks," Mape said, slipping the envelope into his pocket. "They'll appreciate it."

Greg staggered slightly as he made his way to the bedroom. Mape locked the door behind him as he and the kids left.

CHAPTER 56

Cottonwood Cove, Nevada, 1996
(Five days before the killings)

"Greg?" Mape called out cautiously, as he entered the cabin the next morning. Getting no response, he crept slowly toward the bedroom. Everything seemed to be as he had left it the day before. He had telephoned several times, but none of his calls had been answered. The pills must have done their job. Mape was sweating profusely as he entered the bedroom. As a sheriff, he'd seen his share of dead bodies before, but this would be his first time seeing the body of someone he knew and he wasn't sure how he would react, especially when he pressed the pill bottle into Greg's lifeless fingers.

He wiped his face with his sleeve and walked into the bedroom. The bed was rumpled, but empty. The bathroom too was empty. The house was cold, so the stove hadn't been lit that morning. What was going on? He was pretty sure Greg hadn't called 911 and been taken to the hospital, there would be signs. He walked through the house, calling Greg's name then went outside and walked around the house. Sitting down on the sofa with his head in his hands, he muttered, "The moron is indestructible."

Though frustrated, he was also relieved. As confident as he was that his plan had been foolproof, he had still been apprehensive. There was always that fraction of a possibility that he might have been caught, and being in prison for tax evasion was preferable to being in prison for murder. So he was back to Plan A, finding a way to get Greg incarcerated. He was mentally reviewing his one remaining option when the Lincoln drove up.

"Where the devil have you been?" he asked as Greg walked into the cabin. Greg's color had improved since the previous morning, and he was smiling.

"I'm okay now," Greg said cheerfully as he hefted his bulk up the porch steps and went into the house. "I wasn't really sick. Pree was right all along. It was them pills that was makin' me feel so bad."

"So how do you figure that?" Mape asked. This was not a good sign.

"It's true," Greg insisted. "You remember yesterday when you was leavin' how dizzy I was?"

Mape nodded.

"Well, I was about to lay down on the bed but I got real sick to my stomach and ran to the bathroom and puked my guts out. The oatmeal and the pills and everything. I slept for a while, and when I woke up I wasn't dizzy no more, and my head didn't hurt or nothin'. So I got cleaned up and went to Laughlin and took Nita out to a movie and dinner. And other things." His face turned pink as he said the last words.

"That's great!" Mape said, forcing a smile. "And how is the darling Nita?"

"I know you don't like her," Greg said defensively. "But I do. And she likes me too. In fact, on the way home I started thinkin' about how maybe I'll just sign the divorce papers and put the money back into the stock account. Then I'll see what happens with me and Nita."

"What about that little problem called tax evasion?" Mape asked. This was really bad.

"I've been thinkin' about that too," Greg said. "I don't think Pree'll turn us in. She hasn't yet. Why would she? She's got nothin' to gain by it."

Mape listened as Greg laid out a plan that would systematically destroy his future. He had to do something, and do it fast. Otherwise Nita and her son could end up with everything, and all the frustration and stress of the last seventeen years would have been for nothing. Mape suddenly felt very tired.

"You're such a moron," Mape said. "Don't you know the IRS pays for tips on tax evasion? It's a percentage of the money they recover. She stands to gain a lot. But it's your money and your life. Do what you want."

It was a bluff, of course. Mape wasn't ready to throw in the towel just yet. Admittedly, the best of his plans had failed, but he might as well fire the one volley he had left.

"Anyway, you're feeling better," he said, "and that's a good thing. How about you clean up and I treat you to an early lunch in Searchlight?"

"That sounds good," Greg said. He'd been afraid Mape would blow up and stop speaking to him again when he told him about his plans.

The minute he heard Greg get into the tub, Mape hurried to the kitchen and grabbed a knife from the drawer. He unscrewed the cover of the old wall phone, removed it and disconnected the bell mechanism to assure it couldn't ring. He replaced the cover and returned the knife to the drawer. Using his mobile phone, he dialed Greg's number and the phone stayed silent. He had effectively cut off communication between Greg and the woman. She could only receive emergency calls at work, and he knew Greg wouldn't call her at her mother's house for fear Maude would answer.

As they walked to their cars after lunch, Mape said, "It's good that you're feeling better, Greg. I just hope that stuff doesn't come back on you. That happens sometimes."

"I don't think so," Greg said. "I'm sure it was all them pills I was takin'. Pree kept tellin' me that was the problem, but I wouldn't listen to her."

"Well, whatever it was," Mape said, "since you're feeling so much better, how about if you go home and rest, and I'll come and get you in the morning and take you to Las Vegas so you can see Lance and meet my other son Leon? We'll have lunch, then you can go with me and the little ones to take the boys back to the airport. They're leaving tomorrow."

"Really?" Greg asked, somewhat stunned. For some reason he'd always thought Mape didn't want him to meet his older boys. "That would be great."

"I'll be here early," he said. "Put on some coffee and I'll make us some more oatmeal."

"Okay," Greg agreed excitedly. "See you then."

CHAPTER 57

Laughlin, Nevada, 1996
(Four days before the killings)

Mape had felt like a hamster on a treadmill for days, with no way to jump off. He slid out of the bed as quietly as he could and went to the bathroom. He couldn't afford to upset Mirabelle. He needed her help with his last and final plan.

As Mape became wearier, the trips between Las Vegas and Cottonwood Cove seemed to grow longer. This morning, it felt like he would never get there. He kept reminding himself how well the previous day's efforts had gone. He had succeeded in dumping Nita, quite tactfully, he thought. It was lucky he hadn't given the boys Greg's Christmas envelope. He'd been able to use it to soften Nita up, and fixing the phone assured she wouldn't be able to call him to say goodbye or anything. But best of all, he had gotten her key to the trunk of the Lincoln.

Mape could smell the coffee as he walked up to the porch. Good. Greg was already up. Inviting Greg to meet his son had been a stroke of genius. He knew Greg would cancel any plans to see that woman again for a chance to meet Leon. Like that was going to happen!

This morning Mape had dumped a different kind of powder into Greg's oatmeal. As he watched Greg drink his coffee and listened to him drone on, Mape became concerned that the powder wasn't taking effect until Greg jumped up from the table, hurried to the bathroom, and slammed the door. Mape went into the living room and turned on the television to drown out the noise.

"Are you okay in there?" Mape asked after a while, knocking on the bathroom door.

"No," Greg called through the door. "I don't think I'll be able to go with you today. I have diarrhea really bad. Tell your boys I'm sorry. I really wanted to meet Leon."

"They'll be disappointed," Mape lied. "They were looking forward to seeing you. By the way, they said thanks for the money."

"Tell them I hope it was lucky for them," Greg said.

"Listen, Greg," Mape said, talking fast so he could get away from the odor. "I'll be back tomorrow morning to get you, and we'll still go to Vegas for a couple of days. You can see the kids and we'll have a little fun."

"Sounds good," Greg said.

As he pulled on to the road Mape looked across the street at the cinder block garage that housed the Lincoln. He finally had a key to the trunk, but not to the garage. His good fortune was so close, but still unreachable.

CHAPTER 58

Cottonwood Cove, Nevada, 1996
(Three days before the killings)

Mape finished his second cup of coffee and read the comics, waiting for the pill to kick in. This morning, he had put only a couple of sleeping pills into Greg's oatmeal, needing only to keep Greg docile and out of his way while he set his final move into motion.

Greg stood and walked over to put his cup in the sink. He returned to the table and sat down.

"I think I'm having another dizzy spell," he complained, putting his head down on the table.

"I'm not surprised," Mape said. "It's your blood pressure. I'm telling you, Greg, you're asking for trouble when you stop taking your pills cold turkey like that. You have to cut back gradually."

"You're probably right," Greg agreed. "Do you know which ones are for my blood pressure?"

"I do," Mape said, jumping up and removing one of the pill caddies from the drawer. He removed two blood pressure pills and gave them to Greg with a glass of water.

"I'm sure you're doing the right thing," he coaxed as Greg swallowed the pills. "Why don't you put your pill caddies into your suitcase while I clean up?"

"Mirabelle must have taken the kids to the Children's Museum already," Mape said when they walked back into his empty apartment. Greg had sat by the pool as Mape loaded some moving boxes into the Lincoln and two men loaded Mape's leased furniture into a van and hauled it away.

"I'll just go get the mail then I'll put this stuff into storage get us a room for the night. We'll even have time to play a little poker."

"Oh my god!" Mape shouted excitedly as he walked back into the apartment carrying an open letter. "She did it to us. The witch actually turned us in!"

He handed the letter to Greg. "It's from the IRS. You'll probably get one like it tomorrow."

Greg's eyes got wide as he read the words on the paper.

"Does this mean that even if I pay back the money and pay the fine, we still could go to prison?"

"That's what it says," Mape confirmed. Mirabelle had worked magic with her computer. The letter looked official. All it had taken to get her to do it was the promise of the three 'M's', money, Mexico, and marriage, in that precise order. She had demanded two grand in advance.

"Those IRS guys don't fool around," Mape said. "Remember, even Al Capone had to serve eight years in prison for tax evasion."

Greg leaned against the wall, put his head in his hands, and started crying. "What are we gonna do?" he asked. "What are we gonna do?"

Mape patted his friend's shoulder. "I'll think of something," he said. "I won't let you go to jail."

The pills were doing their job.

Finally settling into the motel room, Mape said, "Let's try to forget about Pree and the IRS for now and go next door to the casino and have a good time."

"You go on without me," Greg said. "I'm a little tired. I think I'll take a nap."

Mape was delighted! *This one was going to work!* He would be on his way to Mexico soon. At last!

Mape hurriedly opened the trunk of Greg's car. At last he would know the value of his long sought after prize. He blinked when he first saw the number at the bottom of the page. Was that possible?

Could that little moron be sitting on top of over a million dollars in cash? It was almost too much for Mape to take in.

Excitedly, he put the envelope back into the box, returned the lid and was ready to close the trunk when he spotted the leather pouch and helped himself to three more hundreds from it. In the state Greg was in, he wouldn't know the difference.

Mape was elated by the new turn of events. His luck was finally changing! He had gone into a tailspin on Christmas when the kids mentioned Laria had a new baby, obviously not his, but that was no longer important to him. It wasn't a question of whether or not he would get Greg's money any more. The question now was how fast he could get his hands on it.

He decided it was time to tie up the one remaining loose end. The kids. He dialed Laria's number and told her he wouldn't be able to bring the kids home on New Year's Day, as required, telling her he would instead return them the following Sunday, three days late. As expected, she went into orbit, telling him he had no right to keep them that long, and that the children had to be in school the day after New Year's. Unfortunately for Mape, the conversation ended with Laria informing him she was coming to Las Vegas on New Year's Day to get the children, then hanging up on him.

Mape realized Laria could ruin everything. The minute she found his apartment vacant, Laria would report the children missing, maybe even kidnapped. Worst case, the authorities could be waiting for him by the time he reached the border. Mape figured it would take Laria approximately eight hours to get to his apartment in Las Vegas, but at best would take him at least ten hours to get to Mexico. Assuming they left their homes at approximately the same time, he needed a way to stall her for two hours. He called back and when her machine picked up he left her a message saying he and the children were going to spend New Year's Eve at Greg's house and stay the night. He said she could pick the kids up there, and gave her directions for finding the cabin. Though he calculated that would buy him enough time, to be safe he decided to leave on New Year's Eve instead of New Year's Day.

CHAPTER 59

Las Vegas, Nevada, 1996
(The day of the killings)

As if Mape wasn't stressed enough, Mirabelle complained about having to babysit on New Year's Eve, so Mape took them all to the Tropicana for a little family celebration at the brunch buffet. He reminded Mirabelle that by midnight, they would be on their way to Mexico with more money than they would ever be able to spend, and she got a little nicer.

By early afternoon, Mape and Greg were on their way back to the Cove to pack Greg's things and to pick up the money. Greg had been pouting all morning about having to go to Mexico, so Mape was relieved when he slept most of the way. Just outside of Searchlight, Greg woke up and noticed that the reading on the thermostat of his car was a little high. They pulled into the twenty-four-hour garage where Greg had the car serviced regularly so Ed Avino, the owner and mechanic, could check it out. Mape had played in a few Hold'em tournaments with Ed and Dee, his wife, and nodded in recognition.

"You've got a tiny hole in the radiator," Ed told them. "You won't have a problem getting to Cottonwood Cove and back, but I wouldn't drive it any further. I'm getting ready to close for the holiday, but I can fix it for you first thing Friday morning."

Over Greg's protests, Mape paid Ed an extra hundred dollars to fix the radiator on the spot and to let them borrow his pickup to go to the cabin and get the hatchback. Silently, Greg removed the money pouch from the trunk of the Lincoln and stuffed it into his pocket. Mape removed Greg's gun from under the front passenger seat and put it on the floor behind the driver's seat of the pickup. Mape followed in the pickup as Greg drove the hatchback back to the garage, where Mape paid Ed in advance, moved the gun to the hatchback, and drove directly to the storage facility in Bullhead City where he would, at long last, get his hands on the money.

Opening the storage locker, Mape saw a square, brown leather suitcase and a tan leather monogrammed satchel, both loaded with a hodgepodge of bills of every denomination, as well as a lot of coins. After both suitcases were filled, Greg had begun throwing the overflow into a black plastic garbage bag.

Still upset about moving to Mexico, Greg refused to get out of the car, leaving Mape to struggle with the heavy bags of money by himself. When the money was finally loaded, Mape grabbed three empty suitcases in which to pack Greg's clothes and other belongings.

Back in Searchlight, the garage was closed but the Lincoln was waiting for them, as agreed. Greg drove the Lincoln back to the cabin and Mape followed in the hatchback. Well aware they would be taking the Lincoln to Mexico and would need to load their things into it, Greg stubbornly parked it in the garage anyway, and walked across the street to the cabin. It was cold, and the winds were getting stronger.

Mape backed the hatchback up to the porch and propped the cabin door open with the rock. After a struggle, he finally got the bags of money onto the porch then kicked them across to the doorway. There he laid the suitcase down flat and set the satchel and trash bag on top of it. He left the bags in the doorway to load into Greg's car when they were ready to go. Greg walked past him without speaking and went to the back of the cabin. Mape removed his own luggage and the ice chest from the hatchback and placed them on the porch next to the suitcases with the money. He also removed the tarp he kept in the car to cover items he sometimes carried in the luggage rack on top of his car. He removed the gun and set it on an end table inside the house then reparked the hatchback to make room for the Lincoln.

In the bedroom, Mape began packing Greg's clothes, ignoring Greg, who had undressed and was lying in bed with his back to Mape, weeping silently. He reminded Mape of a beached whale. When he had finished packing and setting Greg's bags by the front door with the others, Mape returned to the bedroom. It was getting late, and he had to get Greg out of bed and into the car.

"A bunch of kids are partying in that big house across the street," he said. "Maybe we'll have a party of our own when we get to Mexico."

"I don't want to go to Mexico, Mape," Greg pleaded. "They talk funny down there, and I won't know nobody."

"Greg, you know we have to go," Mape said, sitting on the bed and taking Greg's hand in his. "It's the only way we can stay out of prison. Besides, you'll know me, and Mirabelle, and the kids. We'll be a family, and we'll learn the language together. We'll help each other. It'll be fun."

"But I'll miss my friends," Greg pouted.

"We'll invite them to visit us," Mape said, wondering what friends Greg was referring to.

"Even Nita?" Greg asked defiantly.

"Of course, Nita," Mape assured him. "Maybe she'll even move down there and you two can get married. How would you like to have a Mexican wedding?"

"But you don't like Nita," Greg said.

"I'm growing to like her, because you like her, and you're my brother." It was time to pull out all the stops.

Greg looked startled.

"I thought we can't tell nobody about that," he said.

"That's in this country," Mape said, pulling Greg up from the pillow and hugging him. "When we get to Mexico, we'll be able to be a real family. I plan to tell everyone that you're my brother."

Greg smiled.

"I'm going to run you a nice bubble bath to relax you," Mape said. Greg smelled terrible. The extra weight and heavy medication had taken a toll on Greg's personal hygiene. "I know you're all tense about our adventure, but I promise you're going to love Mexico."

"I hope so."

After helping Greg into the tub, Mape closed the bathroom door and jumped into action, setting the dining chairs and table against the wall and covering the dining room floor with the tarp. The tarp would reduce the mess and make it easier to carry Greg out, if it actually came to that.

"It's cold in here," Greg said as he walked into the dining room. He asked, "What's the tarp doing on the floor?"

"I noticed a couple of loose shingles on the roof this afternoon. It looks like rain and I was afraid the roof would leak. No sense in letting Nita's floor get ruined."

"That was nice of you," Greg said, smiling.

"I'm going to be a better brother to you from now on," Mape said, holding out his arms for a hug.

Greg hugged him back. "Listen, Mape," he said, "I don't think I'm gonna go to Mexico with you. I'm gonna stay here and try to get the IRS to let me pay back the money instead. Then maybe Nita and me will get married."

Mape could feel Greg's tears against his face.

"I mean, I want to be your brother and all, and I'll come to see you, but I don't want to live there. There's fifty or sixty thousand dollars in that trash bag over there, and I want you and Mirabelle and the kids to have it. You should be able to get set up pretty good with that much money. Things are supposed to be cheaper in Mexico."

"That's very generous of you, little brother, and I understand. I'll miss you though."

"I'll miss you too," Greg said, relieved. He'd been worried Mape would be upset.

"Well, I have something for you too," Mape said. "I was saving it for Mexico, but I guess I'd better give it to you now."

"What is it?" Greg asked. He loved surprises.

"Just turn around and close your eyes and I'll get it for you. No peeking"

Picking up the gun from the table, Mape stuck it into his belt behind him. Hurriedly standing behind Greg, Mape reached his right arm over Greg's shoulder and got a firm grip on his chin to prevent his head from moving. He then arched his spine and leaned back as far as he could to keep as much spatter as possible off of himself. In one swift move, Mape reached behind his back with his left hand, removed the gun and shoved the barrel against Greg's head. He heard a voice behind him shout his name as he squeezed the trigger.

EPILOGUE

Frazier Park, California, 2001
(Four years after the killings)

Heavy clouds had obstructed the natural illumination that night, producing an eerie effect. A faint light coming through the open door enabled the man to make out the steps he used to climb onto the crude wooden porch. The bitter wind, along with the frequent pop of firecrackers and an occasional gun shot, courtesy of impatient New Year's Eve revelers, increased the man's anxiety. He could see a pile of suitcases stacked by the door, which had been propped open with a rock. Men's voices were coming from within, but the howling of the wind prevented him from making out what they were saying. The man crept across the porch and stood behind the open door. A crack between the edge of the door and the door jamb enabled him to make out living room furniture. A lamp on a table at the far end of the sofa threw a dim light into the space behind the living area, which appeared to be empty except for a table and some chairs that had been pushed against the wall.

The man could make out a male figure standing in the middle of the far room, facing the back of the room. No, it was two men hugging each other; or rather, one man appeared to be hugging the other from behind. He strained to hear what they were saying, but the wind continued to drown out their words.

The instant he heard it, a shiver ran down his spine, and his hands automatically flew to his face. The wind made it impossible for the man to pinpoint exactly where the sound was coming from, but it seemed to be coming from the other end of the enclosed porch. He tiptoed into the dark recesses of the porch to try to frighten it away. As he neared the back of the enclosure, he heard it again, but this time it was coming from the opposite end of the porch, near the door, where he had just been standing. Puzzled, he turned to see a woman walk across the porch and through the doorway. As she entered the cabin, he heard her shout, "Mape! Don't!" Then he heard a gunshot from inside the cabin.

Now the woman was pulling on his arm. No, not the woman. Someone else. Someone who was calling him Daddy!

Bob opened his eyes and found himself staring into the eyes of his four-year-old daughter, Lauryn, who was insisting that he get up and make her brother Joey share the Fruit Loops.

"Joey says I have to eat Cheerios, but I want Fruit Loops," she complained.

Wearily, Bob pulled himself up onto the side of the bed and, remembering what day it was, said, "*Shhh*, we don't want to wake Mommy. This is her special day, remember?"

Bob glanced at Laria. Her eyes were closed, but the edges of her lips were curled into the beginning of a smile.

"Oh yeah, Mommy's Day. I forgot."

Grabbing Bob's arm, the child whispered, "Come on, Daddy, before Joey eats all of the Fruit Loops."

"Okay, Kitten. Just let me put on my robe and slippers."

The child's mind immediately jumped from Fruit Loops to another subject, one of her favorites. She whispered, "Daddy, tell me again why you call me Kitten."

"Oh, honey," Bob whispered. "You know that story better than I do."

"But I like to hear you tell it, Daddy. Please."

"Oh, okay," Bob whispered, leaning over to grab his robe from a chair. "It was dark and I was standing on the porch of a man I had gone to see when I heard a cat meowing and I got scared."

"'Cause you're 'lergic and you can't breathe when cats come close to you and you might die, right?"

"Right. I couldn't see the cat, but it's meowing kept getting louder. Then a beautiful woman walked onto the porch, and I asked her to help me find the cat so I would be able to breathe."

"And it was Mommy, and she said, 'That's not a cat, it's my baby crying,' and she opened her coat and there was a little baby in a sling under her coat and it was me and I was so teeny, I couldn't cry good and I sounded like a cat meowing and that's why you call me Kitten!"

Forgetting about her sleeping mother, Lauryn giggled with delight and held her arms out to Bob.

"That's right, Kitten," he said as he slung her over his shoulder. "Now, let's go make Mommy some pancakes."

"And don't forget about the Fruit Loops," Lauryn reminded him.

As their voices trailed off down the hall, Laria opened her eyes. She rarely thought about that hellish night now that the nightmares had stopped, but she had no doubt that the horror would continue to revisit both of them from time to time.

Laria had been angry at Mape that day for not bringing the children home as he was supposed to do. She had stopped briefly in Barstow to change and feed the baby and pick up a burger for herself. That part of her statement had been true. But she had immediately continued on, hoping to find a place to spend the night near her destination so she could pick up her children early the next morning.

When she spotted the "Vacancy" sign, she almost turned into the motel in Cal-Nev-Ari, but she so ached to see her children she decided to continue on to the cabin to see if Mape would let her bring them back to the motel to sleep so they could get an early start the next morning.

She had a little trouble finding the cabin and passed it once, as she had said in her statement. She remembered Mape had said it was across the street from a vacant three-story house. She turned around and drove back and parked in front of the only three-story house she had seen, although she heard music coming from it and it didn't appear to be vacant. If it hadn't been for a small patch of dim light, barely visible in the darkness, she might never have located the cabin. Unfamiliar with the desert, she decided not to chance her car getting stuck in the sand in front of the house, and opted to leave it parked on the street and walked over.

She had to struggle against the wind to get her car door open. Fastening her coat over the baby sling to protect Lauryn, she grabbed the diaper bag, hunched over to brace herself against the wind, and struggled across the wide lot. As she approached the trees, car lights illuminated the outline of a cabin and a car barely visible in the trees. She made her way over to the car to be certain it was Mape's or Greg's before disturbing the people in the cabin. As she drew near it, another pair of headlights revealed it to be Mape's hatchback, so she turned and fought her way to the cabin.

Lauryn had awakened and was crying at the top of her lungs as Laria walked past the walled-in porch of the cabin. As she reached the steps she could see a dim light coming through the open door, so she climbed the steps and looked into the cabin.

Mape and Greg were standing in the dining area with their backs to her. Mape was behind Greg and seemed to be leaning backward. Suddenly Mape raised a gun and put it against Greg's head.

"Mape! Don't!" Laria had screamed at the top of her lungs. She rushed forward to try to stop him, but she was too late. She watched in disbelief as Mape blew his best friend's brains out.

Her scream startled Mape, who jerked his head around to see who had yelled at him, neglecting to release his hold on Greg's chin. Greg's huge, lifeless body fell backward on top of Mape, knocking him to the floor and pinning him to the tarp.

"What have you done?" Laria demanded, letting the diaper bag fall to the floor. "Are you crazy? You've killed Greg!"

"What are you doing here?" Mape asked angrily, trying to push Greg's three hundred plus pounds off of him. But his spindly thighs were pinned under Greg's monstrous buttocks and he couldn't get any traction. "Pull him off of me!" he demanded as Greg's blood dripped onto his arm.

"Where are the kids?" Laria asked. "They can't see this."

"They're in Vegas," Mape said. "They're fine." His voice became quieter, more menacing. "Get him off of me, Laria."

Laria moved to the old-fashioned dial phone on the wall.

"What are you doing?" Mape demanded.

"I'm calling the police," she said.

Mape heaved Greg's body up as far as he could and made a lunge for the gun that had fallen on the floor a few feet away, but the effort was futile. Greg's head bounced as it fell back onto Mape's chest.

Stretching out the long phone cord, Laria hurried over and picked up the gun, forcing her gloved finger into the space next to the trigger. She pointed the gun at Mape and said, "Don't move until the police get here."

"Sweetheart," Mape said in his smarmiest voice. "See those bags over there?" Laria recalled seeing the pile of luggage, but she didn't turn her eyes away from Mape.

"Two of those suitcases are full of money, sweetheart. Cash. And there's more in the trash bag. Over a million dollars. We're rich! We'll be able to go anywhere we want and live the life we've always dreamed of. You, me, and the kids. Even that baby of yours. Think about it, Laria."

Determined not to let Lauryn's crying or Mape's pleading distract her, Laria focused on the situation. Holding the gun in her right hand and the receiver with her left, she tried to dial 911. Her gloved finger barely fit into the holes of the dial.

As she began dialing, Mape heaved Greg's body forward with all of his strength, this time almost getting it into a sitting position. This enabled Mape to rise up, twist his body awkwardly at the waist, brace himself on the floor with his left hand, place his right shoulder against Greg's back, and face Laria. Encouraged by his improved position, he snarled, "You're a dead woman!"

Startled, Laria whirled around and pointed the gun at Mape again. The sudden movement caused her finger to tighten on the trigger and the gun exploded, sending a bullet into Mape's chest. As if in slow motion, Mape's torso jerked, turned forward again, and allowed the weight of Greg's body to push him back onto the tarp.

"Oh dear God! Mape!" Laria screamed, dropping the gun and the phone onto the floor. She made a move toward Mape then stopped herself, unsure if he was still a threat. "Please don't die, Mape. I'm sorry. It was an accident. I'll get help," she cried, picking up the receiver and jiggling the phone cradle to get another dial tone. "Please don't die," she repeated.

"What are you doing?" a man's voice called from the doorway, startling the already panicked Laria. A tall, sandy-haired man in jeans and a leather jacket rushed into the room, his hands obscuring half his face.

"I'm calling the police," she screamed hysterically. "I just shot my husband!"

"I am the police," the man said, taking one hand from his face to produce his badge and ID and hold them out to her. "Detective Robert Kips from Las Vegas Metro. I can help you, but first I have to get the cat out of the room, because I'm really allergic to them."

"What cat?" Laria cried, looking around frantically. "I don't see a cat."

"But you can hear it, can't you? It's right here."

"No, I can't," Laria said, straining to hear the cat.

Just then Lauryn bellowed loudly.

"You didn't hear that?" Bob asked, turning to hurry outside and suck in some fresh air.

"That noise?" Laria called after him. "That's not a cat, that's my baby."

Bob turned back as Laria opened her coat and revealed the squalling child. "She's hungry, and she needs to be changed."

Embarrassed, Bob removed his hands from his face and inhaled. Assured that his lungs were functioning normally, he came back into the room and verified that both men were, in fact, deceased.

"Wait," he said as Laria reached for the diaper bag. "Don't touch that yet."

"I need to feed my baby," she insisted, "and change her."

"I know," Bob said, trying to think what to do. "But we have a bad situation here. I didn't actually see the shooting, but I heard enough to know it was an accident, and I'll be a witness to that fact.

The problem is, since you were the shooter, they'll probably have to hold you, at least until they investigate, and you may be arrested."

"Oh dear God!" Laria said, bursting into tears. "I have three other children. I can't go to jail!"

"There may be another way," Bob said.

"Another way?" Laria asked, wiping her eyes, desperate not to be separated from her children again.

"I need to think it through. But first I need you let me remove your gloves and your coat," he said.

"Why?" Laria asked, wondering if he really was a policeman. "It's cold in here."

She jiggled the baby and the crying subsided a bit.

"Just as a precaution," Bob said, "until we figure out what to do."

Laria had no idea what was going on or why the man was doing this, but she was too weary to object. The man walked around the bodies and into the kitchen and returned with a plastic trash bag. She asked to see his credentials and badge again, noting he had put on plastic gloves. The ID card and badge looked genuine, so she let him remove her coat and gloves, which he put into the bag.

He took off his jacket and placed it around her shoulders. "I have a brand-new windbreaker in my car. I'll bring it in for you to wear home."

He set the bag down and left the cabin, leaving her free to tend to her baby. By the time Detective Kips returned with the jacket, Laria was already nursing the baby, her chest covered with a baby blanket, the empty sling on the floor. Bob dropped wearily into the chair opposite her. The room was quiet except for the sound of the wind and the baby's nursing sounds.

"I just flew in from Pennsylvania this afternoon," Bob said, breaking the silence. "I bought the windbreaker at the airport for my nephew Clyde. He doesn't know about it, though, so you can keep it. I'll get Clyde something else. It's big, so there should be room for the baby."

"Why are you helping me like this?" Laria asked quietly.

Bob hesitated for a long time, reluctant to explain the situation to her.

"The truth is, lady, I could be in a lot of trouble over this myself. My boss thinks I'm at home, sick.

"Then why are you here?" Laria asked.

"Because I'm an idiot," he explained. "When I got home from the airport this evening, I unpacked and took my empty suitcases down to my carport, where I keep my near-new Dodge Ram, which my friends jokingly refer to as my obsession. Someone had scratched the letters *F* and *U* into the door of my truck. I don't know if it was hunger, jet lag, or what, because I rarely lose my temper, but I freaked out. I don't recall ever being so furious before in my life."

"I can understand why you were angry," Laria said, reaching under the blanket and switching Lauryn to the other breast. "But why did you come here?"

"Because the guy who lives here is the only person I know who would do something like that, and I wanted to shake him up a little. Nothing physical. I just wanted to make it clear that he'd better not mess with me or my truck again."

"Are you talking about Greg?" Laria asked. "Greg Crenski?"

"The one and only," Bob said, gesturing with his head toward the bodies in the dining room. "He is – was – a real piece of work."

"How did – do – you know him?" Laria asked, resentful of the disparaging way the policeman was speaking about Greg.

"His wife is a friend of mine."

"You're friends with Pree? So am I. Or at least I used to be, before things got so messed up."

"I met Pree a few months ago when I stopped her husband from attacking her."

"Attacking her? Greg?"

"You do know he paid an undercover officer to kill her, don't you? He got off easy on a technicality. Six months of house arrest and five years' probation. They extended his house arrest two extra months after I booked him for attacking his wife and he threatened to get even with me for it. I'm sure he was the one who scratched my truck. Nobody else I know is crazy enough to do that."

Laria shook her head. "I just can't imagine Greg doing those things."

"Pree said he changed a lot after they moved here. She thought it was the prescription drugs he was taking. She moved out of their house into a trailer park to hide from him. She suspected his friend was keeping him stirred up."

"What friend?" Laria asked, already knowing the answer.

"Mape somebody. I'm guessing that's him over there, which would make you Mrs. Mape?"

"I'm afraid so," Laria sighed.

They sat in silence again while Laria put herself together, wrapped the sleeping baby in the blanket, and placed her on the sofa. She felt reasonably calm and lucid again.

Bob retrieved his leather jacket and helped her into the windbreaker. He picked the baby sling off the floor and put it into the plastic bag, then sat back down.

"I'm still not clear on why you're willing to involve yourself in this mess," Laria said. "Do you really think you'll get fired just for coming over here to warn Greg not to scratch your truck again?"

"That plus lying about being sick might get me a suspension, but not fired."

"Then why are you putting yourself out like this for someone you don't even know?"

Bob had no choice but to tell her everything. "The fact is, I was already here when you arrived. I'd been watching through the door when I thought I heard the cat, and I walked to the far end of the porch in an effort to scare it away. I watched you walk into the cabin, heard you scream, then heard the gunshot. That's when my brain went AWOL. I knew I could get into serious trouble for being here, so when I heard you say you were calling the police, I bolted instead of staying to investigate, as I'm sworn to do. I was halfway across the yard when I heard the second shot. That's when the cop in me finally kicked in, and I came back."

"So what would happen to you if I called the police right now and reported it?"

"For leaving the scene without investigating the first shooting and thereby not preventing the second one? Let's put it this way. In four months, I'll have twenty-five years on the force. For sure, I could kiss my pension goodbye. I might even do some jail time, not to mention the disgrace."

They sat silently across from each other, neither of them knowing what to say or what to do. Finally, Laria spoke.

"My kids will be here in the morning, or at least I hope they will. Mape said they're in Las Vegas."

"If they don't show up by morning, I'll find them for you," Bob assured her.

Laria nodded, and they were quiet again.

Suddenly Laria said, "I can't let the children see their father and Uncle Greg like this. What would happen if I pulled that tarp up over the bodies?"

Bob chuckled at the idea. "That would create a forensic nightmare for sure. For openers, it would mix up the blood and other tissue and obliterate the blood spatter patterns, and who knows where the gunshot residue would end up? The crime scene people would come unglued. This one's already going to be a nightmare for them. With the bodies stacked like that, it will initially appear that your husband was killed first, by Greg. They might never figure out what happened here if the evidence was all jumbled together in the tarp."

It took only a few seconds for the detective's words to sink into both their brains. They looked at each other. They both shrugged. Why not? What did either of them have to lose?

Laria moved the gun next to the bodies. Bob removed the gloves Mape was wearing and rubbed the gunshot residue onto Greg's left hand. He put the gloves into the bag with Laria's coat and gloves and baby sling. They folded the tarp over them, first one side then the other, in such a way as to maximize the mingling of the evidence. The gun was of such a low caliber the expended bullets hadn't exited the bodies; one remained in Greg's head, the other in Mape's chest. Only a few additional adjustments were necessary to make it appear to be a murder/suicide, or so they hoped.

They went over Laria's story one last time. Bob reminded her to turn the lamp back on the next morning, remembering to leave no fingerprints on it. Since the deaths occurred at night, the police would expect the light to be on. Bob turned it off when they left because without the light, the cabin was virtually invisible, making it less likely anyone else would enter it before morning. He left the door open so the cold and dampness would make the time of death more difficult to estimate.

Bob walked Laria to her car and turned his back while she changed into her jeans and Reeboks. He apologized for asking her to throw away her nearly-new walking shoes, but he explained that one microscopic drop of blood or could be enough to do her in.

"That's okay," she said. "It's giving up the nicest coat I've ever owned that hurts. Compared to that, giving up the shoes is a piece of cake."

"Good luck to both of us in the morning," Bob said, exhaustion evident in his voice. "Don't forget, you need to come up with a good story to account for the missing two hours in your timeline."

Suddenly, fireworks exploded down by the lake, and they heard two gunshots coming from the big house. It was 1997.

"Happy New Year," Laria said as she smiled tiredly at Bob and stuck her key into the ignition.

"Let's hope so," Bob said.

"The money!" Laria exclaimed suddenly, jumping out of her car.

"What money?" Bob asked.

"Mape said there's over a million dollars in two of the suitcases and a plastic bag. It was Greg's money. I have to get it and give it to Pree."

"Let's drive over there. I don't think I can persuade my legs to walk that far."

"Won't we leave tire tracks in the sand?" Laria asked.

"So? We've already left our shoe prints. One is as incriminating as the other."

Laria looked horrified.

"Just kidding," Bob said. "In a few minutes, the sky is going to open up and drop so much water we'll have to wade through mud to get to the cabin when we return in the morning. Any prints we leave in the sand tonight will be obliterated."

Loading the bags of money into the back of the truck turned out to be harder than Bob expected. He was jet-lagged and exhausted and the bills were interlaced with coins, making the suitcases extremely heavy.

By the time they drove out of Cottonwood Cove, the wind had returned with a fury. When the rain started, Laria was thankful to be following Bob's truck. Without his taillights to guide her, she would have been hard-pressed to stay on the road.

Bob honked and stuck his arm out of the window to wave as Laria turned off the highway in Cal-Nev-Ari. The rain had stopped. She had passed the all night gas station, made a U-turn, and doubled back, in case the attendant was watching, and was asked by the police what direction she'd been coming from. She filled her tank and drove over to the motel. From that point, things went pretty much as she had said in her statement.

Laria mentally rehearsed her story on the way back to the cabin the next morning. The most difficult part had been walking around the bodies to leave footprints to show that she had gone to the bedroom to look for her children. She was most apprehensive about telling Lieutenant Keebler about falling asleep at the rest stop, to account for the extra time, but it was the best she could come up with. She hoped the part about being awakened at midnight by New Year's revelers would lend a little credibility to her story, since that had actually happened once when she and Mape were traveling home from New Jersey.

Delivering the money to Pree turned out to be a fiasco for Bob. He remembered that residents of the trailer park would be at the New Year's Eve dinner and show, leaving the park deserted until at least 2:00 a.m.

Bob pulled into the overflowing parking lot across the street from the park, turned his truck around, and left it facing the gate with the motor running and the lights off so he could make a fast getaway, if necessary. He knew the gate code from the times he'd visited Pree.

The suitcases were soaked and were even heavier than they'd been at the cabin. Spurred on by the desire to deliver the money and get home to bed, Bob hoisted the wet satchel onto his shoulder and hurried out, getting through the gate before it finished closing. It seemed to take an eternity for the second gate to open enough for him to pass through. Once inside, he power walked down the stone walkway, slowing considerably by the time he reached Pree's trailer. He dropped the satchel onto the step and hurried back to his truck.

He was about to lift the second suitcase onto his shoulder when he saw headlights coming down the road. He left the suitcase on the truck bed, slammed the tailgate shut, and jumped into the driver's seat. As soon as the car pulled into the park and was out of sight, Bob drove through the still-open gate and sped down River Road, leaving his lights off until he was half way to the River Queen. The rest of the money would have to be delivered another time.

Back at the condo, he locked the suitcase and plastic bag of money in the storage compartment of his carport, leaving the plastic bag of evidence in his truck to deal with later. His brain and body had shut down. He showered and went to bed.

Bob felt surprisingly rested when he got the call from the dispatcher three hours later. Arriving at the station to pick up his department car, he noticed the plastic bag containing the items from the crime scene sticking out from under the seat of his truck. Making sure there was no one else at the station, he quickly buried the bag containing the plastic gloves, Laria's gloves, pants, shoes, and the baby sling under several identical bags of trash in the department dumpster. He had removed Laria's coat from the bag at his condo and hidden it in his entertainment center, planning to get it cleaned a couple of times and return it to her when the time was right. He couldn't bring himself to throw away the nicest coat the lady had ever owned.

They had messed up at Pree's birthday party when the lieutenant announced that there was insufficient evidence to charge Laria with any crime. They had each been informed earlier, but that was the first time they had heard the words together. When she looked at him he spontaneously grabbed her and held on for so long that people probably suspected they had become romantically involved during the six days they had been neighbors. Nothing could have been further from the truth. They had both been so emotionally drained that a romantic encounter would have been out of the question. They had held onto each other out of shared joy and relief at the realization that their lives may not have been destroyed after all.

Mape's sister's antics aside, the day of the memorial service had been a good one. Bob had surprised her by returning her coat, which she wore to the service. He came to dinner, stayed a while afterward to play Yahtzee, and seemed to hit it off well with her mother. When Jessica and the older children returned to California the next day, she and Bob made love for the first time, as well as the second and third.

The day after that, they went to Las Vegas to check out Mape's storage locker, which Bob had located through one of his connections. On their way out of the condo, they were stopped by Jean Cress, one of the tenants, who had her two sons, Garrett and Tate, in tow. Laria recognized the boys from the pool, where she had seen the older boy bully the younger kids a few times.

"Go ahead," Jean said sternly, pushing the boys toward Bob.

"Sorry," the boys said, their eyes cast downward.

"Say it like you mean it," their mother insisted.

"We're sorry for scratching your truck, Detective Kips," the older boy said; his brother nodded in agreement.

"They're on restriction for a month," their mother said. "Send me the bill and I'll pay it."

"That's okay," Bob said. "The insurance paid for it. You can reimburse me the three-hundred-dollar deductible, though."

"I'll bring you a check tomorrow," Jean said. "You know this is coming out of your allowances," she said to her boys as they walked away.

After they were gone, Laria and Bob looked at each other, shrugged, and burst out laughing.

Mape's storage unit was nearly empty. Laria set most of his things in a Salvation Army box next to the dumpster. She took a few books and a box of photos and papers back to the condo. That night, while Bob was on duty, she sorted through them, picking out some documents and photos to save for the kids, when she ran across something that gave her quite a surprise. When Bob arrived home the next morning, she showed him Greg's last will and testament, leaving all his worldly goods to Maple Avril Belata.

"What do you think this means?" she asked.

"You're the legal expert, but my guess is that since Greg died first, except for the house, everything Greg owned legally passed to Mape, including the money, the boat, his car, everything. As Mape's widow, it would all belong to you now. Of course, trying to have the will probated and claiming Greg died first would open up a can of worms I don't think you want to deal with."

"No," agreed Laria, "and Pree should get a share anyway. I guess we should just leave things the way they are."

In the end, Laria got more of the cash, but the car, boat, coin, and gun collections, jewelry, and other assets made Pree's share quite a lot larger than Laria's, and many times what she would have gotten if she had been divorced from Greg. Laria decided it was fair enough that her conscience could live with it.

The money brought problems of its own, though. They paid cash for everything they could possibly pay cash for without arousing suspicion. They even used Greg's money to pay for their wedding and honeymoon. They opened college funds for the children and a savings account for themselves, and made cash deposits into them every week.

Laria was forced to start up a home business, taking on the overflow of her former law firm. She occasionally typed a master's thesis or doctoral dissertation for students at UCLA and Pepperdine, for which she required cash. She slipped as much of Greg's money as she felt she could get away with into each deposit. After almost three years, they took the family out to a nice dinner with the last of the cash, and breathed a sigh of relief.

They built their dream home in the picturesque hills above Gorman, California, and Bob's job as head of security at the amusement park enabled him to provide well for his family. Over Stella's objections, Bob adopted the children and proved to be a caring husband and father. Ironically, in the end, Mape had done well for his family after all, just by dying.

Pree never mentioned the satchel of money to Laria or to Bob. On one of Pree's visits, Laria was tempted to ask her about it, but she knew that was a Pandora's Box that had to stay sealed forever.

Voices from the hallway reminded Laria of how truly blessed she was. She pulled the covers over her head, closed her eyes, and waited to be surprised.

CPSIA information can be obtained
at www.ICGtesting.com
Printed in the USA
FFHW021332190319
51149114-56601FF